A Circle Around Forever

by

Robert K. Swisher Jr.

OPEN TALON PRESS

**PUBLISHED BY
OPEN TALON PRESS**

EDITOR: Stephany Tullis

COVER DESIGNER: Arleigh Johnson

PRINT FORMAT: Samantha Fury

Library of Congress - In Publication Date

Swisher, Robert K, 1947 -
A CIRCLE AROUND FOREVER: A novel / by Robert K. Swisher Jr.
Summary: paranormal, love, saga, quest, fulfillment, fantasy
ISBN:....978-0-578-98426-1
LCN:....2021918043

OTHER PUBLISHED NOVELS BY ROBERT K. SWISHER JR.

Historical Fiction: Trade and E-book
Published by Sunstone Press
The Land
Fatal Destiny

Contemporary Western Fiction: Trade and E-book
PUBLISHED BY SUNSTONE PRESS
How Far the Mountain
The Last Narrow Gauge Train Robbery
The Last Day in Paradise
Love Lies Bleeding
The Man From the Mountain

Literary: Out of Print
Published by Samisdat Press - Canada
American Love Story

Young Adult: Trade Only
Published by Echo Press California
The Weaver
Published by Sunstone Press
Only Magic

Humor: E-book and Trade
Conversations With the Golf God

Mystery Series: E-book and Trade
Bob Roosevelt Mystery Series – 4 novels

Contemporary Fiction: E-book and Trade
Hope
A Circle Around Forever

Trade and E-book
Published by Open Talon Press
Vent
Grammar Nazis Are Not Always Rite, Right, Write
Vent Revisited
The Lonely Cowboy
How Bridge McCoy Learned to Say I Love you
Short stories and poetry in literary journals, articles in outdoor magazines.
Reviews by Publishers Weekly, Best Sellers, Library Journal, and many others.

A Circle Around

Forever

Dedication:

For the Lost Ones

June 14, 1966

The tormented ghost of Bertha Adams observed the birth of her great grandson with selfish and evil anticipation. Barbara, the mother to be, the only person able to see the ghost, was overcome with both a sickening dread and a smothering sense of uselessness. She feared there was no creature either living or dead who possessed enough power to protect her child from the diabolical desires of her grandmother's ghost.

The baby did not cry upon his arrival into this life, instead his tiny lips erupted into one enormous smile. A nurse said, "How sweet."

The doctor said, "I'll be damn."

His mother yelled, "Grandmother Adams you get the hell out of here and leave this poor boy alone! He is not your salvation!"

Unable to see the ghost the doctor and nurses were shocked by her outburst.

The ghost floated over and patted the baby boy tenderly on the head. "You are the one who will finally give me the nothingness I seek," she said and then leered triumphantly at her granddaughter before disappearing.

For a brief moment an image of his great grandmother's hateful face engulfed the baby's mind and sad tears erupted from his eyes. It is a curse to be born into this world with a smile and then immediately realize others' intentions will shape your life – even if the intentions belong to a ghost.

And although only an infant the child knew he would never be able to love – his love for others would only bring pain and anguish.

Chapter One

SHANNON

For people who believe like the majority, life can be easy. People feel comfortable around those with the same ideas. It gives them a place in life and makes them feel appreciated. For those born with a gift that sets them apart from the majority, life, more often than not, is lonely. Their gifts are not appreciated, but maybe they are the fortunate ones. They are not ruled by the suffocating and self-centered rules of the majority.

****

As a baby there was always a whisper in the back of Shannon's mind that made him feel safe and protected. A whisper that told him things he could not understand, but even without understanding he sensed the whisper was guiding him in a direction he would be compelled to follow for his entire life.

Shannon also had the sensation there was something around him that was different from his whisper. Something that was deceitful and wanted to harm him, but although the feeling was uncomfortable he accepted it. He sensed there was no harm that could come to him as long as the whisper continued to protect him.

Since the day of his birth Shannon's mother, Barbara, worried desperately over him. She knew she could not confide in anyone. How could she tell people about the ghost of her grandmother that she knew needed her son for her evil desires?

People would think she was crazy – to most people ghosts are nothing but myths and superstitions.

****

Barbara was eight years old when her Grandmother Adams died. During the funeral Grandmother Adams spoke to Barbara from her grave. "One of your blood will be my redeemer. My vengeance is not yet finished. My destiny is not yet fulfilled," she threatened.

The words both frightened and confused Barbara. Was she really hearing her grandmother or was she only imagining things?

Walking away from the grave Barbara felt two hands grab her by the shoulders – turning in alarm there was nobody there. It was only the steady pull of her mother that made the hands release their grip. Barbara refrained from telling her parents. Her reasoning being they might scold her for making up such nonsense.

That night, alone in her room, Grandmother Adams' ghost appeared to Barbara. The ghost was light gray in color with a vague human form and reeked of evil and torment. Her hair erupted away from her head in no set pattern and moved menacingly like snakes. Within her gray form there were thousands of swirling black angry hornets waiting impatiently to be released and inject pain and anguish. What frightened Barbara the most were the ghost's eyes – the eyes were blank empty holes that seemed to devour all they witnessed. There were no other discernable features to the face – no mouth or ears or nose. The ghost's hands were so white it was as though they had never felt the warmth of the sun.

Seeing the ghost Barbara ran fearfully to the corner and covered her eyes with her hands. The ghost tore Barbara's hands from her eyes. "You cannot hide from me, do not ever try," she warned.

After scrutinizing Barbara for a few agonizing moments the ghost said. "Do not doubt me little one, you will have a son and your son will give me the nothingness I seek. If you try and fight my destiny I will destroy you and everything you hold dear. Do you understand?"

Unable to speak Barbara nodded her head. The ghost disappeared.

With deep agonizing dread Barbara realized beyond a doubt the ghost and her threats were real.

Two days later Grandmother Adams' ghost appeared once again to Barbara. The ghost's face, although without true form, was bitter and etched with hate. She pointed a foreboding finger at Barbara but did not speak. The silence filled Barbara's mind with fears she could not define or control. Once again she did not tell her parents.

As she grew older fear of the ghost never left Barbara. It was a fear she suffered alone.

The ghost did not appear again until Barbara was fourteen years old. The ghost gazed silently at Barbara as if she hated her and said nothing. By then Barbara knew about her grandmother's crime which only added to her fear.

When Barbara was sixteen she was walking home from her after school job as a checker at the local grocery store when Grandmother Adams' ghost appeared to her and repeated her threat. "You will have a son and your son will give me the nothingness I seek. If you try and fight my destiny I will destroy you and everything you hold dear."

Trying to be brave Barbara yelled at the ghost, "Leave me alone. You are nothing but a ghost and a ghost has no power over me or what will be mine."

"When the time comes you and all you love will suffer greatly if you do not do as I command," Grandmother Adams warned confidently before disappearing.

It was not until later in life Barbara came to understand the seriousness of her grandmother's threat.

****

Barbara had another troublesome and confusing worry

concerning Shannon. Being a single mother she could not remember sleeping with a man during the time frame necessary to coincide with Shannon's birth. How could it be possible? Was Shannon a god? Or worse, was he destined to be evil?

Despite Barbara's worries Shannon was a good baby, even though most of the time he was distant and remote, as if he was not a part of the world. Looking at him Barbara would say hopefully, "You will be a scholar. You are my little genius."

Six months after Shannon was born Barbara returned to her job as a waitress at a local bar and grill. She hired a babysitter to watch Shannon. Shannon did not fuss when Barbara cooed to him she would be back and she would miss him. He merely looked at her as though he already understood that the majority of one's life is spent doing things they do not want to do but must.

Besides being remote Shannon was not a vocal baby. He did not mumble and sputter bits and pieces of words while Barbara fed him or played with him. He seldom smiled or complained, but always looked serious as though everything he experienced had a deep meaning he must understand.

After two years, even with her coaching and prodding, Shannon still had not made any attempts at walking or speaking, which alarmed Barbara slightly, and she decided if there was no progress within a few months she would take him to a doctor.

Several months later, Shannon was in front of the living room window in their small apartment playing with a cardboard cylinder from a roll of toilet paper. It was a warm August day and the sun was shining brightly through the window. Barbara was reclining on the sofa wearing a light blouse and short pants – enjoying one of those rare moments in time when everything in life seems to be in order. Shannon was looking at her through the toilet paper tube. "Little sailor boy," she said. "How far is it to land?"

Shannon lowered the tube from his eye, looked directly through Barbara and said his first words, "Great Grandmother Adams you are not nice and I am too young to help you." Spinning around, but seeing no ghost, Barbara turned quickly back to Shannon who shrugged his shoulders and said simply, "She is gone but my friend is still here."

"Who is your friend?" Barbara asked both shaken and confused by Shannon's ability to speak in complete sentences and the fact he saw the ghost.

"I don't know. I only hear him in my mind but I know he is good," Shannon replied and resumed playing with the toilet paper tube like nothing unusual had happened.

My poor son, Barbara thought, what dire fate does life have in store for you?

The next week Shannon stood and walked without a teeter or wobble. Barbara worried more – the ghost's threat a constant echo in the back of her mind.

By four years old Shannon had a better vocabulary than most high school students although his voice still sounded like a child. He did not call his mother "Mother" or "Mom" or "Mommy." He explained to her gravely, "Barbara, I feel that I need a friend more than I need a mother."

When Shannon immediately saw the sadness in her eyes he added, "Friends are the most important things in life. They will not forsake you."

Barbara hugged and kissed Shannon and started crying. Shannon stood stoically until she stopped. Then he kissed her on the forehead as if he was sorry for something that he could not explain.

The way Shannon was Barbara knew she could never date or think about falling in love. There was no man that she could trust to know the truth about her son.

As Shannon grew Barbara stopped worrying if he was a god or destined to be evil – it made no difference – he was her son and she loved him no matter what. She did worry about Grandmother Adams' ghost and also about Shannon's sanity.

How could a child maintain a mind that was so advanced? It was as though he had been born with a vast store of knowledge that would take most people a lifetime to learn. She started to wish that he was a normal little boy who broke things, cried and needed attention, threw the trash on the floor, loved to get dirty and track dirt into the house. But Shannon was neat and meticulous. His hair was a deep yellow blond and he kept it combed perfectly. He brushed his teeth twice a day. He folded his own clothes, shined his shoes, left them by the bed each night, and made his bed each morning.

One day Barbara asked Shannon, "How can you possibly know all the words you do without reading any books?"

"It doesn't matter," he replied. "At times it all seems so illogical, but there must be logic to it. What used to be a whisper in my mind is now a voice and he tells me I am unique and not to fear."

"Who is your voice?" Barbara asked.

"I don't know, but I know it does not want to hurt me. Grandmother Adams wants to hurt me, but as long as I have the voice she cannot. The voice did tell me I will be his champion."

"A champion for what?" Barbara asked trying to conceal her dread.

"I do not know but I feel it is important," Shannon replied.

Barbara's worries deepened. What was this voice that Shannon heard? And she vowed if the voice was real and caused her son harm she would do all in her power to destroy it.

When Shannon was five years old, without being taught how to read, he started reading the encyclopedia. He exclaimed happily to Barbara one day when he was reading the D's. "This is refreshing. This is true knowledge not tainted by opinion."

When Shannon was on the G's he informed Barbara he wanted to read newspapers. Barbara started taking him to the library. Besides reading newspapers he read magazines. He would not read comics, or sports magazines, or men's magazines, or publications for women's fashions, saying, "They are all the same. They only try to pull people into vanity. There is already enough vanity." With that statement Barbara knew, to her great relief, that Shannon was not destined to be evil.

When Shannon was almost six years old Barbara received a letter from her mother stating emotionlessly they would like to see Shannon. Her parents were not overly religious, but they were moral in their own eyes, and had abandoned Barbara out of shame when she told them she was pregnant. Against her true feelings, but feeling it was necessary for Shannon to know his grandparents, Barbara wrote and informed them she would bring Shannon to visit.

During their first visit Shannon did not want to sit on his grandfather's lap, or hug his grandmother, or chase the dogs and cats, or want to play in the yard. He explored every inch of the old house that had been in his grandfather's family for three generations. He examined the photographs of distant relatives and breathed in the dust of the old house like the dust held secrets that only he could decipher. "You have given him the mark of Cain," Barbara's mother said thinking Shannon would not understand what she was saying.

"I have given him nothing but love," Barbara replied angrily.

Even with no true feeling for her parents Barbara took Shannon to visit two or three times a year.

After one visit Shannon informed Barbara, "They do not like me. Therefore I do not like or dislike them. There is no need trying to change the minds of people who cannot reason. It is their problem and not of my concern."

When the time came Barbara did not enroll Shannon in kindergarten – fearing how other children would react to how he was.

Life continued. Shannon read countless books on every subject imaginable. Barbara no longer was forced to serve beer and hamburgers and smile at drunks who thought their ideas would save the world. She got a job at Sears working in the dress department, and within three months she was the department manager. With the extra money they moved into a two-bedroom apartment in a nicer neighborhood.

Winter came and with each passing bleak day Barbara worried more. Soon Shannon would have to enroll in first grade. She feared he would be treated like a freak, or that he would mention the voice he heard, or the ghost, and the teachers would think he was crazy. She wished she could pack a few things and leave. They would explore the world and never have to stay in any place long enough Shannon would be forced to attend school. Life would take care of them and give them sanctuary. But Barbara knew there is no sanctuary on earth without money. Her worries became deeper.

It was early morning and still dark when Barbara was jarred from sleep feeling something was terribly wrong. The luminous hands on the bedside electric clock jabbed into her brain like a sharp dagger. Standing in the hall she saw light emitting from underneath Shannon's door. She apprehensively pushed the door open and peered into the room. Shannon was facing into a corner talking calmly to the ghost of his Grandmother Adams. "I do not know if I can help you or if I even should," he calmly explained.

Barbara could not hear the ghost's reply.

"My voice says I must have more understanding," Shannon said.

Barbara burst into the room screaming, "You old witch! Leave us alone! May your soul rot in hell!" The ghost, with a look of contempt on her face, smiled at Barbara and vanished.

Barbara frantically picked up Shannon, rushed to the living room, set him down and kneeled so she could look Shannon straight in the eyes. "You must ignore her, Shannon. You must not let her control you. She is evil. She was evil when she was alive and she is evil now. All she has ever known is hate and all she wants is hate."

Then Barbara told Shannon the history of his great grandmother. How she had killed her husband and died in the penitentiary. The times she appeared to Barbara informing her that Shannon would be her redeemer although she had no idea from what. "You must never do her bidding," Barbara beseeched him.

Shannon looked straight into Barbara's eyes and she could see his mind working to decipher the information. After a few moments he said seriously, "I think the ghost of Grandmother Adams also has a voice, but her voice is different than mine. In fact I feel the two voices are enemies."

Barbara did not know what to say. Then Shannon added, "You must buy me a Bible. My voice tells me I must read the Bible."

Slipping out of her grasp Shannon acted as if nothing had happened.

The next day Barbara bought Shannon a Bible. He read the Bible in five days during which time he was completely silent. When he was finished he said to Barbara, "Now I must read the Koran."

It took him seven days to read the Koran. Then over the next month he studied Buddhism, Taoism and all of the major religions. The day he was finished he stood by the window, looked outside, and his shoulders started shaking. His lower lip trembled and six years of heartfelt uncontrollable sobs erupted from his body.

Barbara was in the kitchen when she heard him crying. Hurrying into the living room she tried to pick him up and hold him but he pushed her away gently stating, "You must not touch me. It is my burden and my burden alone."

Sitting on the sofa Barbara watched her son weep. A chilling loneliness settled in her bones although tears refused to form in her eyes. The sadness was entrenched so deeply into her heart tears could not reach it.

Shannon wept for thirty minutes. He held his arms stiffly by his sides, with his hands tightened into fists, and made no attempt to wipe the tears away. Then, as suddenly as he had started, he stopped crying and wiped his face with both hands. He took two deep breaths, exhaled loudly, and turning from the window he walked resolutely over to Barbara. His face was flushed and his eyes were filled with confusion.

Barbara wanted to tell him everything would be all right but she said, "I will take your pain. Please give me your pain. I will bear your cross and suffer all your misgivings."

Shannon replied sadly, "There is nothing you can do. There is nothing I can do."

"Oh Shannon," Barbara murmured heartbroken. "I am so sorry for you."

Mother and son embraced. To Barbara his arms felt like steel bands that although strong and tenacious would one day snap from their burden. Shannon rested his head wearily on Barbara's shoulder and, for the first time calling her "mother," he said in a far away voice, "Mother there is no redemption. History is only a continuing folly. I fear there is no hope. And even though your mother said I have the mark of Cain I know we all have the mark of Cain."

"No! No!" Barbara pleaded. "Do not believe what you say."

"Life is saved only through death," Shannon continued. "Great Grandmother Adams needs me to become like her, unfeeling and filled with hate, then and only then will she find what she seeks."

Barbara held desperately to her son.

"Please do not worry, it is fine. My voice is my friend and also yours. He wants me to tell you to have faith," Shannon said.

"Faith in what?" Barbara asked.

"I do not know," Shannon replied.

Then, stepping away from Barbara, Shannon said, "My love will only bring pain and sadness to those around me."

"Oh Shannon! That cannot be true!" Barbara said, forcing herself not to cry.

"No Barbara. It is true and I am sorry," Shannon said.

"What can I do to help?" Barbara asked feeling useless.

"There is nothing. At times I think my life is only a dream and I have done all of this before. It is like I have known you before, but with many different names, in many different places, and many different times."

That night in bed a deep loneliness entered Shannon – a loneliness he knew he would carry with him throughout his entire life. He wanted to get out of bed and go tell Barbara he loved her but he knew he must not. The loneliness grew stronger.

Chapter Two

BERTHA

The ghost of Bertha Adams sought relief from her endless existence. She wanted no memory of her life. No memory after her death. She longed to be nothing. She wished to be as devoid of thought and feeling as the darkness between the stars. Her voice told her what she must do to have her wish fulfilled. Once again she must kill.

****

Bertha Cartwright was born on January 4, 1900 in Promise City, Iowa, a town with 285 people. The originators of the town had migrated from Virginia in hopes of becoming a world unto themselves. But even with the name Promise City they could not stop the world around them – discovering too late that isolationism is not a defense and God does not always take care of his followers. As a man said to his wife years later when they were leaving Promise City after losing everything, "Maybe we believed in the wrong God."

When Ruth Cartwright discovered she was pregnant she told her husband, who was a Lutheran Minister, "Reno this fourth child will kill me. I know it as well as I know you love me."

"Now Ruth dear," Reno said. "After three sons we will have a daughter and she will be like the first flowers of spring."

Ruth started her pregnancy as a robust woman weighing one hundred and fifty pounds with a creamy complexion, bright rosy eyes, and long rich black hair. After being in bed for five months Ruth was down to little more than a hundred

12

pounds. Her stomach was so swollen she could barely move. Excruciating pain radiated through every cell in her body. Her once lustrous black hair was now dull charcoal in color and streaked with white. When one of the two ladies Reno had hired to take care of Ruth would brush her hair it would fall out in handfuls. Her hair became so thin her scalp shone through like ancient parchment paper.

Ruth would cry out when no one was around, "I can endure no more. Please God. What have I done to deserve your scorn?"

Reno could do nothing but observe and give what condolences he could. He kneeled at night and begged God to stop his wife's suffering. He offered his soul, his life, his tears, anything for God's blessing. He would leave all he loved behind and go out into the wilderness and bring God to the heathens if only God would stop his wife's misery.

But God refused to listen and the pain only grew worse. But one day his prayers were answered and the pain stopped. The women were all happy. Ruth could hold down small amounts of food and her creamy complexion returned. Reno rejoiced with the confirmation of his faith. Two weeks later the child inside of Ruth began kicking with its feet and hitting with its hands. The thrashings were not little bumps of love but vicious blows – their only intent pain and suffering.

The malicious kicking never ceased. It became so severe that the bruises on the inside of Ruth worked their way through her skin to become dark blotches of hate-filled dried blood on her flesh. With the bruises Ruth started having terrible dreams. In one dream Ruth saw her baby as a grown woman standing in the center of a barren room with blood streaming from her hands – a river of blood that never stopped, so red it resembled fire. Her daughter was chanting, "That will teach you not to love. That will teach you not to love."

Waking up Ruth screamed, "You will not be born!! I will your death!! You must not live!! You must not!!"

Running into the room Reno held his sobbing wife. "Kill

me and the baby," she begged. "We have created a curse. Please. For all that is good. Kill me."

"Now, now. It will be all right. We must trust in the Lord," Reno soothed while tenderly stroking her feverish brow.

"I trust in no God!" Ruth sobbed hysterically before passing out.

Reno was appalled by Ruth's outburst and prayed for his wife's eternal soul. He also begged God's forgiveness for her breach of faith during one of God's tests.

After seven and a half months of almost continual pain Ruth was down to eighty pounds and she lay closer to death than life. It was as though she was being tortured, but the torturer wanted her to feel every pain imaginable, and keep her on the brink of death as long as he could until not even death would stop the pain.

The ladies now kept constant vigil over Ruth. They kept the curtains open to let in light and hope but it was no use. Even with the light the room reeked of gloom.

Ruth's three sons Andrew, who was seven, Thomas, who was six, and Paul, who was five were not allowed in the room. They did not worry about their mother. They believed like their father that God was good and just and their mother was good, therefore everything would be fine. The boys attended school, played, did their chores and life continued. The ladies cooked for them so they were full and warm. What more could be asked from life?

During Ruth's eighth month of pregnancy, as the sun was rising, Ruth bolted straight up in bed and screamed terribly. The baby gushed out of her in a torrent of blood screaming as horribly as her mother. The two women were terrified. As the next scream gurgled from Ruth's lips she fell back dead on the pillow – her face twisted into a hideous grimace.

The two women quickly heated water, cut the umbilical cord, washed the baby and wrapped her in warm towels. Through it all, the baby continued screaming at the top of her lungs. The ladies had no idea that already the baby heard a voice – a voice that only desired its own cravings. "You will be my champion of champions. Through you I will finally defeat my enemy," the voice said.

One of the women hurried to the church and informed Reno of his wife's death. Reno broke into tears and fell to his knees in prayer. The woman then rushed to the store and purchased a pint of goat's milk. Back at the house she warmed the milk, put it in a bottle and tried to feed the baby who, still screaming, refused the nipple.

The baby cried all day. She turned blue at times and still refused the goat's milk. That evening when the child had nursed a little, and was finally sleeping, one of the women said, "Poor little thing. What a wretched way to start a life."

The other lady looked at the sleeping baby and shook her head. "She is the ugliest baby I have ever seen. I pray she receives a precious amount of love."

Two days later Reno informed the two ladies, despite their protests, that they should go home. As soon as they departed he trudged to the baby's room. Standing over the sleeping form his heart was not filled with love – only remorse and sadness. Picking up the child Reno examined her face intently. He looked for any resemblance to his wife, but he could not see either her or himself. Laying the baby back down he said scornfully, "You are not from God," and walked out of the room as the baby awakened and once again resumed screaming.

In his study Reno sat down heavily in his chair. He opened his Bible but closed it. He gazed at the wall and imagined the depths of hell.

The three boys were in their beds trying to ignore the cries. Each boy blamed the crying baby for their mother's death and their minds filled with questions. Did God want one of them to be the instrument of His wrath? Would they only find grace once again by taking vengeance upon their sister?

Early the next morning a widow lady, Mrs. Rebecca Johnston, having heard about the baby and Reno sending the ladies home, knocked on Reno's door. She could hear the baby sobbing in the background. Rebecca was a large boned and stocky woman of Swedish descent who was not afraid of any man or beast. She believed life was a battle that must be fought with resolution and strength. God's job was not to help those in need, He helped those who worked and anybody who was lazy had no comprehension of the world. Rebecca's husband had been a farmer and they were unable to have children. He was strangled to death while plowing a cornfield when his team of mules was stung by bumblebees. They bolted and he was caught around the neck by the reins. Rebecca sold the farm and now did mending and laundry, cleaned other people's homes and canned on the split. She also made the best watermelon and gooseberry wine in the county. She sold it for a dollar a gallon – keeping at least two gallons from every batch for her nightly nip. Rebecca spoke to Reverend Reno Cartwright in her usual straightforward manner, "I have come for the baby. I know of a wet nurse. You and your sons would not be fit for a baby daughter. What have you named her?"

"I have not named her," Reno answered feeling no guilt.

"Then her name will be Bertha for my sister who died at birth. Bertha can carry your last name. I will expect you to give me ten dollars a month for her keep and for you to visit as often as you can." Reno nodded his head and Rebecca swept by him to get the baby. "You poor, poor thing," Rebecca cooed as she picked up Bertha who immediately stopped crying.

As Rebecca left she shook hands with Reno and said, "I am sorry for the death of your wife. But time will heal. Do not forsake your convictions out of pity for yourself. Do not, for all the good in you, blame this child."

Reno did not watch Rebecca leave. He was overcome with the burden knowing he could never forgive his daughter.

When Rebecca got home she emptied a drawer from her chest-of-drawers and made a bed for Bertha. Laying the baby in the drawer she examined the child. Bertha had piercing blue green eyes and her little mouth was twisted and uneven. Her hair was thick and black and her face was wrinkled like she was already old. Rebecca felt odd looking at the baby. It was not fear or apprehension – it was something in between, but it was not good and made her feel uneasy. Rebecca tucked the blanket tightly under Bertha's chin and hurried to get the wet nurse.

Mary's own baby was only two months old but she had enough milk for three children. Mary was 19 years old with long blond hair, mirth-filled blue eyes and breasts that were made for babies. When Mary opened her blouse and touched Bertha's lips with her large and generous nipple Bertha began sucking deeply and a small sigh swept through her body. Mary and Rebecca both smiled.

The day of Ruth's funeral it was ten degrees below zero. The gravediggers had to build a huge bonfire to melt the frozen ground so they could dig the hole. A stiff steady wind blew from the north kicking up snow and ice. The people stood around the grave bundled up in coats and scarves. All that could be seen were eyes filled with frozen tears. On Ruth's headstone was carved: **MOTHER OF THREE – LOVED BY HER HUSBAND – MAKE READY OUR HOME IN HEAVEN.**

Reverend Cartwright stood stoic and upright with his Bible in his hand. The three boys were crying, unashamed of their tears. Rebecca saw no need to take Bertha to the funeral.

Later in life, reading the headstone, Bertha would feel no remorse or guilt over those she murdered.

Chapter Three

BARBARA

Why is it that the lonely need love more than others but are usually ignored?

****

When Barbara was born on March 2, 1944 in Kirksville, Missouri her oldest brother had recently been killed in the Pacific. Her father, already a drinker, started drinking more and her mother and father grew silent with each other and with their children. The older children, for a reason she never understood, ignored Barbara as if she was invisible and had no merit.

By the time Barbara was seven her three brothers and two sisters had left home – more than happy to leave the poverty and neglect behind. Barbara never heard from any of her brothers or sisters again.

What little scraps of attention Barbara received from her parents she cherished, but they did nothing to ease the aching loneliness she always felt or quell her deep longing to feel loved. She dreamed about having a father who would hold her and talk to her and a mother who would brush her hair and teach her how to cook.

Despite being mostly ignored Barbara always tried her best to please her parents. She studied hard in school and wanted to be the first person in her family to go to college, but she knew she could only attend college if she got a scholarship. Even though she studied hard she hated going to school. Her dresses were worn, her shoes second hand and most of the students shied away from her or made fun of her. Though it hurt Barbara deeply she refused to retaliate with words or actions. She held her pain inside and kept her dream of college burning in her mind like a lovely dancing candle flame.

Barbara was eight years old when, by accident, she discovered she had a Grandmother Adams who was in the state penitentiary. Barbara's father's parents died before she was born and no word had ever been spoken about her mother's parents. Barbara was home from school with a bad cough and a sore throat. Her mother was cooking at a truck stop and her father, who could never hold a job for long because of his need for gin, was working at a gas station. The mailman delivered a letter for her mother. The return address was a woman's name, Bertha Adams, followed by a long number and, Missouri State Penitentiary for Women.

Feeling guilty, but also excited, Barbara took the letter to her room. After shutting the door and closing the curtains she opened the letter. The letter was difficult to read. The writing was course and uneven as if the writer's fingers were half frozen.

Dear Daughter:
For all of these years you have never returned one of my letters nor come to visit me in my time of need and distress. Even so I am still your mother and I would have thought that no matter my deeds you would have come out of the generosity of your heart. I am writing to tell you that my years have been filled with anguish and plight. I hope this gives you good feelings. I have been told that I will die within the next few months. Cancer has filled my body. I do wish to tell you that what I did I would do again. I trust your life has been as wretched as mine. You always reminded me of myself and you stole my love. Let me hope I find nothingness in death.
Your mother, Bertha Adams

Barbara was not appalled by the letter. She found it

exciting and glamorous that her grandmother was in the penitentiary and wondered what mysterious crime she had committed. Did she kill her cheating husband in a moment of rage? Did she embezzle money from a rich lover? Did she rob banks with a dashing gunman

Barbara hid the letter under her mattress. She read it late at night and romanticized her grandmother's adventures. The letter was a cherished ring in a lonely jewelry box.

Several weeks later, when Barbara came home from school, Anna, her mother, was in the living room. Her mother jumped up with the letter in her hand and slapped Barbara across the face so hard Barbara saw stars. "How dare you read my letters?" her mother chastised and slapped Barbara again.

Barbara's mother had never struck her. She fell to the floor both in fear and astonishment.

"Your grandmother is evil. You have no business knowing about her. Why do you think I have never mentioned my mother?" Anna hollered.

Then Anna started crying and fell back onto the sofa as if life had finally broken her completely.

"I'm sorry Mommy," Barbara whimpered. "I'm so sorry. I did not mean to make you angry."

Anna cried softly as if there were not enough tears in the universe to rid her of her sadness. Wiping her eyes with her dress Anna said, "Come here. Come sit by me, dear. I should have told you the story of your grandmother before. It is not your fault."

Barbara sat timidly by her mother who put her arm around her. "It is time you knew. You should not be kept from the truth forever."

Barbara felt nervous and apprehensive.

"My father's name was John Adams. He was a very good man," Anna began. "Before he married my mother he was in the Navy. He visited Japan and China. He had been to Scotland and England. He had a great sea serpent with a bright red forked tongue tattooed on his left forearm. He told me it was his guardian and that it had kept him alive during the war. How he got to Corydon, Iowa I do not know. He opened a combination dry goods and grocery store in Corydon and soon had a thriving business. He was friendly with people and never cheated a person when they traded. He also knew who he could give credit to and who he couldn't. He met my mother after she ran away from Promise City."

Barbara was no longer nervous or apprehensive. She was entranced. Her mother had never told her stories.

"I wish to God or the Devil he had never met my mother," Anna said bitterly. "My father had to have known why mother ran away from Promise City, but I suppose his feelings for my mother made his mind lie to him. I did not know for many years why she ran away. It was years after the tragedy before I went back and asked questions."

Barbara's mother looked out the window focusing on nothing. When she started speaking again her voice was low and distant – her words thorns that stabbed without mercy into her heart.

"My mother never liked me. Maybe that is why I have never been a good mother. I loved all of you children but I was never able to show it. Maybe I have been afraid to rid myself of my own pain by not showing feelings for others. I have kept myself shut up tighter than a cupboard, but it was not right for you children or me. It was not good for your father either. He was not always a drunk, but when a wife no longer seems to care what must a man do?" Anna sighed deeply and shuddered before continuing. "My mother used to beat me for no reason. Everything had to be perfect. If I did not brush my hair right she would go into a rage and tell me I was not worthy of her. If I got dirt on my dress she would make me sit in my room for hours. But it was not so much her scolding that bothered me. It was the way she treated my father. She screamed at him all the time for no good reason. My poor father would only look sadly at her and refuse to argue back. There were times my mother would lay in bed for days with the curtains closed and she would not allow anybody in to see her. My father would sit in his chair and I could feel his sadness. As I grew older my father became a mere shell of a man. Dark circles were under his eyes and he seldom smiled. My mother had sucked all the energy out of him. He grew listless and uncaring. He left the store rundown and he began to stay away from home. But who could blame him? I would lay in bed and day dream that my mother was happy. My parents would dance in the living room and have parties where people laughed and joked. I also dreamt the three of us would go on picnics and my mother would hold my hand and tell me what a good girl I was. But it never came to pass. Now I see I have done the same thing with my children. I shut you all out and made you experience the same feelings I had as a young girl. I have been very selfish."

"I love you mother," Barbara said.

Her mother smiled but did not tell Barbara she loved her before she started speaking again. "I was twelve years old when it happened. I came home from school and my mother had destroyed the house. She had cut the pillows open with a knife, ripped the curtains from the window and smashed all the mirrors. She was standing in the kitchen screaming hysterically, "I am ugly! I am ugly!" over and over again. She was tearing her hair out with her left hand and throwing it on the floor. She had a butcher knife in her right hand and she ordered me to go get my father or she would kill herself. As I ran to the store I wished my mother would kill herself. My father and I could go on with our lives. We could go on walks. He would smile and tell me he loved me more than anything else in the world. My father told me to stay at the store and he hurried home. I waited and waited, wishing my mother was dead. After several hours I started to worry and when it was almost dark I ran home. There was a crowd of people in the front yard talking in hushed voices and milling around nervously. I tried to run through them but a neighbor lady grabbed my arm. No matter how hard I struggled she would not let go of me. I can remember in detail all of the peoples' faces in the crowd. They were all deeply grieved and confused. They looked at me sadly but they did not know what to say. The lady who was holding me loosened her grip and I broke free and ran into the house. As soon as I dashed through the door my life was shattered forever. My father was lying on the floor in a pool of blood with a butcher knife sticking out of his chest. His eyes gazed emptily at the ceiling and his face was the color of flour. My mother was sitting in a chair with a policeman on either side of her. She was smiling bigger than I had ever seen her smile. She said calmly to me, 'See what you have made me do. It is your fault. Without you your father would have always loved me. I hate you.' And then I was carried away."

"Oh mother," Barbara said. "I am so sorry."

"I stayed at a friend's house until after the funeral. My father was buried on a beautiful day and all of the town's people attended. My mother's brother had no desire to raise me and my father had no living relatives. I was sent to the Kresh Orphanage in Omaha, Nebraska. One day the head mistress called me in and told me in a soft and caring voice that my mother had been sentenced to life without parole in the penitentiary. I felt nothing, but it took me many years to push the sight of my dead father out of my mind."

Feeling devastated and sad for her mother Barbara buried her head into her mother's side and started crying.

"Now, now little one," her mother said and hugged her. "I know for a fact tears do us no good. They are merely the torment of an uncaring god."

Barbara sat with her mother until her father came home from work. He was drunk as usual. Her mother, without saying hello to him, stopped her story and went to make dinner.

The family resumed its normal existence with little talk and little show of emotion. Barbara did not forget her mother's confession and played it over and over in her mind. The talk had aged her. Her second hand clothes and the taunts of the other children at school no longer bothered her. Life was how it was, and no matter what, things could always be worse.

Two months later her mother came to Barbara's room as she was doing her homework and said simply, "Your grandmother is dead. We will go to the funeral," and she shut the door quietly.

Bertha Adams was buried in Promise City next to her mother and father and two brothers who had died when they were young. Most of the houses in town were abandoned. Those lived in were worn and run down. All of the stores had closed years earlier. The cemetery was overflowing with weeds. Barbara and her parents were the only ones at the cemetery – standing emotionless during the service. After the preacher had gone, Barbara's mother said to the grave, "Despite all your hate, I hope you find rest, but I can never forgive you."

Only Barbara heard a voice coming from Bertha's grave, and although she did not understand, the words made her deathly afraid. The grandmother she never knew said to her, "One of your blood will be my redeemer. My vengeance is not done."

"Are you okay? You look like you have seen a ghost," her mother questioned.

Barbara nodded her head. She was too confused and frightened to answer, but as she walked toward the car Barbara could feel invisible hands on her shoulders that were trying to pull her towards the grave.

Bertha Adams' gravestone read: **FORGOTTEN DAUGHTER OF RUTH AND RENO MAY GOD FORGIVE YOU YOUR SINS**

Chapter Four

SHANNON

We all believe we have free will, but in all truth there is no free will. Maybe what we have is free thought. But thoughts are really nothing. They do not embrace you and they are as fleeting as dreams.

****

Barbara was so nervous her stomach had been upset for three days. Tomorrow Shannon would start first grade. She had been trying her best to tutor Shannon for the role he must play if he was to make school a success. "You will have to act just like the other kids, Shannon. We know you are smarter than they are but they must not know that. You cannot tell anyone about your voice or the ghost of your great grandmother."

"Please do not worry. The voice is my guide," Shannon replied calmly.

"But what is your voice? Has he ever told you?"

"I do not know. But I do know he has deep feelings for you."

Barbara did not ask him how he knew, but she did know the voice was real, and unlike earlier when she thought the voice would harm Shannon, she now felt the voice's intentions were good.

That evening Barbara was in the living room reading when Shannon came in from his room. Shannon reminded Barbara of a one-hundred-year-old man whose mind was weary from too much knowledge, "Are you ready for school?"

she asked.

"I think it will be boring but I know it is something I must do," Shannon said. "I feel the children will make fun of me and taunt me but I cannot expect more from them. They do not really know what they do. I will not let it bother me. One day I will no longer have to go to school. I will be a man before I know it and my childhood days will be a memory that I can learn from."

"Come and kiss me goodnight," Barbara said.

Back in his room Shannon pulled various objects out from underneath his bed and closely examined them. Several weeks earlier, guided by the voice, he started picking up different things from outside and hiding them secretly under his bed. He now had a collection of small rocks that were many different colors. He had saved twigs from trees, pieces of birds' nests, pinches of different types of dirt and sand that he wrapped in newspaper. He had dried snail shells, dragonfly wings, dead ants, and other various bugs, and leaves from grasses and weeds.

One night while Barbara was sleeping his voice said to him. "You have basic knowledge. Now you must understand the earth."

Shannon took a gray rock from underneath his bed and stood by the window. He squeezed the rock and a great emptiness and longing swept through him. The emptiness was so intense it almost caused him to fall down. Without thinking he put the rock in his mouth. As the rock touched his tongue the emptiness left and was replaced by calm. The rock tasted like rain and hope and rejuvenation. It rolled in his mouth like a dream.

Shannon whispered, "I understand."

After the experience each night he would hold and feel the secrets of a different object. By putting it in his mouth he could absorb its knowledge. From the dragonfly wing he felt freedom and the rush of air from flying that was so intense he thought, for a moment, his feet had come off the ground. From a blade of grass he felt serenity and a slow methodical will to please and make other creatures happy. With each of the objects there was also an undertone that something was not right, but there was nothing that could be done about it.

Tonight he waited for over thirty minutes until he heard only the normal creaks of the house and he was sure Barbara was sleeping. Quietly getting out of bed he took a newspaper wrapped pinch of dirt from underneath the bed. Standing by the window he put a tiny portion of the dirt in his mouth. He was instantly consumed with a pulsating fear that made his heart beat frantically. The room started spinning so fast he could not see anything but a rushing colorless blur and he started breathlessly falling down a twisting tunnel that for some frightening reason he felt would end with oblivion. There would be no memory of trees, no memory of birds, no memory of fish. No memory of rocks or oceans. No memory of mankind. Everything that had ever been would be gone forever.

Shannon wanted to scream. "Stop! Stop! We are on the wrong course!" But he had no voice. Shannon stopped falling and he started trembling. Impulsively he stuffed the remaining dirt into his mouth and chewed furiously. The trembling was replaced with the emptiness of a cave so deep and dark not even bats would enter, only snakes and scorpions and blind creatures that did not long for the light. They were afraid of the light, afraid of their own treachery. They were the curse not the redemption.

Shannon's Great Grandmother Adams' ghost appeared. Her form was dark and the hornets within her were in a wild frenzy. Her face was twisted in pain and hate. It seemed as though the pain and hate were in a battle to control her. "You are my salvation," she whispered and grabbed Shannon's trembling hands. "Come with me. I must make you like me."

"No, no!" Shannon pleaded.

But he could not free his hands from her clutches. "You must save me. You must," the ghost screeched and pulled harder. Her grasp was tight and unrelenting and caused Shannon to writhe in pain.

"No! No! Please," Shannon pleaded again. "I must have time. I must. There is much to do."

But the ghost continued pulling. Shannon's energy began waning, and he started feeling weak as the will of his great grandmother filled his mind with swirling dark clouds of hate, mistrust, and a loneliness that was so intense Shannon could only sob and feebly beg, "No! No!"

The door burst open and the light flashed on. "Get away! Get away from my son!" Barbara yelled. "Get away!! Get away!! You will not take him!! Get away you foul creature!!"

Barbara's flaying fists penetrated the mist of the ghost and even though there was no feeling of flesh or resistance the ghost released her grip on Shannon and disappeared.

Shannon collapsed. His breathing was forced and raspy. His eyes were pinched tightly shut like they never again wanted to see light. Barbara fell to her knees, cradled his head in her lap, and saw the dirt circling his mouth. She started rocking him like he was a baby. "She will never win. I will not let her win," she vowed.

Slowly Shannon's breathing returned to normal and his eyelids fluttered and opened. Looking up at his mother he smiled in relief. Barbara helped him to his feet and led him to the bathroom. She ran warm water on a washcloth, wiped the dirt from his mouth, led him back to his room, and tucked him into bed. It was not until then that she asked him, "Why are you eating dirt, Shannon?"

"My voice told me I must know about the earth," he said.

"But what did you learn?"

"I know that although the earth is full of hope she is lonely and crying out for help."

Barbara kissed him on the forehead. "Do not fear little one," she said trying not to show her own fear.

"Barbara, it is deeper than fear," he whispered. "I will be in a war, and although it grieves me, I fear there is nothing my voice or I can do about it."

"What will the war be over?" Barbara asked with despair.

"I don't know."

"You must ignore your voice, Shannon."

"I cannot."

Looking up she demanded of the voice. ""Who or what are you? Talk to me. I am not a child."

But there was no reply.

Barbara left the door open to Shannon's room. She turned the kitchen light on so she could see Shannon's door from the sofa. But, even in her vigil, she knew she could not protect Shannon forever.

The next morning Barbara took Shannon to the first day of school. Mothers were consoling crying children, other children were running around and playing, two boys were wrestling by the swing set, one little girl had her thumb in her mouth. Teachers were wondering which of the new group would be in their class. Barbara and Shannon got out of the car and Barbara started walking with him toward the school. "You must not come with me," he told her. "You cannot protect me from life."

Barbara hugged him. Shannon wiggled free and headed towards the school. Stopping several yards away Shannon turned. Barbara smiled. Not returning her smile he snapped to attention, saluted her like a soldier, did an about face, and marched resolutely toward the school.

Neither of them saw Great Grandmother Adams' ghost in the top of a tall tree by the playground with a gloating smile on her bitter face.

Chapter Five

BERTHA

There is a saying that there is no vengeance after fifteen minutes. But maybe vengeance is better when it takes years to accomplish. When the person upon whom its wrath falls has forgotten their crime and they suffer not knowing why they are being punished. What sweeter vengeance?

****

For the first five years of her life Bertha knew nothing of her mother's death and did not question not having a father. Rebecca was good to her and their time together was enjoyable and without incident, although there were times that Bertha was inexplicably lonely.

Then life started to unravel. It was spring. Rebecca had put the blankets on the clothes' line to air out while she cleaned the house. Bertha was playing in the front yard with her doll Naomi. Naomi was a beautiful doll with long golden hair, a complexion like fresh cream and shiny blue glass eyes. Her lips were raspberry red and turned up into a perpetual smile. Rebecca had sewn several colorful dresses for Naomi, fancy slips and three pairs of different colored felt shoes. Bertha dreamed every night that one day she would wake up and be as beautiful as her doll. Her face would not be wide and flat. Her hair would not be thin and a muddy brown. Her dark eyes would be blue and sparkling. She would not be chunky with large protruding bones and crooked teeth. A voice in her mind told her no one would ever love her because she would always be ugly, but Bertha was still too young to know the voice was real and had merit.

Bertha was changing Naomi's dress when three older boys she had never met stopped at the white picket fence that enclosed the front yard. They all picked up rocks. "You are the reason our mother is dead," a tall bony boy with pimples all over his face shouted.

"You are evil," another boy said with so much venom in his voice the words made Bertha cringe.

The smallest boy hollered, "I will kill you! You witch!" and threw a rock that hit Bertha painfully on the leg.

The other boys started throwing rocks. Bertha was terrified but she did not run. Instead she curled up in a ball with Naomi under her. The rocks pelted her and she started to cry – not so much from the pain but because she could not understand why the boys did not like her. She had done nothing to them. "This is what life will always be for you," a voice in her mind said. "You are born for me. Come to me. We will give each other what we need and no one will ever harm you."

Rebecca ran angrily out of the house with a broom in her hand. The boys did not see her coming until it was too late. She struck the oldest boy in the face so hard the broom handle broke. She hit one of the other boys in the back with the handle. Both boys yelped in pain and all three ran off. "I will tell your father!" Rebecca threatened.

Rebecca took Bertha into the house and washed the cuts from the rocks. Bertha, sobbing, told Rebecca about the terrible things the boys had said. "You play with Naomi until I get back. Do not go outside and don't answer the door or let anybody in the house," Rebecca ordered and rushed out of the house in a great huff. Bertha had never seen her so angry, but she had no idea where she was going.

Bertha brushed Naomi's hair. "Those boys were trying to hurt me not you," she consoled. "Don't be worried. I will get them back," she vowed. It was the first time in her life she felt a tinge of hate and the need for vengeance.

"I will help you with your vengeance," a voice whispered in her mind.

Rebecca stormed to the church. Reverend Cartwright was in his office working on his sermon for the coming Sunday. Rebecca barged in and pointed her finger at Reverend Cartwright accusingly. "It is bad enough that for the first five years of your daughter's life you have not taken the time to come and visit her at least once. Now, today your boys have thrown rocks at Bertha and threatened her. How can you call yourself a man of God when you have no compassion? I have not once come to your house begging you to take on at least a few of a father's duties. Now I am ashamed for not doing so. Bertha is a nice little girl, but she is lonely, and does not know why. But I know why she is lonely. There is a piece missing from her heart – a piece that you, in your selfishness, keep from her. Damn your soul and your heart for your self pity!" Rebecca was so angry she was trembling.

Reverend Cartwright tried to speak but Rebecca cut him off. "If your boys ever again taunt Bertha or in any way try to harm her I will hold you accountable." With that she turned and stomped out of the office.

Reverend Cartwright looked out the window, but did not see the budding maple trees or the pin oaks still covered with last year's brown leaves. He did not see the freshly sprouted green grass, the red peonies blooming, or the last of the red and yellow tulips that lined the walkway to the church. All he could see was his wife's worn and haggard face as she pleaded for her own death and the death of her baby. "My soul may rot in Hell," Reverend Cartwright said bitterly, "but I cannot love the child." He resumed writing his sermon pretending Rebecca had never interrupted him.

That evening he gathered Andrew, Thomas, and Paul, in the living room. "You know you have done wrong," he admonished them before making the boys bend over. He whipped them with his belt until they cried. "You will have nothing to do with your sister," he ordered when the whippings were over.

The boys sat on the porch drying their tears and mending their pride. "I will see that Bertha pays for this," Andrew, the oldest, swore. "Now she has even caused our own father to turn against us."

"We will have to make a plan against Bertha, one that father will not find out," Thomas said.

Paul, the youngest, said nothing, but his mind was burning with ideas about what he would do to Bertha.

Chapter Six

BARBARA

Duty binds people into nations. Duty has to be followed. Without it there is no pride. So say the leaders of all nations even though they no longer lead their soldiers into battle. Where is their pride? Where is their realization of duty? Does it hide behind a user's mask? Are our leaders so old and weak they cower behind the folly of their words?

****

Barbara's heart felt like it was being squeezed in a vice as she watched Shannon walk like a little soldier into the school. He had saluted her. He knew school was his duty and it was something he would have to endure, but there would be no happiness in it. Barbara knew her son had never really known happiness. One born like Shannon would probably never find it. Driving away from the school Barbara prayed he would not have to live his life burdened by duty. "My poor, poor child," she murmured.

Barbara called in sick for work and lay on the sofa. She had not slept well in months. As she shut her eyes her thoughts drifted back in time. "I wish I would have gone on to college," she said. "Maybe then Shannon would have never been born."

When Barbara was eighteen, high school was almost unbearable. Her mother and father barely talked. Her father came home drunk almost every evening. Her mother would serve dinner and then go to her room to read. Her father would fall asleep on the sofa with the television on. Barbara would go to her room to study but it was difficult to concentrate. She felt alone and helpless, and she knew that because her grades were not good enough to get a scholarship she would never have enough money to go to college. All the other girls were dating. Even the plain ones had boyfriends, but nobody would ask her out even though she was not ugly. In fact she was cute and well developed, but the boys shied away. At times she thought the ghost of Grandmother Adams somehow frightened them away.

Although the ghost had not appeared to Barbara since she was sixteen her fear concerning the ghost became more intense. She now fully understood the ghost's threats. "Please leave me alone?" she pleaded at times.

One Saturday morning Barbara and her mother were in the backyard when Barbara noticed how worn and frail her mother looked. Barbara was overcome with a deep sadness as she realized that her mother's life had been joyless. None of her brothers and sisters wrote home or visited or even sent cards at Christmas. Barbara hugged her mother. For a mere instant her mother's eyes sparkled and she smiled but the smile quickly vanished.

"I have to tell you something," Barbara said apprehensively.

"You're not in trouble at school are you?" her mother asked.

"No. Something is bothering me that I should have told you years ago but I have been afraid."

"Well tell me child," her mother said impatiently.

Barbara was hesitant. Her mother might think she was crazy but she finally confessed, "I have seen the ghost of Grandmother Adams many times."

"Oh child!" Anna gasped.

There was a weathered picnic table in the corner of the yard. Anna grabbed Barbara's hand and pulled her quickly toward the table. "You must tell me everything," she said in a high pitched and nervous voice. "You should have told me sooner."

They sat opposite each other at the table and her mother's eyes beseeched Barbara.

"Grandmother Adams spoke to me from her grave," Barbara said. "She appeared to me that night and said to me 'You will have a son and your son will give me the nothingness I seek. If you try and fight my destiny I will destroy you and everything you hold dear.' She has appeared to me several times since but not for several years. Now I feel that she is watching me all the time, waiting. I also think that somehow she keeps boys from asking me out."

Anna was silent for a long time. "I have seen the ghost of my mother," she finally confessed. "She came to me five minutes after she died in prison. She was filled with rage and she cursed me for stealing the love of my father from her. She vowed she would destroy all that I loved, that someone of my blood line would be her redemption, and that I would die in as much misery as she did. But I met her rage with my own. I returned her hate. 'You destroyed me when you killed my father,' I confronted her. 'I have no heart left, no desire for life. I live out my days waiting for the end and when it comes I will embrace it.' I admonished her for all she had done and I told her I knew of her secret. Besides killing my father I know she murdered two of her brothers even though I cannot prove it. Then her rage and anger grew in such intensity her image began to twist and whirl until there was no shape or form. I could hear her voice as she disappeared in a torrent of wind. 'Remember my words. I will destroy all that you love.'"

"Have you seen her again?" Barbara asked, both terrified and relieved her mother had also seen the ghost.

"No. But I feel she watches me."

"Then we will have to destroy her before she causes harm," Barbara said. "There has to be a way."

"I know of no way," her mother answered despondently.

"I will find a way," Barbara said with determination.

"I fear for your yet born children," her mother said. "I

think you will have to find a god or a man that is like a god to destroy your great grandmother."

"Oh, mother!" Barbara lamented.

The next day at the library Barbara read everything she could about ghosts. She read about exorcisms. But how could she go to a priest and tell him her problem when the ghost did not exist within her? And she was overcome with the feeling she would never be able to defeat Bertha.

From then on Barbara lost all interest in school. What good was an education if her grandmother's ghost would shadow her all her days?

After graduation the majority of the class departed for college happy to be away from a small town and planning never to come back. Those who remained in town got jobs at the grocery store, Sears, the gas stations, worked on farms or drove everyday to Kansas City where they sold cars, drove trucks or worked with construction crews. The ones who were lucky had a relative that worked for the county and got jobs driving snow-plows in the winter and working on the highways during the summer. They would receive good benefits and a steady retirement if they lasted thirty years.

The only entertainment in town was two bars. Barbara got a job at Slimm's Bar and Grill and joined the ranks of people telling off-color jokes, participating in drinking contests, and blaming the state of their life on others. Barbara drank to ignore the constant thought of her grandmother. She and her mother grew more distant even though Barbara still lived at home and paid a small rent. She could not afford to live anywhere else on the money she was making. She and her mother never discussed the ghost of Grandmother Adams. Each was locked in her own shell. Each was defeated and lost. But they both would learn one cannot ignore the world or a ghost. Neither will go away.

After three years working at Slimm's Bar and Grill Barbara had had enough. Besides being tired of the same faces, the same stories, the same gripes and complaints, and the same worthless men hitting on her, she also hoped by moving the thoughts of the ghost would go away and maybe the ghost would not follow her. She packed her bags and bought a ten year old Pontiac from a friend for two-hundred and fifty dollars and moved to Kansas City where she rented a small apartment in a not-so-nice part of town. With her experience as a bartender she immediately found a job at a bar.

Sadly, it was no different than Slimm's. There were different faces but with the same stories, the same gripes, and the same lost hopes and dreams. But this time Barbara rarely got involved. She would listen to the stories, nod her head like she understood, and then forget everything when she was home. There was the occasional man she treated to her bed but there was never a hint of love. She vowed she would never marry a poor man, but she dreamed every night of falling deeply in love. She would say at times, "I wish for a love as big as the sky."

"What wasted years those were," Barbara said to herself as she got up from the sofa and headed for the kitchen. "Dreaming about a love as big as the sky. How could I have been that stupid?"

But everything had changed with the birth of Shannon. She now had a reason to live and love even though Shannon's unexplained birth, what he was, or what his voice was, and the ghost of her grandmother all combined were beyond normal worry. She realized that even if she had attended college, in time there would have been a child, and nothing would have been different.

As she passed Shannon's room Barbara could sense the presence of her grandmother. "I know you want my child," she said. "I know you think you will win. But I will make sure that not even the end of the world will give you rest. You will exist forever in your own hate and agony – long past any living thing. Your pleas will fall on the emptiness of space and you will not even be able to hear your own echo."

In the kitchen Barbara made herself a cup of instant

coffee. Her mother's words from long ago suddenly roared through her brain like a marauding tornado. "I think you will have to find a god or a man who is like a god to destroy her."

Barbara's fear for her son intensified and she cried out, "You are not a god, my son. Please, for all that is good, never think you are a god."

Chapter Seven

KATRINA

People become burdened by life. Their desires force them to chase frantically after what they have been taught life should be. They seem to forget that life, in all truth, is nothing but a short dream – a dream that far too often becomes a nightmare if they cannot find their own true path while living.

****

On Shannon's first day of school he was assigned a desk. He smiled timidly at the girl sitting in the desk next to him. She smiled back and shyly looked away. A feeling Shannon had never experienced rushed through his body. It made him feel happy but also confused. He could not take his eyes off of the girl. The girl looked back at Shannon with a puzzled expression. Shannon was also puzzled. Everything from her blue eyes, light brown wavy hair, and smile, seemed familiar – as if he had known her before. "My name is Katrina Payne," she said confidently.

"I am Shannon. I think you will have an influence on my life," he said.

"I know you. I have known you for a long time," she said and looked away again.

Barbara was nervously waiting for Shannon after school and was relieved when he walked out of the building looking like any other first grader.

Riding home Shannon informed her about his day. "I tried my best to not act smart. I pretended to not know all of my

40

ABC's and that reading is difficult for me. The teachers are not hard to fool but at times I have to catch myself to be like the other children."

"I'm so proud of you," Barbara said.

"I hope you will always be proud," Shannon replied.

"How could I not be proud of you?" she asked.

He did not answer her question but said, "I met a girl today. For some reason I think I will know her for a long time and she and I will be friends or maybe closer than friends. She makes me feel safe when she smiles and I don't know why, but I feel like I have known her many times before."

"I would like to find a man that makes me feel safe," Barbara replied jokingly, but also perplexed by Shannon's statement.

"You will one day," Shannon said simply. "You will find the greatest love of all time. I know it for a fact. Your love will be larger than the sky."

Barbara was amazed that Shannon had used almost the same words when she used to dream about love. "The only person I will ever love is you," she said.

Shannon smiled even though he knew better.

When Katrina's mother picked her up after school she did not tell her mother about meeting Shannon. In her young mind she knew there were connections beyond the definition of words that bound Shannon and her – there was something about them that was timeless. She knew she must never fail him and there would come a time she would be asked to lay down her life for him. The thought did not make her afraid but filled her with an inner peace.

That night Shannon lay awake in bed long after Barbara was asleep. He thought about school but mostly he thought about Katrina. Not the little innocent girl she was now but years from now. He knew she would never lose her innocence. She would be one of those blessed in life that could smile through it all and accept whatever befell her. "In your times of need I will help you and in my times of need I will need your help," he whispered to her mental image. Then a deep sadness covered him. "I will never be able to love you, Katrina. No matter my feelings I cannot permit it."

Then he called out softly, "Great Grandmother Adams show yourself to me. I know you are here."

The ghost appeared at the foot of his bed and Shannon sat up. Great Grandmother Adams started to speak but Shannon said fearlessly, "You will not speak. You will listen."

The ghost's eyes flared like billowed embers and her form twisted in anger but she did not speak. "I and only I can save you," Shannon began. "I am not the way I am because of you. You have no merit in my life. No matter what excuse you have for your deeds. It is not enough. All beings, no matter their actions, deserve rest. Life has a plan for me that I must follow, and although I do not know where it leads, I know that you are part of that plan. I also know you cannot make me hate."

A sordid smile creased Great Grandmother Adams' lips. "Do you not think I can force my will upon you?"

"I do not fear you. I do not fear death. The only thing I fear is myself."

Great Grandmother Adams' glare bore through his veins, and swept through his heart, but she could not find even a tiny crack of weakness that she could exploit. When Shannon's eyes remained locked with hers Great Grandmother Adams uttered in a low mocking laugh. "You think you have found a soul mate, and she will save you, but love will not save you. It will only devour your heart and leave you empty and forlorn and filled with bitterness. Never think you can escape. If need be, to get what I desire, I will destroy what you love the most." And she was gone.

Shannon shut his eyes. "Katrina Payne. What a beautiful name," he thought, but he was instantaneously filled with a deep dread for her that he knew was because of him.

Chapter Eight

BERTHA

Many search for love. They think love is like food and that it will nourish them and make their days blissful and carefree. But for many what they find instead is a stale loaf of bread that leaves them empty and unnourished. They have not found love. One can not search for love.

****

Before the three boys threw rocks at Bertha she never questioned her life. No one ever mentioned her true mother and father or that she had three brothers. Her complete life was centered on Rebecca who she called mother.

Although Rebecca knew she did not love Bertha she tried her best to be a good mother. She took Bertha to church every Sunday and raised her in a loving and gentle way.

When Rebecca came back from lambasting Reverend Cartwright she took Bertha by the hand and led her to the kitchen table. Bertha placed her doll, Naomi, in another chair. Rebecca poured them both a large glass of iced tea. Bertha could tell she was troubled. "I must tell you about your history Bertha and you must be strong," Rebecca said in a serious tone that Bertha had never heard before.

"I am strong," Bertha said bravely.

"You have always been a good girl," Rebecca said. "You have been a joy to my heart and given me great pleasure in life." And she proceeded to tell Bertha about her mother, her father, her family, and the fact that the three boys who had thrown rocks at her were her brothers.

43

As Rebecca talked the voice in Bertha's mind taunted her. "I am your only salvation as you are mine," it said over and over again.

Hate filled Bertha. It encased her mind and settled into her being. Rebecca saw the change in Bertha's eyes and cried out in dismay, "No! No! You must not let other people's actions govern you."

"I hate them all," Bertha swore bitterly. "What they did was not right. It was not my fault my mother died."

"Please child. You have a good home with me. God has smiled on you and given you an opportunity many children would not have had. Do not blacken your heart."

"I hate my father and brothers," Bertha yelled and grabbed Naomi and ran to her room crying.

Rebecca did not chase after her. She thought how easy it was to ruin a life and was deeply sorry she had told Bertha the truth.

By her window Bertha glared through her tears at the houses down the street. The houses were all painted white – some with yellow trim, some with red and some with blue. The picket fences stood in neat lines and the flowerbeds were masses of gently swaying spring flowers. But Bertha refused to see the good will in the cleanliness and neatness of the neighborhood. Her father was walking with her three brothers behind him. Everything around her father and brothers turned black. There were no flowers, no picket fences, and no neat houses. "I will make your life miserable," she vowed to her father.

"Seek vengeance," the voice said to her. "Seek vengeance."

Bertha watched her father and brothers until they turned the corner. She sat on the floor and rocked the doll, saying sweetly, "I have been nice to you and you are a good little girl. You should be happy for your life and the fact you are pretty."

Then she screeched, "But you killed your mother!!" And she started ripping out the doll's long blond hair.

"Your father hates you!!" she wailed as she poked out the dolls' eyes.

"I hate you!! I hate you!!" she screamed as she ripped the arms off the doll.

Hearing the outcry Rebecca rushed into Bertha's room. "You are not my mother!!" Bertha shrieked at her. "I hate you more than my family."

Rebecca was mortified and she knew nothing would ever be the same again. She left the room without speaking and shut the door quietly.

Laying on the bed the vision of her birth flooded Bertha's brain. She heard her mother's screams, smelled and tasted her mother's blood as she came into the world. She saw the ash white face of her mother's pain-filled grimace as she died. She heard her own birth screams and remembered the day and night with no food and how hunger gnawed at her stomach.

She felt her father's hands pick her up and saw him gaze at her like she was nothing. She deserved neither food nor love. To him she was a wild beast that should roam the forest and live off of carrion. She heard her father's words, "You were not sent from God."

She remembered the sound of the door as her father left the room, and although she cried and cried her father and her brothers ignored her. "I am your only friend," the voice whispered. "I will never abandon you."

"Who are you?" Bertha asked without fear.

"I am to you what you are to me," the voice replied.

"But who are you?" Bertha asked again.

"All will become known to you in time," the voice replied. "Just know that I together we can defeat all that opposes or oppresses us. You will be my champion."

For the first time Bertha realized, even with her voice, she was alone and would always be alone. Her father had cursed her and his curse would poison her life and take away any possibility for love or joy. She got out of bed and hurried downstairs. Rebecca was sitting in the living room. She fell into her arms. "I'm sorry for being so mean. You are my mother. I love you," she said softly resting her head on Rebecca's shoulder, but her eyes glared emotionlessly at the wall.

Rebecca patted Bertha on the back. "In time all will be fine," she lied not believing her own words.

It will only be fine when I have my revenge and not until Bertha thought.

Even though she was only five years old she was no longer a little girl and her voice gloated over his victory. Bertha's brothers never bothered her again. They would pass each other on the street at times, but neither Bertha nor the boys would acknowledge each other, although they could feel the other's mutual dislike.

Bertha started school. Unfortunately she did not outgrow her homeliness but grew more drab and ungainly. By the time she was in the sixth grade she was taller and heavier than anybody her age. She had large bones, big hands and a nose that occupied most of her face. Her eyebrows were thick and bushy and her eyes had turned from dark to black. She was built more like a boy with a large neck, square shoulders, a stocky trunk, and straight masculine legs. Her voice was coarse. Because of her size her mere appearance intimidated the other children so badly she was friendless. Because of all this she became a bully – bloodying the nose of anyone who offended her.

Even with her disposition, and because Promise City was a small town that prided itself on community, Bertha was still invited to birthday parties and other gatherings. The adults hoped and prayed their kindness would change her. In the back of their minds they felt a great empathy for her because she had been abandoned by her family, and although they did not chastise Reverend Cartwright, they could not understand his actions. The majority of people agreed it was a sad situation.

The town's people could see the drastic changes his wife's death brought upon Reverend Cartwright. He no longer walked with his head held high, but with slow short steps. His gaze was always toward the ground like he had abandoned all hope for the future. His once black hair was streaked with premature gray, and his eyes wandered when he talked, as if everything anybody said had no importance compared to the troubles that were buried in his own heart.

The only time he seemed at peace was when he gave his sermons on Sunday. They were not loud damnations of mankind with all their vices, but soft pleas that God would understand how weak all mankind had become with the overbearing load they must endure. One Sunday during his sermon he looked out at the faces of his flock and pleaded, "Why must we all bear a cross?"

Bertha kept hidden her bully-side or her coarseness to Rebecca. She was always polite and continued going to church although she hated church. To her it was only filled with bigots who felt that because they knew God they were better than anybody else. She could not understand how Lutherans were better than Catholics or Baptists better than Presbyterians and so on. There could not be that many gods. Bertha used her time in church to plan vengeance on her father and brothers.

Following the advice of her voice Bertha was meticulous with her planning. Starting in fourth grade she began sneaking around her father's house and watching the comings and goings of the boys. Over several years, without ever being observed, she learned the routines of each of the boys. Every Saturday during the summer Paul got out of bed several hours before sunrise and rode his bicycle to Grand River to go fishing. He always fished alone. No more than a mile from town a bridge spanned the river. It was made from large creosoted timbers with spaces between them. Horse drawn wagons and a few automobiles made the bridge rumble and shake as they crossed. Paul would fish the deep hole that had been dredged out to set the pillars for the bridge. The bank was not dirt. Instead rocks had been piled deeply on the bank to ease erosion. The water hit the pillars and caused backwashes and eddies that circled endlessly. Several times Bertha explored the fishing hole. The water was so deep she could not see the bottom and extended for over a hundred yards until it narrowed into a fast moving chute between two sandbars.

Bertha patiently bided her time. There was no rush. She would follow the boys to the far corners of the earth if she had to. Her pursuit of vengeance was far past being an obsession. It was her true essence.

****

Time passed. Andrew was now nineteen years old and was working on a wheat harvest for the summer. He was trying to decide if he wanted to join the army or go to college in the fall. Thomas was eighteen and worked for a farmer cleaning out the barns and doing most of the dirty jobs the old farmer no longer wanted to do or possessed the strength to accomplish. Paul, who was seventeen, did odd jobs, but every Saturday morning he always went fishing regardless of the weather.

On a Thursday morning in July, when Bertha was twelve years old, Rebecca received word that a dear friend of hers, who lived twenty miles away in Corydon, was dying from cancer and wanted to see Rebecca one last time. She arranged for a friend to take her in his buggy that afternoon. She still did not trust automobiles. "I will not return until Sunday evening," Rebecca informed Bertha. "You're old enough to take care of yourself and I trust you to not get into any mischief."

"I will be good. I will clean the house and wash the windows while you are gone. I will pick the dandelions out of the yard," Bertha assured her.

That afternoon Bertha waved happily to Rebecca as she rode away. When Rebecca was out of sight she rushed into the house and changed her clothes. She put on a pair of denim overhauls, work shoes, and a blue long-sleeved cotton shirt. She started immediately cleaning the house and then washed the windows. People passing saw her working and were impressed.

That night she rehearsed her plan in her mind over and over again. Her voice rejoiced.

Friday morning, as people walked by the house, they saw Bertha on her hands and knees in her work clothes furiously weeding the yard and the flower beds. She would stop, say "Hello" or "It is a nice day" and smile warmly. The people commended her on her hard work.

She finished in the late afternoon having weeded all but one of the flowerbeds in the front yard. Her hands were black with dirt and her clothes soiled. She then picked up several dead branches that had fallen out of the maple tree. One was over ten feet long and three inches around at the base. Chopping it into two-foot lengths she stacked the wood by the garbage incinerator and placed the biggest one carefully on top and said to herself, "Paul, tonight will be your last."

She then made supper. When it was dark Bertha closed all of the curtains and paced around the house. At ten o'clock she turned off the lights downstairs, rushed upstairs, and turned on her bedroom light for only a few minutes before turning it off.

An hour later Bertha crept out of the house, fearing even the slightest noise would raise suspicion from the neighbors. She inched the back door shut, picked up the big branch she had carefully placed on top of the pile of wood, and made her way slowly through the darkened town avoiding houses with dogs. Once outside of town she cut through a cornfield until she came to the Grand River Bridge.

It was a beautiful night. Fireflies dotted the corn fields, frogs sang their shrill love songs, and the stars were so bright they looked like they could be picked out of the sky and put in a jar. After sliding down the steep grade by the bridge Bertha leaned against the concrete wall that supported the bridge. She could barely see the dark muddy water as it slowly made its way to Missouri but she visualized the huge, greenish-blue catfish that lived in its depths – primeval fish with whiskers and fins as sharp as spears and mouths as large as coffee cans that would eat anything dead and rotten.

Swarms of mosquitoes bit Bertha's face but she did not slap at them. Erie sounds came from the river that to her were no more frightening than the meow of a kitten. She held the stick tightly in her right hand and practiced swinging the stick – each time faster and harder. The swish of the stick through the dark sticky night air made her tingle with anticipation. "There is no love for thy neighbor," the voice encouraged her.

Bertha began playing back the memories of her three brothers taunting her and the look of disgust on Paul's face as he hurled the first rock. She felt the sting of the rocks, but most of all she felt the pain that filled her heart. Why? Why? Then she made her mind go blank and she became one with the dark, the river, and the sound of the mosquitoes. There was no passage of time. There was nothing but the slow steady beat of her heart and the voice. "One day you will be my champion," the voice whispered. "This is only your first deed. Soon you will know the power and the why of me and you will discover you are nothing without me."

The horizon was beginning to turn a black purple when Bertha heard the bicycle start to cross the bridge. It caused small bits of dirt and pebbles to splash into the river. She held her breath. The bicycle progressed. Each timber rattled and groaned. The bicycle stopped. Footsteps echoed through the purple haze.

One step, two, three, four, five – Paul, fishing pole and a can of worms in hand, inched past the concrete retainer wall. The stick cut through the air. Filled with hate it smashed across Paul's forehead. The blow shattered his skull and forced bone fragments into Paul's brain. Paul crumbled to the ground. The stick once again thudded into Paul's skull. A shove and he was in the water. Face down his body was caught in an eddy and slowly turned in clockwise circles. His arms were extended straight out from his sides. His eyes stared blankly into the dark water. Bertha threw the stick as far down river as she could – past the circling water and into the current where it would immediately be carried away. Water filled Paul's nose and mouth. It crept into his lungs and his body sank. Suspended halfway between the top of the water and the bottom of the river the last moment of life departed. He could not feel the catfish as they began nibbling on his nose and ears.

"My will be done," the voice sang proudly as Bertha dashed up the incline from the river and darted across the road. She ran as fast as she could through the cornfield. In town she slowed to a quick walk through the alleys – constantly alert for an early stroller or somebody in a backyard. As the horizon turned from purple to a glazed blood red she slipped through the back door. She stood by the kitchen window and watched the sun rise. Bright and brilliant it brought hope once more to the earth. The birds were chirping merrily in the trees when she began weeding the final flowerbed in front of the house.

A couple walked by. Bertha waved happily at them and they waved back.

Bertha wondered if she would kill Andrew or Thomas next.

That night when Paul was late for dinner Reverend Cartwright was not worried. The fishing must be good. But in the morning when Paul was not home he ran frantically to the bridge and discovered his son's body caught on a sandbar downstream. Several hours later a farmer, who was bringing produce to town, found Reverend Cartwright hugging his lifeless son and weeping uncontrollable. He was so distraught it took two men to tear him away from Paul's body.

The town mourned the drowning and wondered how many times the backwash had rammed Paul's head against the bridge pillar.

Rebecca attended the funeral but Bertha refused to go. Andrew returned from his job on the wheat harvest crew. Reverend Cartwright, Andrew and Thomas stood by the grave. The death ravaged Reno. It added years to his life. After the funeral Andrew joined the army. He wanted nothing more to do with the town. Thomas could not cry. His anguish was too deep for tears.

From her bedroom window Bertha watched her father and brothers return from the cemetery. She felt no glow of victory – only the anxiety of an unaccomplished task. "One is not enough," her voice taunted.

"I know," Bertha replied. "It is only the beginning."

"My champion to be," her voice whispered.

"Champion of what?" Bertha asked.

"Of all that is and ever will be," her voice replied.

Chapter Nine

BARBARA

If a person is lucky there are periods of time when their heart is at ease. Life takes on a rosy glow with no fear of death or the impending fate of heaven or hell. The days go by contentedly and he or she enjoys the simple things – the simple things that more often than not are overshadowed by necessity. For a period of time the lucky person has made simplicity a necessity. Sadly most soon forget.

****

For Barbara the last five years seemed to have been nothing more than a long day and she found it hard to believe she was thirty-four years old. Shannon was now twelve – a good looking young man but not strikingly handsome. His hair was still honey blonde, and his features were soft but not feminine. His blue green eyes were mysterious and deep. People looked into them and felt slightly ill at ease. He was thin, but his muscles were tight and strong because he did one hundred sit-ups and one hundred push-ups every morning. He informed Barbara, "The body has to be taken care of as well as the mind."

Although nothing out of the ordinary had happened during the past five years, to Barbara's sadness, Shannon still did not show a great deal of emotion. He never laughed or cried or told Barbara he loved her. He never hugged her. It was as though he had no control over his life and all of his emotions were caged inside of him – a cage that Shannon himself kept locked.

53

To Barbara's relief Grandmother Adams' ghost had not reappeared. She knew Shannon talked a lot with the voice that spoke to him, but Shannon did not divulge any of the conversations, and Barbara had stopped trying to figure out who or what the voice was.

In school Shannon hid his intelligence by holding a solid B average. The previous summer when school was out he read all of the core requirements for college courses from English to Psychology to Biology. He studied evolution from both scientific and religious points of view including Creationism. He followed this with numerous theology books and then astrology. He then studied astronomy, which he enjoyed, and Barbara bought him a telescope. Sitting at night on the back porch Shannon explained to Barbara the various constellations and stars. To Barbara it was interesting but the stars to her were simply something to be admired.

"It does confuse me that some scientists say that space has no end," Shannon told her one night. "If there was a beginning how can there be no end?"

Barbara did not have the faintest idea, but she was filled with wonder by the fact that a star hundreds and thousands of light years away could be extinct while it was still visible in the heavens. "Maybe when we die we are like extinct stars and our life rays go on forever," she speculated.

"I have wondered if a soul is only light," Shannon answered. "A light that travels endlessly from one life to another life until it finds good."

"Do you think you have been alive before?" Barbara asked.

Shannon hesitated before answering. "At times I feel I have been many things at many times, but the strangest feeling I have is that I have been alive since the beginning of mankind."

"I think I am only what I am," Barbara said.

"That would be a good feeling," Shannon stated.

******

Shannon was on his way to school and Barbara was getting ready for work. Life was fairly easy now. She had received several raises and had five thousand dollars in savings. The previous year she purchased a "new used car" as she called it and a new living room set. She had even been asked out a few times but had refused. Shannon inquired one night why she never dated? Barbara replied she really was not interested but thought it best not tell him it would be impossible with Shannon the way he was. Shannon had stated. "People are only looking for somebody like themselves even if there is no such thing. We are all little orbs unto ourselves. All you can learn is to share and let the other be what they need to be."

Barbara countered, "How about the love you told me I would find that would be bigger than the sky?"

"It will happen," Shannon replied like there was no doubt.

"And how about Katrina Payne? Is she an orb unto herself?

"That's different," he answered seriously without expounding on his statement.

Barbara smiled. Ever since the first grade Shannon and Katrina had been best friends. They were closer than brother and sister. They walked to school together, ate lunch together, and walked home together each day. At least twice a month Katrina would come over for dinner on a weekend.

Katrina was a polite girl. She was pretty, not the least shy, and talked like a person twice her age. Barbara knew that even though she was young Katrina loved Shannon dearly. At times she was confusing to Barbara – even verging on being eerie. There was a look in Katrina's eyes when she talked to Shannon that implied she knew more about Shannon than he did himself. It was as though Katrina knew what Shannon was going to do, and although they were different in many ways, they were completely at ease with each other. They understood at an early age that they both had individual needs, but also understood they were special to each other.

Shannon visited Katrina's house often. The relationship did not bother Barbara or Katrina's parents. Katrina's father, Sam, was a psychologist for the Veterans Administration and her mother, Danyella, was a high school math teacher. Barbara had met them several times although they did not socialize.

"Your son is very intelligent," Sam said. "It seems at times that he tries to hide how smart he is. I don't understand how Katrina gets better grades than he does."

Danyella said, "I love to watch them. They are so cute. Shannon is such a little gentleman. Wouldn't it be wonderful if they stayed friends all the way through college and then got married? It would be a fairy tale."

Barbara felt no need to tell Danyella she had no faith in fairy tales.

Barbara did worry that if Shannon and Katrina ended up going their separate ways Shannon would be crushed. Little did she know?

Barbara drove to work. The Sears store was crowded as usual but Barbara liked the crowds – so many faces with so many different wants. As she punched her time card the general manager rushed up to her and Barbara knew immediately something was wrong. "We just received a call from your father," he said urgently. "You have to go home. Your mother is in the hospital and she wants to see you."

Barbara felt no emotion over the news. Even though she took Shannon to see his grandparents a few times a year there were no close bonds, and the burden of Bertha's ghost they each bore separately.

Back at the apartment Barbara called Katrina's father at work and told him the situation. "Shannon can spend the night," he said adding with a chuckle, "Of course they will have separate rooms."

During the drive to Kirksville Barbara thought about her life as a little girl and for the first time in years she wondered where her brothers and sisters were. She wondered how their lives had turned out. She wondered how many of them were married and how many divorces there had been. She started crying. She wished she knew her family, but she knew it would never happen. She cried for several minutes and then stopped. What was the use?

Arriving in Kirksville was always a shock to Barbara. It was strange to return to a small town where everybody knew each other and what each other did. In one way the thought of it was comforting. In another way she liked the obscurity of a large city. In a city nobody cared who you were or what you did. In a strange sort of way everybody was lonely and accepted it.

The hospital had not changed since Barbara was born – a reception area and two wings. Her mother's room was barren. The floor was white tile with not even a print on the walls. There was a TV in the corner, two chairs, and a bed with a blue curtain that could be pulled around it. The blue curtain reminded Barbara of a death mask for the poor. Her mother was sleeping. A blanket was pulled up to her stomach and her arms were parallel to her sides. She was wearing a cotton nightgown with little strawberries on it that seemed out of place. Her gray hair rested on the pillow like wilted flowers. Her cheeks were indented and underneath her eyes were folds of blackened skin. They reminded Barbara of a fighter who had never won. Her thin lips were white from lack of circulation. Her fingernails were brittle and cracked.

Barbara hoped she would not die this way. A death-dealing accident with no pain would be more humane – one moment life, the next moment death, with no knowledge of the transition. She wondered if there was a heaven. If one made it to heaven did their spirits sit around and talk about their lives on Earth? Or was God's one true mercy to remove all remembrance of one's life on earth?

Anna's eyes fluttered but remained shut. Her brow wrinkled and she looked worried. "I will destroy you. I will destroy you," she wheezed. Her words were mere puffs of invisible smoke. Taking a deep, troubled breath, Anna suddenly bolted upright in bed – her eyes were filled with fear. She screamed. "You are the devil! Get away from me!"

Stretching her arms toward the ceiling Anna beseeched God. "Be my wrath. You who needs sacrifice do not let her find what she desperately seeks. Punish her for time beyond eternity. I demand justice for my father's death."

"Mother, it is okay. Please relax? I am here," Barbara said, holding her mother.

At first Anna resisted but she finally recognized Barbara and relaxed. She let Barbara push her back down. Barbara brushed the hair away from her mother's face and said soothingly, "It's okay. Everything will be fine. Rest."

Rolling her head to the side Anna said weakly, "In my will I have left Shannon all the money I have – three thousand dollars. You will put it in an account in his name and you must tell him about it. He can only use it for the journey he must take."

"What journey?" Barbara asked.

"A voice came to me telling me Shannon will go on a journey and that I would be part of it. I know the voice is real."

"Oh, Mother! What am I to do?"

"I don't know child. You can only live and see what life brings. I have not told you but Bertha's ghost started appearing to me once again a few months ago. It would be at various times of the day. At first she would not say anything. She would appear with a menacing sneer on her face and point at me. Then she started saying things. 'I will see you die and I will spit on your grave. You will be like I am now after I am nothing.' Last week she appeared to me and said, 'you must know there are many like me but I am the most powerful of them all.'"

"I don't understand," Barbara said. "I don't understand. What purpose does Shannon have in all of this?"

"I must tell you," her mother said gravely. "Shannon's purpose is to die for love."

"How do you know this?" Barbara demanded.

"It came to me in a dream that was more real than life."

Bertha's ghost appeared over the top of the bed and smiled triumphantly at Barbara. "I will defeat your son. He will become like me," she gloated.

Barbara struck furiously at Bertha, but unlike before when she chased the ghost from Shannon's room, her blows did not cause the apparition to leave. Instead Bertha laughed a deep guttural laugh that originated from a place where no joy could possibly live. Then, with one final laugh she vanished.

Barbara wanted to ask her mother more about the journey Shannon would take, but Anna was dead. Her eyes were wide open with fear as if in her last moments she had seen all that was hideous on earth. Barbara started to cry. Not out of love for her mother, but sad that her mother had led such a lonely life.

At the very moment of Anna's death Shannon was eating dinner with the Payne's. "I must go outside," he said solemnly and went to the backyard. Gazing up at the sky he said with no sense of loss or emotion, "You will find rest grandmother and I know you will help me." Then he returned to the table.
Mr. Payne looked at him questioningly.

"My grandmother just died. I had to give her solace," Shannon said.

Katrina stood and hugged Shannon. Not hugging her back he said, "It is okay
Katrina I am not sad. My grandmother held a great amount of pain inside of her. For her, death is a blessing."

"I understand," Katrina replied. "She was without love."

Listening to the children Mr. Payne was both alarmed and confused. "Do you get premonitions often?" he asked Shannon, trying to sound casual.

"At times," Shannon replied.

After dinner Shannon and Katrina were in the backyard. "There are times when I know what is going to happen in the future," Katrina said. "I think about something and then several days later it happens."

"Does it frighten you?" Shannon asked.

"No, but it is not something I wish for," Katrina said. "It is something I have no control over."

"I wonder at times if we have any control over anything." Shannon stated. "Most of the time I feel like I am merely floating through life and it is a meaningless journey."

"You have a destiny and I know you hide many secrets. Maybe one day you will be able to tell me what they are," Katrina replied.

"I think you have some idea of what they are but won't tell me," Shannon said.

"If I knew I would tell you," Katrina replied, concealing a deep sadness.

Standing by the kitchen window Sam and Danyella watched Shannon and Katrina. "There is something about Shannon that both enthralls and scares me," Sam said. "I look at him and although he looks like a young boy I know he is not a boy. He is ageless like a stone. It is like he has been a part of the world from the beginning – searching and seeking but he does not know for what."

"Oh Sam," Danyella said. "He is just a boy who is very intelligent. Don't read more into it than there is."

Sam put his arm around his wife's shoulders. "I also think Katrina will have a role in his life that none of us can imagine."

"I hope so," Danyella said.

Sam did not reply. He knew he had no power to stop his daughter from whatever course she would follow, but he dreaded her interaction with Shannon.

Four days later the sun was shining brightly when Barbara and Shannon left for the funeral. It was drizzling and cloudy in Kirksville and Barbara thought it was fitting. Only ten people besides Barbara, her father, and Shannon attended the funeral. Only the family followed the hearse to the cemetery. Her father, smelling like gin, sobbed like a baby. Barbara noticed Shannon was distracted and paid no attention to the preacher, but gazed over his grandmother's headstone toward a dense stand of elm trees. When the service was over, as they walked toward the car, Shannon turned twice and looked back at the trees. "What is over there?" Barbara asked.

"I will tell you on the way home," Shannon replied.

At the church they had ham sandwiches, orange Jell-O with marshmallows, and coffee or tea. The old and tired looking people told Barbara how sorry they were for her loss. Barbara's father stood in the corner. His suit was wrinkled and hung on his bones like a shroud. His eyes were vacant and Barbara knew there was nothing she could do. He would die in a bar, drunk, grieving over his life. She held no love for him. There was not even enough care for him to grieve for his misery. When it was time to leave she hugged her father and kissed him on the cheek. Shannon shook his hand.

Barbara felt neither pity nor remorse over her mother's death as they drove home. It was raining harder and the steady back and forth of the windshield wipers were erasers that destroyed the bad memories. In many ways she felt relieved. A sad and dark part of her life was finished, and now she could get on with other aspects of her life that had always been blackened by her mother's remoteness.

"My mother left you three thousand dollars," Barbara said to Shannon. "She told me there is a journey you must take and you can only spend the money for the journey."

"I have never thought about a journey," Shannon said.

"Has your voice mentioned a journey?" Barbara asked.

"No," Shannon replied simply.

"I am sorry your grandmother was the way she was," Barbara said.

"She was not a bad woman," Shannon replied. "It is sad she was not strong enough to battle her pain."

"What did you see in the trees at the funeral?" Barbara asked.

"I saw your mother's ghost. She told me she would always be by my side and that I must be strong and never to fear. She will do her best to protect me. She also wanted me to tell you that she was sorry for not being a better mother."

They were silent for a while. Then Shannon asked for the first time in his life, "Barbara, do you know who my father is?"

"I knew you would ask me one day and I have dreaded the day," Barbara said unable to hide her shame.

"There is nothing to be ashamed about," Shannon said.

"I don't know who your father is, Shannon. I do not remember being with a man."

"My voice told me he is my father and I know he loves you deeply," Shannon said.

"That can't be so," Barbara gasped. "I have never even heard your voice or know who or what he is."

"He will reveal himself to you in time, although he has never told me what he really is. I have asked many times. But I do know my father is not a god and that neither of us is blessed."

"How can I love what I do not know?" Barbara asked.

"How can I be what I am?" Shannon replied.

Chapter Ten

SHANNON

There are many people who cannot face the real world and hide behind fantasy. They are the ones who will always proclaim they cannot stand a person who tells lies, although they live in a lie.

****

Shannon could not tell his mother all that Anna's ghost had told him at the funeral. How could he explain to his mother that during the twenty-minute service his grandmother told him the story of her life after her father's murder? She had not wanted love, or understanding, or pity, only that Shannon would know her story.

"The orphanage was not a bad place," Anna's ghost stated. "When I was turned over to the orphanage there were twenty-four girls and thirty-five boys between the ages of six and eighteen. The boys and girls were divided into separate dormitories. We had a bed with two blankets, a footlocker at the end of the bed and a three-drawer chest of drawers between each bed. At night one of the older girls became the housemother after the staff went home. Our clothes were donated but they were always nice and clean. Since we were all orphans a common thread of loneliness bound us together. We had a big playground with swings and teeter-totters, a baseball field also used for football, and many toys to play with. We attended the public school and were treated kindly by the teachers. At times a few of the kids at the school would taunt us about being from the orphanage, but we stuck together, and refused to let it bother us. Mrs. Fisher was the head mistress of the orphanage. She was a big woman whose husband was small and thin. His name was Ray and he did maintenance work around the building. He was very kind and played Santa Claus at Christmas. We knew it was him but we never let on. We ate in a large dining room and had to recite grace before each meal. At night Mrs. Fisher would come into each dormitory and we would say the Lord's Prayer with her. The one thing we dreamed about was getting adopted by a good family who would love us. But once a child was past six or seven years old the chances were slim. Most people only adopt babies but, at times, couples would come to the orphanage to adopt older children. We would stand in a long line trying not to show how desperate we were. The couple, led by Mrs. Fisher, would walk by us. It always made me feel like a cow or a horse at auction, but oh how I dreamed I would be picked. But I never was. The occasional boy or girl who was chosen would leave us and then in a week or so the bed would be filled with another lonely heart. I never made any close friends. I never really got over the sight of my murdered father. I was at the orphanage from the time I was twelve until I was eighteen. When I was eighteen Mrs. Fisher found me a job in Kirksville working at the drug store. The day I left she gave me several dozen letters that my mother had written from prison. She explained to me, 'When you were younger it was not time to give you these but now is the time. I wish you all the best in your life.' And, with tears in her eyes, she hugged me good-bye. Her husband took me to the bus station, bought me a ticket to Kirksville, and gave me one hundred dollars. I had a suitcase with two dresses, two pairs of shoes and two towels, some undergarments, plus what I was wearing. I had no dreams and no aspirations for the future. I was alone in the world but I was not afraid. As the bus traveled across Iowa I read my mother's letters and when I was finished I tossed them out the window like she had tossed my father and me out of her life. Little did I know that I would never rid myself of her curse – not even after she died. I lived in a small room over the drug store. It was different being around real people – seeing couples and children, watching people go to church and socializing. Mr. Owens owned the store and he and his wife were good to me. I got a free lunch with the job and she would give me leftover pies and cakes and cookies. I worked hard and saved my money, but I was shy and stayed to myself. I did not really know how to act with men. Our activities had been tightly monitored at the orphanage although we did have dances and parties. A few boys and girls did sneak out of the dorms and meet on the football field but we were strictly regulated. I never had a boyfriend and was very seldom asked to dance during one of the dances. Pretty was never a blessing of mine, and others could feel the darkness I carried inside, even though I tried to not let it show. I met my husband at the store. He was working on a bridge crew outside of town. He was tall and handsome and he smiled a lot like my father. We went for walks, and to the movies, and one day he asked me to marry him. I don't know why I said 'Yes.' I really did not love him. Maybe it was because I was ready or maybe it was because I wanted to be like the other ladies who married and had children. Whatever the reason I got married. But it brought me no joy or friends. I felt emptier because whatever I was looking for never materialized. I was thinking about leaving my husband, through no fault of his, when our first child was born. Then it was too late. Looking back I should have probably left. Children raised in an unhappy family are worse off than children raised by one parent who is happy or at least demonstrates care. My husband loved me dearly, but he felt the unfulfilled longing in my heart, and he started to drink. I now feel it was my mother's will overpowering me, making me do her bidding, making me feel her aloneness, making me feel like she did when my father fell out of love with her and showered his love on me. But my death has brought me a form of contentment. I know my father is at rest because I have not seen him. I see vague outlines of other ghosts as they travel around seeking whatever will redeem them and give them peace. I am not like them. I know my purpose is to protect you. What the reason is I do not know. But at least in death, unlike during my life, I have found a purpose to follow. I really do not know what your purpose is. I have no idea why you were born the way you were. But I do know that my mother wants to destroy you. But I feel she is only the instrument of something bigger and stronger than her - something lonely and forlorn that it is trapped by its own dark desires. You must take care of your mother. She is deathly afraid for you and she is not as strong as she seems." Anna stopped speaking.

Back in Kansas City Shannon went to his room. Barbara ran a hot bath. Inching into the steaming water she tried to relax, but what Shannon had told her on the way home troubled her deeply. The last five years of tranquility were shattered. Now she felt desperately helpless. There was no one to help her. Her mother was dead. Her father was a self-pitying drunk. She had no doubt her mother's words were true and Shannon would go on a journey. She also completely realized she held no power over the ghost of her grandmother.

Barbara wet a washcloth and laid it over her eyes, but even the washcloth could not shut out the world. Tiny dark molecular dots darted in dizzying uneven patterns beneath her eyelids, molecules begging for release, for freedom, trapped in a world where they groped endlessly to see the real light, caught forever between dusk and dark. Barbara felt empathy for the darting dots and wondered if they had a life force or a soul. She wondered if they knew they were caught in her eyelids – a part of her, although not a part, each sharing the same fate. And she wondered what would happen to them when she died. "What am I to do?" she begged desperately as she wrapped her arms around herself, as if her own embrace would bring her comfort. But there was no answer.

Barbara removed the washcloth from her eyes. The bright light made everything fuzzy for a few moments. When she regained her vision she gasped. Bertha's ghost hovered at the end of the tub. "I destroyed your mother. She will wander aimlessly through time with no form and no salvation," Bertha leered.

"Then leave my son alone," Barbara demanded. "What more do you want?"

"Shannon will come to know what I have only tasted of," Bertha replied.

"What? What will he know? You must tell me," Barbara pleaded.

Bertha's laugh was sinister and gloating as she disappeared without answering.

Barbara was so still not a single ripple dented the water. "Oh mother. I wish I had loved you," she sighed.

Her mother's ghost was in the corner of the bathroom but remained unseen. "It is not your fault. Maybe in time I will be able to make up for the scars I cut into your heart," she said sadly.

Shannon was at his desk. He knew Barbara was terribly worried and upset. He also knew there was nothing he could do to relieve her worry. He went to the window. Even though he could not see the horizon through the other apartments he liked the dusk. The birds sang one last flourish of song. The earth sighed in relief – another day gone – another day of survival.

Undressing for bed Shannon suddenly felt like he was on fire. Then he started shaking from an intense cold. He was so cold his flesh was ice. Before the cold became unbearable it stopped and a treacherous wind picked him up and started spinning him hundreds of miles an hour. The wind tore at his eyes and sucked the air out of his lungs. Then the wind stopped and it was alarmingly calm. Shannon was suspended halfway between the floor and the ceiling. His arms were outstretched as if he was beckoning the gods. His head was tilted back. He felt neither dread nor fear. He felt nothing. He was in a void where no feeling could exist. Then slowly, micro-inch by micro-inch, he settled back to the floor. He felt as though his complete being had been examined – every tissue of his body – his mind, his heart, his beliefs and his desires were gone over and catalogued. A sharp excruciating pain stabbed the palms of his hands as if rusty spikes were being driven through them. Jagged red holes appeared in his palms. One large drop of blood dripped from each of the holes and splattered on his feet with the weight of sledgehammer blows. Shannon collapsed to the floor from the pain. He struggled to get up, but invisible hands gripped his shoulders and pushed him flat on his back. Other hands grasped his ankles. He squirmed but could not move. Then a piercing, sharp pain, sliced through his side and a bright crimson cut appeared on his abdomen, but it did not bleed. He thrashed his head from side to side. He wanted to call out for help but was unable to make a sound.

Barefoot and wearing only a blue terry cloth bathrobe Barbara knocked on Shannon's door. When there was no answer she slowly opened the door. Shannon was curled up on the floor in a fetal position repeating over and over again as if in prayer, "It is useless. It is useless. It is useless. Why do you torment me?"

Barbara threw herself on Shannon. Shannon's arms circled her – clinging to her. Barbara sobbed. Her tears ran down her cheeks and onto Shannon's face. Bertha's ghost appeared in the corner of the room. She was furious and started to speak but her words were not allowed to materialize. Barbara felt another force enter the room and she was engulfed by a deep feeling of love and compassion. Bertha's ghost withered, fought to remain, grimaced while pointing her hand at the unseen force, and then vanished.

"Who are you?" Barbara asked. "Show yourself to me!"

There was no reply.

Standing, Barbara self-consciously tightened her robe around herself. She started to help Shannon up, but he refused her aid, and stood on shaking legs. "Oh Shannon," Barbara sobbed when she saw the bloody holes in his hands and feet and the cut on his side. Grabbing his hands she held them to her face. Her tears fell onto his palms and the holes from the spikes vanished. Barbara knelt at his feet and gently touched the wounds. They healed instantly. Shannon held her by the shoulders. His grip was strong as he pulled her to her feet. The cut on his side disappeared. Shannon ran his fingers gently over Barbara's cheeks and wiped away the tears. "I felt a great love that is not yours," Barbara said deeply shaken.

Shannon helped Barbara to her bed and smiled at her like a father smiles at a child. "Please do not worry!" he said softly. "It is what Great Grandmother Adams wants. She wants you to worry. You must spite her."

"I don't know if I have the strength," Barbara replied.

"You do. I know you do." Shannon bent over and kissed her tenderly on the forehead.

"Why can't my love protect you?" Barbara asked sadly.

Shannon did not have an answer.

<h1 style="text-align:center">Chapter Eleven</h1>

BERTHA

Murder is not really vengeance. The murdered person only feels pain for an instant before death. True vengeance kills slowly by eroding the heart and soul of the victim until he or she is nothing but an empty shell and pleads relentlessly for death. True vengeance waits for the cry of desperation.

******

Bertha witnessed the toll Paul's murder took on her father and she relished his dismay. It was as though Paul's death rekindled the pain Reverend Cartwright felt over his wife's death. Both pains together were almost too much for him to bear.

After Paul's murder Bertha dramatically changed. She stopped being a bully at school. She no longer struck other children or bossed them. When they called her names because she was big and plain she merely smiled. She worked extra hard around the house for Rebecca who was teaching her how to cook. Surprisingly Bertha was a good cook. It came naturally to her. There was no need for her to measure salt, pepper, cinnamon for pies, or the amount of sugar for cookies. She pinched and poured. Whatever she cooked was delicious.

From Rebecca's lush garden Bertha learned how to can vegetables and make both sweet and sour pickles. What surprised Bertha was the fact that when she was cooking or canning she did not think about her hate for her brothers or father. She even ignored her voice.

"One day you could be a world famous chef," Rebecca told her. "You might have discovered your place in life."

But once the cooking was done, and Bertha was alone, she resumed scheming on ways to kill Thomas. She thought about poisoning him, but there was no way to get close enough. She dreamed about finding him alone and stabbing him, but he was normally with a group of other boys.

After graduating from high school Thomas was accepted to the veterinary school at Iowa State and would be leaving soon. Bertha could not stand the idea of her vengeance going unfulfilled. "You must kill him," her voice taunted.

A few days later during lunch Bertha overheard a group of girls talking about Thomas's new girlfriend. He was seeing Ida Cranford, a senior whose parents owned a farm several miles south of town. Bertha knew where the farm was because she and Rebecca would go there in the fall to pick apples from their orchard. Rumor had it that Ida's parents always visited people on Saturday nights while Ida stayed home. Thomas would sneak out to the farm and stay for several hours. Because they were devout Catholics Ida's parents would not allow their daughter to date a Lutheran. Also Reverend Cartwright, if he knew, would not condone his son dating a Catholic. This did nothing but enhance the young couple's feelings for each other.

Over the last several months Rebecca had not been feeling well. Although she was still active, she was always tired, and it took great effort on her part to complete the tasks she must do each day. Right after supper she would go to bed and read for a short while before falling asleep by eight. When she woke in the morning she felt as if she had not slept at all. She started drinking two glasses of her homemade wine in the evening instead of one.

"You should go to the doctor," Bertha told her keeping with her guise of being a caring person. Truthfully she held no feelings for Rebecca – not even gratitude.

"I have never been to a doctor and I never will," Rebecca

replied disdainfully. "My parents did not go either. Doctors only want your money and they don't know anymore than I do. God will take me when it is my time and I won't argue with His decision."

Bertha started taking Rebecca's second glass of wine up to her bedroom. "This is so nice of you," Rebecca said. "It saves my tired old bones a trip." Rebecca had no idea Bertha was putting drops of laudanum, which she had stolen from the drug store, in her wine. Rebecca did wonder why she was sleeping deeper than she ever had in her life.

The next Saturday night, while Rebecca was in a deep drug induced sleep, Bertha left the house and made her way to the road that led to Ida's house. No more than a quarter of a mile from town she hid behind a stand of tall weeds in the ditch and waited. About an hour later she heard whistling and Thomas walked briskly by headed back to town. His dark image radiated love and his whistling was lively and carefree. The happy tune unnerved Bertha and she had to control herself to not run out from her hiding place and scream her hate at Thomas.

Her voice taunted her. "Why should he know love when all you have known is loneliness? Why should he enjoy life while blaming you for your mother's death and carry no guilt of his own? Why should he forsake you like you are nothing?"

Then her own mind spoke to her. "You are ugly and plain. No man will ever love you. You will never be embraced, or kissed, or given flowers, or taken to a dance. No man will lay you down in his bed and tell you he worships you. You will never have children. It would have been better if you were never born."

Bertha started running – not after Thomas but in the opposite direction. She tried to outrun the voice in her mind but it would not cease. It kept tormenting her. "You will never be loved. You will never be loved. You will never be loved. You are ugly. How could somebody love a person so ugly?"

"Stop! Stop!" Bertha screamed and crumpled to her knees

in the middle of the dirt road. But there was no relief. The stars and the moon and the planets also mocked her. "You are nothing. Nothing will love you. Nothing will love you."

"I hate you all," she screamed. "I hate all that is living and will ever live."

She started bawling. Her tears were so vile they would not soak into the dirt. The earth was unwilling to accept them. Bertha cried and cried until there were no more tears and then she retched violently. All that remained good in her spewed out onto the earth in choking torrents. Finished, she stood, and dried her face with trembling hands. She plodded through a black wasteland back to her house. Nothing in life would ever have color. Nothing in life would ever hurt her. She would destroy everything that tried, and she would destroy anyone around her that loved. Love was the basis for all pain – all cruelty. She would be an enemy of love.

The voice smiled but did not speak to her.

Creeping into the house Bertha heard Rebecca's contented snoring. In bed Bertha could not sleep. Her eyes were wide open – glaring into the coal dust ceiling. The creaks and groans of the house were like distant spirits trying to talk to her but she ignored them. What consumed her was the image of Thomas smiling and so in love the world was a wonderful place to be. "When I kill you I will take your smile," she vowed before rolling over and falling into a deep sleep filled with misty distant echoes that she could not understand.

Thomas's love consumed him. Ida was the wind, the green grass, the trees and the color in every flower. They had it all planned, right after her graduation they were going to run away and get married, they could not let their parents beliefs come between them. She would work while he was going to college, and when they had children, they would let the children decide what religion they wished to follow.

Reverend Cartwright did not notice how happy and carefree Thomas was nor did he have any idea of the treachery Thomas was planning. He was too self absorbed with his own pain.

At school on Monday Bertha watched Ida eat lunch. Ida's eyes were bright with excitement and love. She laughed and joked with the people around her and Bertha hated Thomas more.

That night Bertha sat on the porch after Rebecca was in bed. She was overcome by the deepest sadness she had ever experienced – so deep it momentarily overrode her hate. She asked herself, why must I be alone? What destiny controls me? Why has my ugliness gone beyond my skin and corrupted all of my thoughts and desires? There are times when I do not want to hate. There are times when I want to ignore my thoughts but I am not strong enough. It is like a creature filled with pain, without form or substance, controls me. I have no free will. I am only a puppet being pulled through each day as if what I see or feel or desire does not matter. Nothing will make any difference in my life, and when my life is done, the creature will latch onto another unfortunate victim and fill them with its desires.

Bertha contemplated killing herself. What would be better? A life filled with loneliness? Or nothingness? With nothingness there would be freedom from all feeling and thought.

In the kitchen she picked out a large kitchen knife and carried it tenderly to the backyard. The moonlight crept through the oak branches, shadows danced in the yard. The shadows called to her. "We will love you. We will protect you. With us you will feel nothing."

The knife in her hand was warm. It cared. It loved her. It was her answer. "Let me taste your blood," the knife whispered. "Let me show you the path you must follow. I am your destiny. Do not deny me."

Gripping the knife firmly in her right hand, Bertha held out her left arm with her wrist upward. The veins pulsed with the beat of her heart. "We give you life and hope," they whispered.

"You give me hate," Bertha answered. "You give me injustice. You give me pain and turmoil and loneliness. You give me nothing."

Resting the edge of the blade on her wrist she pulled the knife lightly over her skin. A trickle of blood oozed from the slight cut. The blood was devoid of all hope. A gigantic image of Thomas's face appeared in front of her. The face smiled at her. "I have what you will never possess," it taunted before disappearing.

After gazing at the blade for a few moments Bertha stole back into the house and put the knife away. Her sadness was gone - her hate once more triumphant. On the way to her room she licked the trickle of blood from her wrist.

"I am your destiny," her voice said.

"I understand," she replied. "I will be your champion. But who are you."

"In time I will tell you," the voice replied.

The following Saturday night Bertha dripped an extra drop of laudanum in Rebecca's wine and put the bottle in her pocket. When Rebecca was sleeping soundly Bertha took the knife she had cut her wrist with from the kitchen and left the house. A sliver of moon dotted the sky. There was not enough light to throw a shadow. The trees were mute from no wind. On the way to her hiding place Bertha shattered the laudanum bottle with a rock, scooped up the pieces, and tossed them into the night. The tall weeds where she hid were cool and refreshing. The knife in her hand was soothing like a crucifix. No sounds disturbed the night – no cry from an owl, no frogs, no scurrying of field mice, no chirping of bugs. Bertha became one with the night. She waited patiently for her prey. She was calm and at rest – a lioness observing her domain. "Predators do not fear," Bertha whispered. "They control all that is around them and find contentment in their power."

A merry tune whistled through the darkness. The sounds of long quick strides followed, bouncy and joy-filled. Holding her breath and gripping the knife firmer Bertha glanced at the gleaming blade. The whistling grew closer, the steps quicker. Bertha's muscles tensed like taunt barbwire. The song was upon her – a melody flying to the stars, bringing smiles to the heavens.

"Thomas, why do you love?" Bertha beckoned through the dark.

Thomas stopped in his tracks, peered into the darkness, but he could not see anything.

"Thomas, how could you forsake me?" Bertha hauntingly asked.

The voice sounded vaguely familiar but Thomas could not place it. "Who is there?" he demanded.

There was no answer.

"Who is there?" he demanded again.

Hearing something move in the ditch Thomas squinted as a dark form stepped from the weeds. He took two tentative steps toward the figure.

Bertha rushed toward him. Before Thomas knew what was happening she buried the knife to the hilt in his throat. Blood shot out in a rushing stream, covering Bertha's arms and chest. The crimson shower filled her with joy. Thomas clutched the knife in disbelief and sagged to his knees as if prayer would save him. "You! You? Why? Oh Ida!" he managed to say before falling face forward to the ground dead.

Bertha rolled Thomas over and yanked the knife from his neck. With two quick slashes she cut his lips off and laid them on his chest so they formed a frown. "You will never smile again," she gloated before she ran into the field like a rabid dog.

Her voice smiled with satisfaction.

Back home Bertha washed the blood from her hands and arms and the knife in the rain barrel. She tipped the barrel so that the water spread onto the grass. She took her clothes off and put them in the incinerator and then went as silent as possible into the house. She put the knife away. Lying in bed, the sheets cool on her skin, she could see Thomas's face as the knife entered his neck. Everything he dreamed, all that he loved, would never be. "Now father," she said. "You will truly know how you have made me feel."

In the morning Bertha was up before sunrise and before Rebecca stirred. She got a box of matches and took the burnable garbage to the incinerator. She put her bloodied clothes on top of them and started a fire. "Ashes to ashes, dust to dust!" she said happily before going back inside to prepare breakfast for Rebecca.

A farmer discovered the body early in the morning. "My God!" the sheriff commented when he arrived. "Who would be so evil to do this?"

The funeral was a somber affair. Ida wept uncontrollably thinking she would never find love again. Reverend Cartwright was so distraught he could not stand. He sat on the ground with his head bowed and cried silently. Andrew, in his military uniform, stood behind his father somber in their shared grief.

Rebecca attended the funeral but Bertha refused saying, "Blood means nothing."

Andrew left town right after the funeral.

Police were called in from all over the state to investigate the murder. Everyone in town was questioned but no knife was ever found. The murder made the Kansas City newspapers because of the gruesomeness of the crime. After several weeks the authorities decided it must have been a crazed transient who killed Thomas, even though nothing was taken from the body. "An act of God," the Catholic priest proclaimed during the Sunday sermon.

Three weeks later Reverend Reno Cartwright was found dead in front of the altar at the Lutheran church. He had been on his knees praying when he keeled over from a massive heart attack. His hair had turned snow white. His eyes were frozen open as though begging for pity. All the people of the congregation believed he died from a broken heart.

Bertha and Rebecca both attended the funeral. Bertha

wore her best dress and nice shoes and had a black lace hanky pinned in her hair. During the service she relived her deeds. Surprisingly she did not feel triumph or vindicated. She felt hollow. She looked at her father's casket and started crying. She put her arms around Rebecca, and buried her head in Rebecca's side, and let the tears flow. "Now, now, child," Rebecca soothed. "It is all as it should be. We have no control over what life has in store for us. I have always felt in my heart that your father loved you but never knew how to show it."

"I would have been a good daughter. Why couldn't he give me some of the love he felt for my mother?" Bertha cried.

After the service Andrew spoke to Rebecca. "I will pay my father's money for Bertha," he said distantly to Rebecca.

Then he said to Bertha, "I am sorry for our sins against you. I hope in time you will have a happy life and find someone who loves you."

He placed his right hand softly on her head and his touch was like warm spring rain. Bertha smiled shyly. For one brief moment she felt safe and needed and forswore forever her vengeance on Andrew.

Chapter Twelve

BARBARA

We all seek love. But to truly love one must be unselfish. Who of us is not selfish?

****

Barbara tried not to show how hopeless she felt. Each day she fought desperately, but each day she lost ground. Ever since the holes appeared on Shannon's feet and hands, and the cut on his side, Barbara had been lost in a whirlwind of questions for which there were no answers. Barbara once again wondered if Shannon was a demon or evil, but she decided it was not possible. If it were true she would have seen the signs. She convinced herself there was not an evil or hateful bone in Shannon. There was only need – a need that he could not communicate because he did not know what it was.

Barbara knew with certainty that the voice he heard had an unrelenting power over Shannon – the voice that at times she cursed – the voice that Shannon said was his father – the presence that had surrounded her with love in Shannon's room and forced Bertha away.

It was Friday afternoon. Shannon was visiting Katrina and was supposed to be home by six. Barbara was on the sofa trying to banish all the questions that tormented her mind. Then, like a tiny cloud floating across the face of the sun, she had the feeling she was being watched, but she felt no malice from the presence. It was as though the presence wanted or needed to help her.

"Are you here, Mother?" Barbara asked tentatively.

There was only an eerie silence.

"I know you are here," Barbara said.

A warm breeze swept through the room and brushed tenderly through Barbara's hair.

The breeze circled through the room once again, cooler than before. The lamp on the end table rattled but Barbara was not afraid. "I know you are here, Mother."

A faint image appeared on the sofa – translucent gray, interlaced with silver threads. No characteristics could be made out – only an outline of the figure. The image filtered in and out of focus, struggling to be seen, as if other forces were trying to stop it from being visible. A thin frail voice emitted from the form. "You were chosen as Shannon's mother because you never knew love. When love comes you will not forsake it out of selfishness, or pride, or the need to control."

"I don't seek love anymore Mother," Barbara said. "One day it was no more but its passing left a void in me. It's not a feeling I can describe and I don't think it will ever completely disappear."

"I was always lonely," Anna said. "The orphanage reeked of it. It was in the paint on the walls, in the food. It came out of the showerheads and filled the pores of my skin. I thought it had gone away. But it never left. I only buried it deep in my heart and stopped reaching out. I hope your loneliness will never return and you forget the void within you."

"We never knew each other Mother," Barbara said. "We never talked about what my dreams were. We were so distant."

"I don't know if parents ever really know their children. I don't know if people truly ever know another person. We can only judge others by what we know of ourselves. Strange, I did not know myself until after I died."

"Oh Mother! I wish I could hug you," Barbara said.

The image rose from the sofa no more than a mist. It lost all shape and form. The mist settled around Barbara for several moments, and then was gone as though inhaled by the earth. Barbara felt refreshed as though the mist had absorbed some of her worries.

Suspended near the ceiling an invisible Bertha seethed. She had watched everything and felt the kinship between mother and daughter and she was repulsed. What did they know of loneliness? She wanted to pour all of her bile and hate into Barbara and fill Barbara's mind with so much worry and grief over Shannon her mind would break into fragments so small nothing could be salvaged. Barbara would inhabit a barren land of no thought, no comprehension, only a deep fear that could never be driven away or explained. But Bertha knew it was not yet time.

Barbara remembered how happy she was when she first moved to Kansas City. But now she understood where a person lives does not in reality make a great amount of difference. Miserable people were miserable wherever they were. There might be a few weeks of happiness but soon the same old gripes and misgivings would resurface. A person was in the world and the world, in the realm of endless space, was a small place.

Barbara went to Shannon's room and tentatively removed his Bible from the bookshelf. She needed help. Maybe there was no God, but believing in something, even if it was not true, was better than not believing in anything. Sitting on Shannon's bed she began reading Genesis. "And in the beginning..." As she continued she was pulled into the words. In a short while she grew tired and fell asleep more deeply than she had in weeks – a sleep with no questions or doubts and not even a trace of fear.

When Shannon got home Barbara was still sleeping on his bed. Shannon realized he had never seen his mother while she slept. Barbara's thin lips were relaxed, almost smiling, as if she was riding the crest of a good dream. For the first time Shannon realized how pretty his mother was, even though her face was getting a few wrinkles, and there were dark worry circles under her eyes. "If only you could sleep forever," he said. "If only you could live in dreams."

Shannon thought that maybe life was just a dream. Maybe a creature grander than any creation slept on a distant planet and mankind was his continuing dream – a continuous cycle of nightmares and good dreams, and one day the creature would awaken, stretch and yawn, and mankind would vanish, having never really been more than a figment of the creature's imagination.

Shannon kissed Barbara tenderly on the forehead. She smiled slightly but remained asleep. In her dream a golden angel with wings of pure white hovered over her. The slight breeze from his slowly flapping wings soothed her and kept all harm away.

Chapter Thirteen

KATRINA

If there is a God will He judge mankind by the actions of the majority? Would He destroy all man, the good and the bad, so a future creation would not be cursed by mankind's destructive nature? If He did the good people would understand. That is why they are good. They think about more than themselves.

****

It was the weekend after Shannon's sixteenth birthday. He now had a driver's license and Barbara at times would let him use the car. Over the last four years there had been no incidents with either Bertha or Anna. Even so Barbara could not completely overcome her worries and imagined she was living through an uneasy truce.

Shannon and Katrina were going to drive to the Missouri River for a picnic and Barbara and Katrina were in the kitchen making sandwiches. Shannon was outside cleaning the car. He disliked anything to be dusty, out of order, or not placed in proportion to its surroundings. Books were lined up square to each other on his desk. His clothes hung in order with all the hanger hooks pointed in the same direction. His bed was made so the blanket hung exactly the same distance on each side. His pants were pressed, his shirts ironed, and his shoes shined immaculately.

Katrina, at sixteen, was a lovely girl. She had deep blue eyes dotted with golden specs that turned topaz when the light hit them. Her hair was almost peach-colored, extremely thick and glossy, and cascaded to the middle of her back. She was slim with long graceful arms that melted into her hands. Her hips were narrow and her legs moved confidently. From the top of her head to her toes everything was in rhythm with nothing gangly or out of place. She had the air of a confident and caring nurse that the patients completely trusted. Katrina smiled a lot, and was friendly, but there was a deep side to her – a side she kept secret even from Shannon.

Shannon and Katrina had grown closer with each year, although Shannon never attempted to kiss or in any way grow intimate. Katrina's young body was budding. Passing thoughts of sex and passion romantically dashed through her daydreams. There were many times when she wanted Shannon to kiss her or do any of the things boys tried to do to girls. She acted astonished when other girls talked of sleeping with their boyfriends, but she secretly wished for the experience – knowing she loved Shannon, knowing she would always love him. She did wonder what Shannon felt for her. Although they were close and together as much as possible sometimes she felt she was merely a distraction. But she would hold her love within her for as long as she lived if it had to be that way. Many other boys asked her out but she refused content to be with Shannon, "The Freaks," many people called him.

Barbara was cutting a tomato. "I haven't noticed how pretty you have become," Barbara said to Katrina. "You are a woman now."

Katrina smiled a rosy smile. "It is hard to believe it has been eleven years since Shannon and I were in first grade," Katrina said, sounding like an old woman fondly discussing her life with a dear and trusted friend.

"I think you will always be with my son," Barbara replied.

"I know I will always be with Shannon," Katrina said, trying to cover up a trace of worry. "He might not want me at all times but I will not forsake him."

Barbara wanted to ask Katrina if she was sleeping with Shannon but she did not. If they were Barbara hoped they were smart enough to use protection. But, if they were, she also wondered if Shannon was a good lover. Could he give enough of himself to be caring? Or did his mind always keep him so far away he could not lose himself in anything enjoyable?

"I am not sleeping with your son," Katrina said casually.

"What?" Barbara stammered in disbelief.

"I have to tell you, and please don't think me strange, but at times when people think about Shannon I know what they are thinking," Katrina said without alarm but matter-of-factly.

"You know?" Barbara probed afraid to mention the ghosts.

"I know Shannon is a special person and he has great wisdom. I know he tries to act normal but he is years ahead of any one of us. And even though I have not told Shannon, I know ghosts follow him wherever he goes. I don't see them, but I feel them, and at times I get glimpses of what they are thinking. One of them despises me and I feel she wants to harm me but she is afraid. She needs Shannon for something but I don't know what it is. But when she is around her hate saturates the room like she needs everyone to feel her misery. The other ghost is sad over the fact she did not know how to show love or affection when she was alive. That one likes me and she knows I mean no harm. But the strange thing about her is that I sense she is not a complete ghost. She is caught in a void and is more like a presence. It's very difficult to explain."

Barbara sighed knowing she had to tell Katrina the truth. "Your feelings are true. There are two ghosts. Shannon's Great Grandmother Adams ghost is evil and for some reason she needs Shannon's help to gain the redemption she desires. The other ghost is my mother who is trying to protect Shannon."

Katrina did not reply, but seemed relieved with the information.

"But if you know then you must have been sent to help him. Nobody outside of the family has seen or felt the ghosts," Barbara said.

"I hope I can help him," Katrina said. "Although at times I think he was sent to help me. I don't know what from, but at times it worries me terribly."

"I trust he will not break your heart," Barbara said.

Without warning Katrina hugged Barbara – a caring and understanding hug. "I hope he doesn't break both of our hearts," she said softly.

"Have you told your parents about what you know and feel?" Barbara asked.

"I don't think they would understand."

"I don't think anybody would understand. If you ever want to talk to someone you can always talk to me," Barbara said.

"I know," Katrina answered.

Barbara finished cutting the tomato. At the same time she wondered if Bertha would ever appear to Katrina. If she did appear would she try and destroy the girl to make Shannon do her bidding? The thought frightened her. She realized with a jolt that she now had both Shannon and Katrina to worry about.

Barbara waved as Shannon and Katrina drove away. "You don't know how lucky you are, Shannon," she said.

"Your mother is a wonderful person," Katrina said, sitting next to the door. Whenever she sat close to Shannon it seemed to make him nervous as if any form of human touch was a threat or something he could not understand.

Shannon pondered Katrina's statement for a few moments. "Barbara has a great heart," he finally said. "She has so much kindness in her she does not know what to do with it. You also are very kind and will only grow kinder. It is a great gift. One that I do not know I will ever possess."

Katrina had never asked Shannon if he knew his father, or who his father was, but the question seemed to escape from her mouth without her thinking. "Do you ever miss your father?" she asked immediately sorry for her words.

Shannon, much to her surprise, answered simply. "My

father and I talk all of the time," and added nothing more on the subject.

They drove the rest of the way to the river in silence. To their relief there was nobody at the picnic area. Three huge cottonwood trees grew by a picnic table. The leaves were large and deep green. Hundreds of cotton-enclosed seeds drifted through the air, each a new world of its own, searching for life and all its meanings. No more than thirty feet away the muddy Missouri River flowed sluggishly by. A blue, long-legged crane stood in the middle of a mass of vegetation on the edge of the river waiting patiently for a minnow, while large yellow carp rolled clumsily in the shallows.

Katrina spread a red and white checkered tablecloth on the picnic table and set out the food. A tugboat came into view pulling a barge filled with scrap metal. Two men ran around on the deck and Shannon waved at them. They returned the wave.

Katrina opened a bag of potato chips, put a sandwich on each plate, and then opened two sodas. Shannon ate slowly, not looking at Katrina. Unlike most girls it did not bother Katrina when she was being ignored. There were times when Shannon was talkative, times when he let his emotions run slightly unchecked and spewed on and on about things Katrina did not understand, or probably would never understand, and there were times he was silent.

Shannon finished his sandwich and nibbled on a potato chip. He always ate his food one dish at a time. If he had meat and salad and a vegetable he ate one at a time in no certain order, but nothing was started until one dish was eaten. He finished his potato chips, sipped on a soda and then said to Katrina, "If man is hungry he can never grow in wisdom. He would not have the leisure time to think."

"I suppose you are right," Katrina said. "But if that is true then why are some well-fed people stupid?" she asked with a wry smile.

Shannon shrugged his shoulders and returned her smile.

He then grew serious. "I know you feel the ghosts that follow me," he said. "I see you look for them at times. You cannot see them but you know they are there."

"I feel them," Katrina admitted.

"They will not harm you. I promise you that. Please do not fear."

"I only fear for you," Katrina said, not telling Shannon she had had the same conversation with his mother.

They fell into a deep silence. Katrina admired the floating cottonwood seeds. She looked at her hands. She then looked directly into Shannon's eyes. Her eyes were tinted with worry. "You know that I have loved you since I first saw you in the first grade," she said. "I dream about you. I dream about getting old with you. I dream of our children. I dream about your touch, the feel of you beside me at night. I dream about holding hands with you and you telling me you love me." A crystalline tear rolled from her right eye. "And, as I have told you before, I feel like I have known you forever or even beyond forever. I feel like we always have been."

Shannon brushed the tear from her cheek. He knew her feelings for him were honest and true, not taking or deceiving. "I fear my life will only bring tears to those that are close to me. No matter how I feel for you I must not succumb to my feelings. There is a force that pulls at me and I do not know what direction it wants me to go. I only know I must follow. At times I feel like I have two hearts pulsing in my body, two minds going in separate directions, and they will never be one. I feel like I am standing in the eye of a hurricane but the hurricane is a living being. I am surrounded by millions of people who look at me with beseeching eyes while the hurricane swirls around me filled with confusion and destruction. As long as I don't move I will be fine and the people around me will be fine. I know one day I will have to venture into the storm. It calls me to the challenge and one day I will not be able to refuse."

"For you I am like this river. I never really question my

course. I will go with you where ever I must and accept it without question," Katrina said.

"The tempest and the calm," Shannon mused. "Which one wins?"

"Neither," Katrina answered, "if they do not follow their own path."

Shannon and Katrina once again drifted into their own thoughts and were silent.

After a few moments Shannon's eyes grew blank as though he was in a trance. He walked to the edge of the river being pulled by a force he could not control. Katrina followed quietly behind him. Small clouds hung motionless in the sky like wise old men that were observing something that puzzled them. Three large buzzards circled below the clouds. Shannon held up his arms to the clouds. Tilting his head back he shut his eyes.

Tranquility settled over Katrina like a fine, hand-woven, silk shawl.

Shannon's body miraculously started to glow. A liquid gold outlined him – gold like fire, the rays were short and pulsed with the beating of his heart. Shannon stepped onto the water. He did not sink through the shallow water into the oozing silt bottom filled with decay, but stayed on top of the water – one with the water, not intruding on its majesty. The golden rays surrounding his body grew longer. They cracked and popped – warning all to stay away. Shannon demanded in a voice that ripped through the crackling and popping, "Why is there loneliness?"

There was no reply.

"Why is there loneliness?" Shannon demanded again.

Katrina was in awe.

"Why do you test me?" Shannon demanded.

The white clouds grew angry and turned instantly into black swirling tempests – lightening streaked through their centers in protest.

Slowly, inch-by-inch, Shannon started sinking into the

water, until at waist level his feet hit the decaying muck of the river bottom. The clouds formed into one dark cloud directly over Shannon, but the rest of the earth remained bathed in sunlight.

Katrina tried desperately to move and pull him from the river, but a force held her in place and she could not move.

The clouds unleashed torrents of rain. The lashing raindrops crashed in a tight circle around Shannon, but spared the rest of the river as it flowed tranquilly and unconcerned.

Shannon, to Katrina's amazement, started laughing. His laughter was louder than a cannon blast reverberating down a canyon. "Go from me if you will not answer me," he commanded.

Instantly the clouds vanished as if they had been nothing but a mirage.

Bright fire burned in his eyes as Shannon turned and looked at Katrina. He splashed out of the water and urgently embraced her. Her breasts were warm and reassuring on his chest. Katrina started sobbing. "I don't understand. I don't understand," she repeated clinging to him.

Slowly Katrina's anguish was absorbed by Shannon's embrace. She shuddered as if a deep chill had been chased away by a roaring fire. Shannon stepped slightly away from her. He held her face between his hands and kissed her tenderly on the forehead and said sadly, "Now you know why I cannot love you."

Katrina ran her hands fleetingly over Shannon's hands, then pulled his hands from her face and turned them palm up to kiss each of his palms. "My Shannon," she said. "You can love."

"I know I cannot love. My love is a curse. It would be better if you would leave me, but I am not me without you."

"We are the beginning," Katrina said not knowing why she said what she did, but she found deep solace in her own words.

Chapter Fourteen

BERTHA

The worst thing about vengeance is that the avenger becomes the perpetrator. It is a vicious cycle with no end that in time births wars and feuds, and forces the innocent into battles they do not know the cause of, but are still consumed by.

****

At times Bertha would walk to the cemetery and stare at the graves of her two brothers and father. She would say vile things about them trying to rekindle the flame of hateful passion that had driven her to destroy them. But, the hate she felt was more an ember than a roaring fire. The graves were mere bumps on the ground covered with green grass and a few dandelions. Her brothers and father were gone. It was that simple. They were either in Heaven or Hell or they were nothing.

Bertha's voice had been silent for many months but, unknown to Bertha, he observed her at all times, patiently waiting. In school the other children now avoided Bertha. She did not know it, but there were many people who thought she had killed her brothers and she was looked at suspiciously and whispered about. Bertha once again became a bully and tried to antagonize the other children but they would only run away. They would not even call her names or taunt her with insults.

Rebecca scoffed at the rumors as malice without merit. But Bertha did trouble her and, although she had always been a caring guardian, she began to feel sorry for Bertha – for both her lot in life and the way she looked. "Frumpy," Rebecca called it.

When Bertha was sixteen her life was miserable. She missed having something to hate even though there was something else inside of her she could not define that needed. It was a strange and foreign feeling. Also no boys asked her to the dances or wanted to walk her home. No girls asked her over to their house for sleepovers or parties.

Being shunned Bertha did not go into her own play world. She fantasized no friends. She had no inclination to read books and live through the characters. She had no desire to play. After school she sat by the window looking out at the world and concentrated on nothing. She no longer cooked and when she did the food was bland – her dishes were devoid of flavor like she was devoid of being.

When Bertha was seventeen her voice rekindled her hate. "You must hate," her voice said. "It is your destiny."

Rebecca and Bertha were eating supper when Bertha snapped bitterly at Rebecca. "I know you don't love me you old witch."

Rebecca was mortified and her fork clattered to the floor.

"The only reason you ever took care of me was because of my father's money and now my brother sends you money every month," Bertha continued caustically.

Rebecca was too shocked to reply.

"Don't even try and make excuses. I know you think I am ugly. I know you think I will never be worth anything and I am only an embarrassment to you. I know you dream about the day I will be old enough to leave and take care of myself."

"I have always thought the best for you," Rebecca stammered.

"You lie. You only think about yourself," Bertha said and jumped up and threw her plate against the wall. Rebecca cringed in fright.

"I hate you. I have always hated you and I will be happy the day you die," Bertha screamed and stomped from the kitchen to her own room. She opened her window and hollered to any who could hear. "I hate all of you. I hope you all rot in Hell."

Then she tossed herself on the bed and glared at the ceiling. After a few moments her breathing returned to normal and she smiled. Once again she had life. "Thank you voice," she said.

Rebecca was so shaken she could not get up from the table. She did not cry but she felt used and abandoned. All of her intentions had been for nothing. Even if she had never truly loved Bertha, her heart had been good, and she had never meant any harm for the child.

Rebecca felt extremely weak. Perspiration broke out on her forehead. She stood, but had to hold onto the table for support. Her breathing came in tight irregular gasps. She moved on trembling legs toward the door. She wanted to lie on the grass and feel its freshness on her arms and legs. She wanted to see the evening sky and be comforted with its promise of dreams. She wanted to hear birds singing happily before it grew dark.

She made her way feebly down the back steps. Standing in the yard it was with great effort she kicked off her shoes. The grass was wonderful on her bare feet and she remembered being a little girl and running around the yard with her dog. "He was such a good dog. I loved him so," Rebecca said.

She thought sadly of the day her dog died. Her father had dug the hole in the rich black dirt and she tenderly placed the dog in the hole with his dish and collar.

She pictured her husband riding a horse to come courting and how he smiled shyly as he handed her the single white daisy and said, "This is for you but it is not as pretty as you."

She had wanted to jump with happiness but she demurely took the flower and replied simply, "Thank you."

Rebecca crumpled face down onto the ground without feeling the impact. "I am so tired," she murmured to the soothing grass.

The wind stirred and gently caressed her. The last thing she heard was the distant singing of a bird.

Bertha found Rebecca in the morning. "You deserve your fate," Bertha said to the still body. "You were no different than all of the others."

When the morticians moved Rebecca hundreds of crickets scampered for cover. They had spent the night underneath her body, enjoying the last of her warmth.

The rest of the day Bertha stayed in the house and closely examined everything. The framed print of four young girls looking tranquilly at birds, a painting of a sea captain standing on the bow of his ship wishfully looking back at his crying wife waving from the dock, the old and frayed imitation oriental carpet, the blue edged dinnerware, Rebecca's bed and the cracked and yellowed photograph of Rebecca and her husband standing in front of a large garden – the corn tall and proud behind them.

Bertha felt no connection with the house that had protected her and kept her warm. She felt no bond with the woman who had raised her. In the morning she packed two suitcases with a few of her clothes, took the small amount of money Rebecca kept in a cookie jar, and started walking the twenty-eight miles to Corydon, Iowa. With each step, she buried her life in Promise City deeper and deeper into the decaying blackness of her heart.

"Now you will truly become mine," her voice said. "You will be my champion of champions."

Chapter Fifteen

BARBARA

Worry is always with mankind, no matter what culture or belief. Man worries about death, disease, hunger, war, status. The list is endless. Even those in life who have been fortunate with money and possessions worry. Worry is a thread that holds all of life's garments together. Love does not have the power to overcome worry. Love creates its own worries.

****

Barbara started reading the Bible before going to sleep every evening. It both soothed and bothered her. At times she was filled with belief, but then at other times she thought it absurd and childish, and she could not understand how God could be so cruel. How could He demand a man to kill his son? How could He not intervene with the death of his only son? She wondered if Jesus dying on the cross had really changed anything. Even with the confusion reading the Bible made her sleep better at night, although her fears over Shannon and Katrina did not diminish.

After Shannon came home from the picnic he was changed. Shannon's eyes became more distant than ever, as though they only saw whatever was going on in his mind, and not what was in front of him. When Barbara and he were together he seldom talked. Barbara would say something simple to draw him into conversation. "Have you had a good day? How is Katrina?"

He would only mumble, "Okay" or "She is fine," and retreat deep within himself once again.

To Barbara it was as if she no longer existed. One day she was a mother and friend and the next day she was a stranger, a person who would never be confided in again, a person who could not be trusted.

What Barbara did not know was that Shannon's voice was constantly speaking to him.

Besides her worry over Shannon and Katrina, Barbara at times, unlike earlier, was desperately lonely. It was not a loneliness based on the need for a man or a friend. It was a loneliness she could not define. She would be doing fine, and then the loneliness would sweep into her so deeply she had to force herself not to cry. She did not feel pity for herself. Shannon's condition or why he was the way he was, left no room for pity, but the loneliness was so intense she had no idea what to do. One day it attacked her at work as she was inspecting the way a new line of dresses were showcased. She was suddenly tumbling into a deep bottomless pit, and the people who walked by her seemed to be only hollow shells that were incapable of reaching out and helping her. She was lost in a limbo of loneliness that would never go away or lose any of its intensity. And although the loneliness would pass, either by itself or by her will, with each attack she grew weaker. She wanted to believe Bertha's ghost was behind it, but Bertha had not appeared in years.

Barbara also noticed a difference in Katrina after the picnic. Katrina no longer moved with confident grace but she seemed to shuffle. Barbara also noticed that when Katrina looked at Shannon it was not with the happiness of friends, or the confident glow of young love, but with a deep reverence that was stronger than love but also frightening. Barbara wondered if something disappointing had happened between them during the picnic.

Neither Shannon nor Katrina told Barbara what happened during their picnic, not even talking about it to each other, but they both knew life between them had changed and it caused a lingering sadness between them. Even though they were inseparable they both knew life would force them to take different paths, and the separation might not allow them to ever reunite.

Katrina's father saw, but could not pinpoint the changes in Katrina. Outwardly she seemed the same. She was still a good person but the young girl was gone. Although she did not look different, she was different. "Oh Sam, don't worry so much," Danyella told Sam. "She is starting to understand she is a woman. It's nothing. All women go through it."

"There is more to it than that," Sam said. "It has something to do with Shannon. I don't know if I trust him anymore. At times I think he is evil and that he will destroy Katrina both physically and emotionally."

"There is not an evil bone in Shannon," Danyella replied.

"There is evil in all of us," Sam said.

****

Barbara was glad to be home from work. It had been a taxing day. Collapsing on the sofa she kicked off her shoes, and for a mere split second she relaxed before she was overwhelmed with an excruciating bout of fear. The fear was so severe it felt as though her insides were being squeezed in a vice and made it difficult to breathe. The room started spinning and she lost her equilibrium. "Mother! Mother!" she pleaded. "Help me! Help me please!"

A cool breeze rustled the curtains and Anna appeared. Anna was now deep gray – the gray of a thick fog bank, so thick that when it came to shore houses would be obscured and car headlights could not penetrate it. Anna's face was a blur and Barbara could not make out her eyes, nose, or mouth. You must not fear, Barbara," Anna said firmly. "You must not grow weak. It is very important."

"It would not be as hard," Barbara said. "If I only had an idea of what life has in store for Shannon?"

"No creature knows what the future holds for them," Anna said. "Why should you be any different from the rest? Because you are Shannon's mother does not make you special on the face of the earth."

"My burden is heavier than most women," Barbara said.

"You must be strong," Anna said.

"Your burden overwhelmed you in life. How can you preach to me now?" Barbara demanded.

"Death is a great teacher," Anna said without remorse.

"Do you think Shannon has been sent to change the world?" Barbara asked, hoping for an answer.

"He has a mission," Anna said.

"Let some other child have his mission!" Barbara pleaded.

"It is impossible," Anna said.

"Do you ever see Bertha?" Barbara questioned.

"She is always around and for some reason she is getting stronger. I try to follow her but I cannot keep up. I do know we are different entities. I feel like I am only half of a ghost while Bertha is her own entity – not a true ghost, not a true spirit, but complete and powerful with what she is. I do know there are many like her."

"There is so much hate," Barbara said more to herself than to her mother.

"I am fortunate. I know I am what I am to protect Shannon. The why of it I do not know. But it is not my place to question the why. I am like a soldier going into a battle that does not know the reason for the battle. I am sorry I can do nothing for your worry or your fear. I can only watch and wait, wait for what I really do not know, but when it happens I will know." Barbara sighed. "It all seems so hopeless at times."

Anna swirled and an edge of her grayness swept over Barbara's hand. Then, like a dream shattered by the dawn, Anna was gone.

Barbara remained still for a few moments. The touch of her mother lingered on her hand and she no longer felt afraid. Rejuvenated she changed out of her work clothes.

Shannon and Barbara ate in silence but it did not bother Barbara. She looked fondly at Shannon and thought, "You have your life. I can only hope for you and grieve if it does not work out."

Shannon looked up from his plate and smiled slightly.

For a brief atom of time they were both at rest.

Chapter Sixteen

SHANNON

Why is it we hurt those that need love the most? Do we reach a point where we take love for granted and forget it is a gift? Do we discover too late that once love has been saddened it is never the same?

****

Driving back from the picnic Katrina stared out the window immersed in a world of her own thoughts. Shannon felt as though Katrina was on one side of a wide canyon and he was on the other. For the first time in his life he felt truly alone, but he was unable to think of anything to say that would bridge the gap between them. He stopped in front of Katrina's house and opened the car door for her. They faced each other, but Shannon had to look away from her eyes, still unable to think of something to say. Katrina kissed him on the cheek and said quietly, "I will never forsake you," and walked quickly toward her house.

Katrina did not turn and wave before she entered the house.

When Shannon got home he told Barbara he was tired and headed directly to his bedroom. Shannon sprawled on his bed fully dressed. "I love you Katrina but I cannot tell you," he said. "I am possessed and haunted by ghosts. How can I love when I do not know myself? But you are with me in all that I do. I am so sorry your love for me only causes you pain."

Bertha appeared at the foot of the bed. The hornets inside

100

her were quiet. Shannon stood and showed no surprise at seeing her. He merely gazed into her vacant eyes. Bertha met his eyes and held them. She tried to penetrate them but could not. "How does it feel to forsake love my lost one?" she taunted.

"I have not forsaken love," Shannon replied.

Bertha moved to within a few feet of Shannon. "Now you will wander the face of the earth like me and you will come to know loneliness and despair. When you call out there will be no one capable of helping you. You will discover that your gifts are a curse and not a blessing. There are no gods that will come to your rescue. You are all alone and will always be alone. There is no love for you that can be sustained. The only person who understands you is me. As you are my salvation I am also yours. The day will come when you will plead for me."

"How can you understand anything when all you have done is hate?" Shannon asked, feeling pity for Bertha.

"Hate does not suffer like love," Bertha replied. "It was love that...that...that...that..." But Bertha could not finish her statement and felt momentarily confused by what she had almost said.

Shannon wondered what truth she had almost divulged. "I will never stoop to your level," he said.

"You will hate one day. You will want to kill and destroy. Your heart will turn black when you find out what you seek is unreachable and that man in all truth truly only desires to possess and destroy all that is around him," Bertha said returning to her normal self.

"I will never turn to hate," Shannon replied.

Bertha's form pulsated. "You feel the beginnings of hate already. You feel the sting of loneliness over your precious Katrina. Your childhood is gone. Now you will start understanding parts of the knowledge you have always possessed. The knowledge will break your spirit and nothing but death will help you."

Shannon was instantaneously overcome with anger more intense than he had ever felt before. He struck viciously at Bertha, but she was gone before the blow landed. Her last words reverberated scornfully through the charged air, "To lash out is only a beginning."

Shannon called out in anguish. "Where are you my voice? You come to me when I do not need you, but when I need you to you do not answer my questions. Why must you test me?"

There was no answer.

Shannon fell onto the bed, black clouds surged through his body – clouds filled with hail and lightening, their only goal to destroy and bring havoc. Rolling over Shannon buried his face in the pillow and tried to chase the clouds away, but they only became stronger and formed into a nightmare vision of an enormous army of men with emotionless faces. They all had rifles on their shoulders and were marching into a hail of machine gun fire. The men firing the machine guns had no eyes or noses, only large grim smiles on their empty faces. Row upon row of advancing men were mowed down like they were mere ants, but still the men marched into the bullets as though they had no purpose or meaning in life. The men marched on until there was a mountain of dead men. Blood saturated the ground and formed a large red lake that covered many of the men. The machine gun fire stopped. The smiles on the men firing the machine guns vanished and eyes appeared on their faces. They looked around and saw there were no more men to kill. They fired the machine guns on themselves until only one man remained. His smile returned as he turned the machine gun toward himself. He bent over and pulled the trigger. One last bullet barked. And then all was insanely quiet. There was no whisper of the wind, no buzzards to pick the flesh from the bones, only the silence of death – a mountain of dead men and a sea of blood.

"How many men have died in your name or whatever name they have called you?" Shannon demanded of his voice. "How many men will it take to satisfy your need?"

There was no answer.

"Is silence your pride? Do you find joy in watching our sufferings?"

There was no answer.

Shannon felt like he was in a vacuum. He was confused and lost. "What can I do?" he begged.

"What should I do?" he humbly asked a few moments later.

A light breeze filtered through the room. Anna appeared. She was glowing silver. "You must go out into the world and see all you can see. You must forsake all those that have loved you but you cannot abandon them."

"I fear the world is a dark and uninviting place," Shannon replied.

"You will discover what is in your heart and your purpose," Anna said.

"How can you be an advisor?" Shannon asked.

"Your voice guides me," Anna answered and vanished.

In bed Shannon tossed and turned knowing he now had a mission and realizing with both relief and sadness he would be leaving his mother and Katrina behind.

In the morning Shannon did not go to school. He needed to be alone with his thoughts until he would meet Katrina after school.

Shannon and Katrina were holding hands as they walked. For both of them, their clasping hands became one – what one felt the other felt. But they were both silent. It was only after going several blocks Katrina said, "You are going away. You do not have to hide the truth from me. I understand."

"I must go. I have no power over my life," he said simply.

"You must promise me you will not leave without saying good-bye," Katrina said.

"I could not do that. It would be cruel for both of us."

"You have seen your great grandmother's ghost again," Katrina said.

"I think I am becoming a ghost," Shannon replied softly.

"But yes. I have seen her ghost."

That evening Shannon could not look at Barbara for fear she would know his thoughts. He knew he could not tell his mother he was leaving. He would have to write her a letter. There was no way she would understand. He would be a thief stealing away in the night with no regard for the people he had stolen from.

Shannon stopped going to school and spent his time at the library. He met Katrina after school to walk her home. She never mentioned his absence from school. They talked little both trying to ignore the parting they knew was approaching. Shannon did tell her he was teaching himself many of the languages of the world.

Shannon learned all of the Arabic dialects. He learned all of the Native American languages of North America. He learned the many forms of Spanish spoken in South America and Mexico. He learned Japanese and Korean and Chinese, Cambodian, Laotian, Taiwanese, Vietnamese, and the languages of Africa. He learned remote island languages. Lastly, Shannon learned Hebrew, but even with the differences in all languages he felt they all came from one source. He then began studying the pagan religions, spirits and Shamans, curses and totems.

When he was finished he realized with certainty he would be leaving soon and a leaden heaviness entered not only his heart, but also his body. That afternoon as he walked Katrina home he asked her, "Will you go for a walk with me this evening?"

"It will be our last for awhile," she replied simply.

Shannon withdrew from the bank the three thousand dollars Anna had willed him. He then visited a jewelry store. Barbara was not home when Shannon got home, but there was a letter from the school. He opened it and read: "Your son has been truant..." He tore up the letter and tossed it in the garbage.

During dinner he could not look at Barbara, feeling he was betraying her with his leaving.

Barbara had no desire to invade his silence and after supper she read the Bible. Her son was gone from her. His path was his own and now she must find hers.

That evening Shannon and Katrina went for a walk at a park not far from Katrina's house. Several people were exercising their dogs while two boys tossed a football. They sat on a bench under a tranquil red maple. "You are beautiful," Shannon said. "You were beautiful the first day I saw you."

Katrina smiled – the warmth and depth of it making Shannon smile. "I will miss you," Katrina said. "And I really don't know how I will stand not being with you."

She almost started to cry, but choked the tears away, and smiling once again added, "Life is so silly to be so serious."

"I will not be able to communicate with you," Shannon said.

"I will know if you are okay. I always know how you are. I feel your pain, your loneliness, and I know you love me. It is not a question. It is only that you do not know what love is or you do not accept it. The world burdens you. Maybe you fear love will make you weak, too weak to tackle your challenge. But I know you love me, and I love you, and as long as I feel that way I will not want for another."

"I am like a heavy chain to you," Shannon said. "Your love for me only brings you longing and pain."

"You are wrong, Shannon, it also brings me strength."

Shannon removed a small box from his pocket and said, "Hold out your hand, please?"

Holding out her hand Shannon slipped a delicate gold ring on her left little finger. Engraved on the ring, no bigger than a tear drop, were two tiny hearts connected to each other. "I give you as much of my heart as I can," Shannon said.

Katrina kissed the ring. "I want you to make love to me, Shannon."

"You know I can't," he said, "although I want to."

Shannon wanted to kneel at Katrina's feet. He wanted to pray his love for her. But he could not.

Katrina knew there was no need to ask Shannon where he was going, knowing he had no idea what his destination was.

They saw a couple talking and laughing – their laughter the song of golden bells.

"It is time," Shannon said as he stood and held out his hand.

Katrina held his hand as they headed back to her house. In the front yard Shannon kissed her on the forehead. "When we turn away from each other please do not look back," he said. "Then there is no true goodbye."

Katrina nodded. They embraced, savoring the warmth, the touch, the beating of two hearts. Releasing her, Shannon turned, and Katrina started toward the door. Neither looked back as the distance between them grew – neither of them cried. Crying would come later.

That night Shannon wrote a letter. In the morning, after Barbara was gone, he packed one suitcase, folded the letter once, laid the letter on the kitchen table and he left, shutting the door quietly behind him.

Finding the letter after work Barbara read:

Dear Mother:
What are we but walking ghosts? Each of us search for meaning while trying to survive in this world, while all the time knowing that only bones are in our future. The fate of millions rides on my shoulders. The absurdity of life confounds me. When death comes I might welcome it, but then there is Bertha to confuse the issue. At times I think earth is the real hell, and we have lived and failed in another world, letting our greed and selfishness curse us from one hell to another. I must go find what I do not know. When my journey is over I will return. My heart is heavy with the parting. I have no doubt the ghosts of Bertha and Anna will go with me. Do not fear my heart is always with you. Please stay in touch with Katrina. I have hurt you both but my sorrow will not help.

Your devoted son, Shannon

After putting the letter in her jewelry box Barbara opened her Bible and read: "In the beginning God created the heaven and the earth. And the earth was without form, and void..."

She set the Bible down.

"Poor Katrina," she sighed.

Chapter Seventeen

BERTHA

L ove cannot be pursued and even longing does not make it happen. It is illusive and free with no desire to be cornered and tamed. People that proclaim they are in love, when they know they are not, soon learn the hard way how vicious and unforgiving tainted love can be.

* * * * * *

Bertha walked deliberately away from Promise City towards Corydon. With the death of Rebecca she felt liberated and free. Several people stopped and asked her if she wanted a ride but with a proud tilt to her chin she replied, "No, I am off to find myself."

"The best of luck," they would say.

With each footstep Bertha planned her future. "I will meet a man and I will marry. I will have children. I will not look back on my life or ever again be consumed by hate. What I did was not wrong. It was justified. I hold no guilt."

Bertha traveled twelve miles the first day. For the first time in her life she truly looked at the world around her and was able to see past the hate-filled confines of her mind. The day was peaceful, not too hot or humid, with just the right amount of wind. There were no clouds to diminish the carefree sun. She was amazed how beautiful the countryside was – the cottonwood trees and maples, even the spiny juniper trees that the farmers hated because they spread quickly into all the fields. All seemed to be a part of a grand plan. Grazing herds

108

of milk cows gazed docilely at her as she passed. Yellow and red-winged blackbirds flew out of stands of cattails, scolded her but at the same time amused her and made her laugh. Her laughter sounded foreign to her ears. Rabbits darted in and out of the bushes not really concerned in what direction they were going. A covey of quail marched across the road in single file, chirping to each other, telling jokes that only they could understand.

As evening approached Bertha stopped in a large stand of walnut trees not far from the road. In her haste to leave Promise City she had not brought food or water or matches, but the pangs of hunger and thirst were in their own way refreshing, almost cleansing. Taking some of her clothes out of her suitcase Bertha spread them out for a bed and rolled up a dress into a pillow.

The night came softly. Bertha watched the stars through the tree branches – her demons were gone, abandoned in Promise City. As she shut her eyes the sounds of the night became one with her. She heard the creak of the branches as the wind kicked up – the patter of leaves touching leaves, and she imagined the leaves were hundreds of laughing lovers. She wanted a man to rip her clothes off – to be so filled with passion he was a beast. She wanted to feel the force of him – the demands. She would let him ravage her, enjoying the animal sounds and smells until they were both nothing but a knot of desire, until there was no world, no day, no night, no dreams, nothing but lust.

She opened her eyes and she was sweating. Her thighs ached for release. A voice crept through the darkness. "You will never know passion," the voice said.

"Come out where I can see you," she demanded.

A dirty gray shape of a man appeared from the trees, floating barely above the ground. The edges of the form were smooth. There were no appendages and no vague outline of a face. "I will never let you love for what you did to me," the shape said.

Bertha recognized the voice. "I would kill you again, Paul," she answered. "Ghosts mean nothing to me."

Another dirty gray form appeared, slightly larger, but its edges were jagged and spiked. "I curse your life," it said. "I will do my best to fill your days with dread and I will make sure there is no person on the face of the earth who will love or even remotely like you."

"I would kill you again Thomas and neither one of you can harm me. I am not afraid of your threats. I command you to go away," Bertha ordered with no fear.

The forms instantly vanished.

"Nothing can harm me," Bertha said to the night. "I am not afraid of any man or spirit or god."

"Nothing will harm you as long as we are together," her voice said.

"You must tell me who you are," Bertha said with no trace of kinship in her voice.

"It is still not time," her voice replied. "But you know I am all that you can trust."

For the first time in her life Bertha was confused by the voice. If the voice was her only friend why would he hide his identity? And what if she no longer wanted to be his champion? Her desire now was to find herself and live a normal life.

Before the sunrise she was headed confidently toward Corydon.

Mr. John Adams enjoyed a good life in Corydon. His dry goods store was doing well and the community respected him. Many of the single eligible women eyed him admirably. A tall and good-looking storeowner John was a good catch. John, though, was not interested in marriage. He held the love for his first wife religiously in his heart. The sight of her dying pale and thin from pneumonia, after only six months of marriage was an agony that never left him. He made a vow to himself he would never tell the story to another person.

After his wife's death John withdrew his savings and

boarded the train in Philadelphia with no destination in mind. His parents were dead and, with no ties and being a proud man, he scorned the idea of pity or sympathy. When the train stopped in Kansas City he got off the train and headed north. A few days later he was passing through Corydon, Iowa. Here nobody knew him. Nobody asked where he came from or what he did? It was a pleasant town of two thousand hard-working people that was surrounded by farms. John opened a dry good store. After only one year he had made enough money to buy a large two-story home with a wrap around porch. The house looked majestic surrounded by several gracious elm trees. He sent for the few possessions he owned in Philadelphia and spent his leisure time planting flowers and shrubs in the yard. During the spring, summer, and fall, his yard was a profusion of color. Outwardly, to everyone in town, John was happy and content.

Only at night did John stop his facade. He would eat alone and afterwards sit in his living room reading and fighting off the loneliness and sense of loss over his wife. Her memory was imbedded in the marrow of his bones and filled his mind with tears and sorrows.

During his five years in the Navy, while he traveled the world, she patiently waited for him. Her letters were his life songs. Her pretty face and petite body was a photograph in the back of his mind during all the years. Then his discharge, the happy tear-filled reunion, the joy of the marriage, and then her death, as if it was all pre-destined – arranged by the gods for no other reason than their amusement over man's frailty.

John was alone in the store the morning Bertha Cartwright entered. It could have been his loneliness. It could have been the fact Bertha was large-boned and plain, dark haired with dark eyes, so unlike his pretty and petite wife. It could have been the dirt and grime on Bertha giving her a lost waif look, or it could merely have been he was tired of being alone. No matter the reason Bertha made him smile and he said to her, "Good morning. It is a fine day."

"It is a fine day," Bertha replied.

After asking her name and discovering she was looking for a place to stay he helped her with her suitcase to a boarding house that was owned by a Mormon widow named Mariah Smith. Mariah fussed over Bertha. "My dear! You need a nice room and a bath."

Bertha's room was on the second floor and had a grand view of the park. After setting her suitcase down John asked her if she would like to go to supper that evening. "I would love to," Bertha replied.

Going back to the store John felt happy and his smile was not forced.

To Bertha the room was beautiful with its lace curtains and white bedspread covered with flower imprints. There was an oak chest-of-drawers, a small table, a red velvet chair and a mirror on the back of the door. She unpacked her few belongings, set her brush and comb on the chest-of-drawers, and, taking a clean dress headed down the hall to take a bath. Relaxing in the tub she thought about John. The first sight of him had sent electricity through her body, leaving her almost breathless. No one had ever smiled at her the way he did. She could not say for sure but she thought maybe she loved him at first sight. But the thought also frightened her. What if he would abandon her? What if her love was refused?

Her answer made her shiver. "I would kill him," she said truthfully.

Early in the afternoon Bertha put on her best dress – light blue but plain, cleaned her shoes, did her hair, and waited anxiously for John.

With the knock on the door she jumped out of her chair almost giddy with anticipation. Taking three deep breaths she straightened her dress and answered the door trying not to show how excited she was.

Holding a yellow rose in his hand John said, "For you. I hope you like roses."

"It's lovely, John, thank you."

On the sidewalk John offered his arm. She draped her arm gently through his. All the people they passed smiled and Bertha relished the look of envy on the ladies' faces. She was living a dream – a wonderful dream that she hoped would never end.

"And what brings you to Corydon?" John asked once they were seated in the restaurant.

"My father died several years ago and my stepmother hated me," Bertha replied.

"Life has a way of getting better," he said, sounding like the father she never had.

The evening was the happiest Bertha had ever experienced. She loved hearing about John's days in the Navy and all of the wonderful parts of the world he had visited. She could visualize in her mind the ocean stretching far beyond the limitations of her sight, the sounds of seagulls, the grandeur of Hong Kong and Singapore, the cold mists of Ireland and Scotland. She lived them all through his words.

"I have never been anywhere," she said. "Your life has been so exciting."

"Well, maybe we can change that," John smiled.

John escorted her back to her room. At the door he kissed her hand. "Come by the store tomorrow," he invited.

"It would be my pleasure," she replied.

Standing by the window Bertha watched John as he walked away. "Life is only a matter of distance," she said and readied for bed.

Across the street the ghost of Paul and Thomas floated above the treetops. "Now we have our purpose," Paul said to Thomas.

Thomas did not reply.

Bertha and John's romance was a whirlwind. They dined out. They took walks every evening and had Sunday picnics in the park. They were invited to all of the important people's houses where there was talk of John running for mayor. Bertha started working in the store. But even caught up in whirlwind romance John never made any improper advances toward Bertha. He was polite and chivalrous. Bertha knew if she pressed the issue he would be offended. So she stayed demure and submissive, bowing to his every beck and call. One day she told John she wanted to cook dinner for him at his house. "I would love a home cooked meal," he said.

Her early training from Rebecca shined through. Filled with her good feelings the food was delicious. "That is the best roast beef and potatoes I have ever eaten," John said after dinner.

She could see the delight in his eyes.

That night, on the way to her room, he proposed. She agreed immediately and he slipped a gold band with a tiny diamond on her finger and they kissed. His lips were soft and warm, gentle and caring.

After proposing John was at home sitting in a rocker on the front porch. The town was resting – the majority of the house lights were turned off. The angry cry of a distant tomcat hissed, then quiet. A few bats circled, embraced by the dark. Paul and Thomas were suspended in a tree watching John. John visualized his first wife on the day of their marriage. She was radiant with happiness – her eyes were childhood dreams, her smile a rainbow that would never end. Their first night together he lay in bed and she stood with candle light behind her and slowly undressed. Her skin was like milk and took his breath away. They made love tenderly. Slowly, not driven by lust, or passion, but so filled with love they only sought peace and tranquility and an escape from the world.

John sighed. "I will never forget you. You were the only love of my life."

There was no thought of Bertha in his mind.

Paul and Thomas absorbed his loving and sad thoughts. They vowed no harm would be bestowed on John by them.

The wedding was held in the park on a glorious June day. A Baptist minister performed the service and after the ceremony there was ice cream and cake and a dance. Bertha did not hear the ladies' gossiping about how John could have found a better wife or the men wondering why he had married such an ugly woman. Bertha wore a white dress decorated with imitation pearls and felt beautiful. She danced the first dance with John and then she danced with each of the men – swinging merrily and happily to the bouncy tunes.

Going to her new home after the party the living room was overflowing with presents and John had flowers and candles in the bedroom.

No sooner had they entered the bedroom when Bertha's body was consumed by passion. She ripped at his clothes – tearing two buttons off of his shirt. John was shaken but he did not protest. Bertha undressed quickly. She did not kiss him, murmur she loved him, touch him gently, but she pushed him onto the bed and attacked him. She groaned and moaned. She got on top of him. She forced him into her and drove up and down like a wild beast. It took less than a few minutes and she screamed and fell off of him like she had been shot with a rifle. She slept and John lay staring distantly at the ceiling while thinking about his first wife.

In the morning they made love slower but Bertha was gangly and awkward. She also felt inadequate and also sensed, ever so slightly, there was a memory holding John from completely giving himself to her.

Eating breakfast she said, "I know I have offended you."

"Why do you say that?" he replied trying to sound casual.

"I feel at one time you loved another and you loved her more than you do me."

"I have never loved another," John smiled, showing no trace of deceit.

Bertha knew he was lying and a corner of her heart turned black. A seed of hate sprouted and her voice whispered, "Your love is only an illusion. It is only I who will never forsake you."

Chapter Eighteen

BARBARA

How can we say we truly know ourselves when we wake up each morning a different person? Another day of wisdom or stupidity added to the complexities of life. What can we really know except that we are, at least for the moment, what we are, and that we will change?

****

Shannon's leaving did not stun Barbara. Anna had told her he would go on a journey, but she was saddened he had not told her face-to-face. But then, she supposed, she would have cried and carried on and made it more difficult for Shannon. She knew Shannon had taken the course of action he thought would cause the least anguish. She also knew he would not write or phone. Whatever journey he was on he must do alone. She only hoped it would not destroy him.

Two days after Shannon departed Bertha appeared to Barbara. Barbara was in the living room reading her Bible. Bertha materialized in the middle of the room. Her face was as clear and vivid as though she was alive. "And now the sheep has been led away," Bertha said mockingly. "And now the mother of the lamb has been cast aside."

Anna was in the corner invisible to both Bertha and Barbara.

Barbara, with the Bible in her hand, stepped defiantly within arm's length of Bertha. "You cannot get to my son through me. If you harm me he will never help you in your pursuit. Don't treat me like I am stupid and don't taunt me. It will not do you any good. I do not fear you or death."

Bertha laughed a demeaning laugh. "You are wrong. I can destroy you anytime I wish. I can crawl into your mind and fill your thoughts with demons you cannot conquer. In time the demons would make you plead for release, but they would not release you until you begged me to make them stop."

Barbara's mind was instantly ablaze with a tortured vision of Shannon. Shannon was ravaged by fear and naked. He was picking his way through a dark land that was strewn with jagged boulders. Horrible, contorted faces that possessed every pain and evil in the universe dove at him and shot through his body. They left blistering red welts as they entered and exited. Shannon stumbled and fell under the bombardment. "Why? Why?" he screamed but there was no answer.

Barbara crumpled to the floor and moaned, "Stop, stop, make it stop."

Bertha's laughter slashed through the room.

Anna observed.

The vision in Barbara's mind vanished. She lay trembling like a dog that had been beaten so cruelly it had lost its spirit. Her eyes were clamped shut as if she never wanted to see light again. Bertha's face was a mere few inches from Barbara's. Her breath was the odor of burnt cinders. "Open your eyes and look at me," Bertha ordered.

Barbara opened her eyes obediently.

"Do not tell me, little one, that I cannot destroy you," Bertha said. "Do not ever believe good can overcome all adversity. Shannon needs me like I need him. But I will win." And she vanished.

Barbara fumbled through the pages of her Bible and found the passage she needed. "And he stretched himself upon the child three times and cried out, 'O Lord, my God, I pray thee let this child's soul come into him again.'"

"Oh God, oh God, oh God," she prayed.

Anna prayed with her.

The pain slowly waned in Barbara's mind. Still shaken she called the Payne's. Katrina answered. "Katrina, you must come and see me. It is important," she stammered and hung up before Katrina could reply.

Katrina was frightened by Barbara's voice and ran to her house.

Katrina frantically rang the doorbell. Barbara let her in. Katrina was shocked at the sight of Barbara. Her face was ashen and she seemed to have aged ten years. "I know something happened when you and Shannon were on the picnic," Barbara said meekly. "You must tell me. I need to know."

Katrina told Barbara about Shannon standing on the water. How he had beseeched the sky with questions but there were no answers. She told her about Shannon not going to school and learning many of the languages of the world. And she showed Barbara the ring Shannon had given her. When Katrina was done all Barbara could reply was, "He is not a god. I know he is not a god. Pray he is not a god."

"I love him so," Katrina said and started to cry. "But even I do not know exactly what he is."

Embracing they cried for themselves and for Shannon.

When they were done crying Barbara told Katrina about Bertha appearing and the visions that had attacked her mind. "You must take care, Katrina," Barbara said with deep concern. "Now that Shannon is gone Bertha might try to harm you. It would be good if you chose a college far away and moved away from this area."

"I cannot leave you," Katrina said. "Maybe the two of us together are strong enough to withstand Bertha."

"No. You must go."

"I would die for Shannon," Katrina said. "I would sacrifice myself if need be to save him. Whatever calls him is more important than you or me. Whatever his destiny is I know it is true and good. There is no evil in his heart."

"I know he loves you," Barbara said.

Katrina smiled slightly. "I know. It is a great blessing, even though he cannot tell me."

"I also know he will never love another," Barbara said.

"Our love is blessed," Katrina replied. "There is no love stronger than ours."

Anna listened to Katrina and Barbara, then like an unheard and unfelt breeze on a remote mountaintop, she departed to pursue Bertha.

Katrina and Barbara embraced again by the door and Katrina went back home.

Barbara paced nervously around the house. "Shannon, Shannon, you must take great care," she murmured.

She fell into bed so exhausted she wished she would never wake up, but even in sleep her mind could not rid itself of the horrible faces that shot through Shannon. She knew their only desire was to destroy all that was good within him.

On the way home Katrina was deep in thought. She had the feeling she would not see Shannon for many years, but his heart was in the ring she wore. "Whenever you need me you know I will come," she said to the sky. "Our hearts are never apart."

Katrina was deathly afraid for Barbara. She was worried Barbara would not be able to take the strain. She might crack into a million tiny pieces so small she could never be put back together. Katrina had seen the unraveling in Barbara's eyes. Her eyes had been intense – darting with doubt and insecurity, and blazing with madness. To help Barbara Katrina would do as Barbara wished. She had her pick of four colleges and she would choose one out of state.

When Katrina got home her parents were in the kitchen. "I haven't seen Shannon lately. Did you two have a fight?" her mother asked.

"He ran away from home. I just came back from Barbara's, she is very upset," Katrina answered and headed to her room.

"Well, at least that is over," Sam said. "I never did trust that boy. I always felt he was disturbed and would hurt Katrina in the end."

"She didn't seem too upset about it," Danyella said. "I always thought they were such a nice couple."

"Another fairy tale bites the dust," Sam said. "Young love never has a chance. Life gets too complicated."

"It is so sad," Danyella said.

"When she goes to college she will meet a nice young man. One with his feet on the ground and who is not a dreamer," Sam said.

Danyella's heart was heavy as she thought. "I know you love Shannon, Katrina, but you will find another love, and you will use it to heal the hole in your heart."

She had no realization there are some pains in a person's heart that do not wish to be healed.

Chapter Nineteen

SHANNON

Many men have abandoned their homes to wander the world in search of truth. They think a new land with new people will answer the questions that haunt them. Most wanderers end up destitute and crazy, lost in some deep abyss in their minds they cannot escape from. They seem to forget truth only rests within oneself.

****

Shannon did not know where he was going but he was prepared. He had read all the great books, he knew many languages of the world, he understood the various religions and beliefs, he had studied governments, the history of civilizations, geology, and the formation of the planets and the universe, and mankind's evolution. He had read newspapers and magazines until he was tired of their constant advertisements to buy more – needing possessions did nothing for his search.

Leaving home he was deeply saddened and lonely, but he reasoned his way, at least momentarily, out of his loneliness. Barbara and Katrina loved him. With you both loving me I can never truly be alone, he thought.

Following a feeling that guided him, Shannon took a bus to downtown. For the first time in ages his voice spoke to him. "Right at the moment I cannot tell you your calling, but I can warn you it is grave and dangerous, and you will go through many tribulations and trials. You must always remember I will be with you. Free your spirit to the wind and trust your decisions."

"One day you will have to tell me my purpose," Shannon said.

The voice was gone.

Shannon rented a cheap room not far from the bus station. The room was shabby, but not dirty, with a single bed and a small chest-of-drawers with a Bible in the drawer. The bathroom was small with one thin towel and a wash rag. Shannon wondered if any of the people who had stayed in the room ever found their dreams. He counted out his money and divided it into four stacks, putting each one in a different pocket.

Shannon then explored downtown Kansas City. After being raised in an apartment in a nice section of town downtown was an alien world. The car and bus exhaust was suffocating and the people marching like ants to and from work were disconcerting. He could not understand how any person had an identity in such a throng. He thought of the billions of people that inhabited the earth and he wondered if it really mattered if he knew who or what he was or if he had a purpose?

Shannon discovered a book store and he browsed the travel section for over an hour, devouring the information on various countries and cities until he picked up a book – *The Wilderness Areas of North America* – and he was compelled to buy it. The photographs of the various mountain ranges enthralled him although he had never been to the mountains or even given them a passing thought.

It was getting close to dark and Shannon was hungry. He saw a diner. The diner smelled of dirt and grease. The patrons reeked of too much work for too little money. Cigarette smoke hung in the air like decaying dreams. There was a long counter and four tables. Everybody sitting at the counter gave him distant glances when he entered. Sitting at a corner table Shannon felt totally out of place and tried to hide his ill feelings by reading the book, but it failed to work.

When he ordered a hamburger he paid no attention to the waitress nor did he acknowledge her when she said, "Enjoy."

As he ate the hamburger Shannon tried to ignore the other customers. Without warning the customer's emptiness entered Shannon and he became each person, one at a time – sharing their lives, their endless string of dead end jobs, their disasters that led them to the dirty diner where they could mix with others of their kind. Shannon experienced such a deep loneliness, coupled with a sense of defeat, tears spilled from his eyes and cascaded down his cheeks.

The young waitress seeing Shannon crying handed him a napkin. "It's okay, hon, we have all been there. Dry your eyes," she said. She was pretty in a rough sort of way and had dyed blond hair – the dark roots glaring out unashamed. She wore deep-blue eye makeup which gave her a clownish air, numerous silver earrings in each ear, and a too tight, low cut white blouse.

Shannon smiled meekly, acknowledging her for the first time.

"What is your name?" the waitress asked.

"Shannon," he replied feeling better.

'I'm Millie," she replied with a, 'what does a name really matter,' tone to her voice.

Out of the customers sitting at the counter all but one turned around and stared at Shannon for a moment. An older lady said to a man next to her, "Some dumb kid that ran away from home and now misses his mommy," before she resumed eating.

"He'll get over it," the man grunted in reply.

Shannon dried his eyes and the waitress sat at the table with him. "I've been on my own since I was 16," she said trying to reassure him.

Shannon was at a loss for words, feeling bad that he had ignored her when she took his order. The waitress smiled. A man at the counter hollered at her, "Millie, get off your duff and bring me some more coffee."

"Get it yourself you lazy jerk," she snapped back. "I ain't your mother."

The man, not protesting or seemingly upset, went behind the counter and refilled his cup.

"People treat you like dirt when you're a waitress," Millie said to Shannon making a mocking face. "Bring me this...I need this...The coffee is too hot...The coffee is too cold...Never saying please... An endless give me...Give me."

Shannon smiled slightly amused by Millie's rendition of customers.

"If I ever have enough money to go to some fancy place to eat I will be polite to the waiters and waitress. I know how tough of a job it is," Millie said.

"I guess we learn by doing," Shannon said.

"You're cute when you're not crying," Millie said and winked at him.

For the first time in his life a dart of desire flamed through Shannon. It was so strong even Millie sensed it and gave him a knowing look. "I get off my shift in twenty minutes. Would you walk me home? It scares me at night. I live only a few blocks from here."

Her eyes were appealing and captivating.

Shannon, as if another person was talking, replied, "Yes, I would like that."

Millie resumed working. Shannon tried to read his book but he could not stop from glancing at Millie.

An older woman entered. Putting on an apron she said to Millie with a wry grin, "Another day in Paradise."

Millie came over to Shannon's table. "Hamburger's on me," she said.

Shannon started to protest, but Millie shook her head. "This place makes more money than the Pope."

Shannon took her hand when she held it out – a shot of desire flashed through his body and made him momentarily dizzy. Going outside they were followed by the knowing glances of the patrons.

It was dark, but the cars still groaned bumper to bumper down the street. Sirens blared in the distance. "Would you like a beer?" Millie asked Shannon.

"I'm not old enough to drink," Shannon replied slightly embarrassed – not telling her he had never had a drink.

"This place doesn't care. They're only interested in the money."

Millie took him to Big Jim's, a dark musty bar with red booths and black laminated tables. There were only a few people in the bar. "George!" Millie hollered. "Bring us a big pitcher and two glasses!"

Millie slid into the booth and Shannon started to sit on the other side. "No. Sit by me," Millie said patting the seat beside her.

Shannon sat as far away from her as he could. Millie scooted closer to him, slid her arm under his, and pressed her breast into his side.

The bartender banged the pitcher down heavily with two iced glasses. "Five bucks," he said gruffly.

Shannon paid while Millie poured the beer. Holding up her glass Millie said enticingly, "To you and me."

The first swallow of beer was cold and not too offensive. The second was good and Shannon chugged the rest of the beer, poured another and topped Millie's off.

Millie laughed and leaned deeper into him.

Bertha, unseen, was on the other side of the booth. "Now you will know treachery and deceit," she said. "Now your love will begin to decay. You are one step closer to me."

Anna, also unseen, observed. Neither ghost knew of each other's presence.

"I came here from Detroit," Millie said. "My mother was a bitch. I never knew my father. Mom would bring strange men home almost every night. I can still hear her groaning and moaning with men like she was a sow. I was sixteen when I ran away to Kansas City. I've been waiting tables in various restaurants and bars ever since."

"My mother worked in a bar for awhile," Shannon said. "You could find a better job."

"I must like the low side," she said. "Every time I get a better job I blow it and end up in some dive getting my ass pinched and making lousy tips."

As Shannon poured another beer Millie put her hand on his thigh. Her touch was fire. Leaning over Millie kissed Shannon on the neck and lava pulsed through his veins.

Bertha smiled.

Anna whispered, "Be careful."

"Would you like to come to my apartment?" Millie asked her breath hot on his neck. "I need somebody tonight."

"But I don't know you," Shannon said shyly. "And I am leaving tomorrow."

"No strings," Millie giggled. "What more do you want?"

With no warning Shannon felt like he was spinning. The walls closed in on him and there were two Millie's coming in and out of focus. He was being pulled out of the seat by a force he had no control over but managed to grab his book. Millie's sensual laughter danced in his mind. He was outside with no sensation of moving. The cars speeding by shimmered like great multi-colored beasts. The tall buildings were tabernacles to defy God, a testimony to the holiness of man, proclaiming man would never kneel to God again.

Bertha and Anna followed Millie and Shannon. Bertha was happy while Anna kept her emotions in check.

The apartment smelled old and tired. The light was dim. The drab furniture was sad and forlorn. The sounds of cars crept into the room like the muted cries of ancient beings.

Shannon sat in a chair. The room bobbed and weaved as if the floor was a restless ocean. Millie was in the middle of the room, masked by the dimness with a sly smile on her face. Taking off her shoes there was pure passion in her eyes – cat eyes – laughing, playing with Shannon. She removed her hose and tossed them carelessly to the side. Behind her an unmade bed beckoned. Millie slowly unbuttoned her blouse and let it slide from her shoulders. The bra came off – breasts inviting, tantalizing. She played with them, molded them and ran her fingers over her nipples, all the while smiling. Slipping out of her dress and panties she turned slowly in a circle. "Do you like what you see?" she asked calmly.

Shannon's throat was dry. His lungs burnt and ached. He felt as though he could not breathe. His groin was on fire. He could not think or reason. Nothing entered his mind except the vision of Millie's body. He unbuttoned and removed his shirt. The heat was unbearable.

Bertha rejoiced. "Go on. Destroy your love," she coaxed.

Anna said nothing. Her will was not Shannon's.

Millie and he were on the bed – Shannon's clothes discarded. Tongues probed. Hands explored. Shannon was inside of her. His passion ruled him. Up and down. Her hips rose to his and then release and darkness and sleep. Sleep deeper than he had ever slept that neither gods nor devils could invade.

Bertha laughed. Anna turned away but not in disgust.

Shannon woke. For a moment Shannon had no comprehension of where he was. Millie's peaceful breathing next to him was confusing. Katrina's beautiful face appeared above him. The face was not upset. It did not reject him. It was not sad but it was deeply disappointed. "What have I done?" Shannon groaned as his deceit flooded over him.

As Shannon was getting out of bed Millie sat up. Shannon searched for his discarded clothes and put them on quickly. As he finished dressing Millie said, "How about a token fifty dollars for the memories?"

Handing her one hundred dollars he was unable to look Millie in the eyes, but he was both sad and sorry for her feeling she would never be more than what she was now. Millie yawned. "You'll forget me. Don't worry. Lock the door," were her last words.

Shannon grabbed his book and hurried from the room.

Anna followed. No sooner had the door shut than Millie slowly melted into the air and then disappeared. When Shannon reached the street he started running. There were no cars – only the lonely rumble of a street washer and a stray dog trying to knock over a garbage can for another day of pitiful survival. Shannon was empty – his insides had been cut out and thrown to wolves. He ran faster. Bertha appeared in front of him. "Run! Run!" she shouted. "You cannot out run your guilt. You will carry the scar forever. You abandoned your love. Your veins are full of deceit."

Shannon fell to the curb and threw up – the bile in the gutter was his selfishness and uncaring passion.

Bertha vanished.

Shannon stumbled to his room and fell onto the bed. Katrina's face appeared once again. "I will not forsake you," the face said. "Do not worry. Now sleep. Sleep. Never forget I love you."

"What have I done? How can you forgive me?" Shannon cried.

Katrina's face disappeared without answering.

"I am nothing," Shannon moaned. "I am nothing."

He passed out. Sounds of Millie moaning, the fire of her breasts, Katrina's understanding, his betrayal, his guilt, his selfishness, all invaded his sleep.

"Even with your knowledge you are still a child," Anna said. You have many more trials to come. Some you will pass and some you will fail."

She placed her hand on Shannon's forehead. "Sleep and bury your sorrow. Do not look back. None of us are without deceit."

Shannon's breathing slowed and settled but could not dispel his disgust with himself.

Anna remained by his side until early morning.

Chapter Twenty

BERTHA

When a person murders in the name of love and devotion is it considered murder? The Crusaders professed their love for God and killed thousands, sparing neither women nor children. The Muslims professed their love for Allah and killed thousands, also sparing neither women nor children. Both still kill each other today – neither one thinking of it as murder. Can both sides be right? Or were God and Allah both lying when they proclaimed, "Thou shalt not kill."

****

Bertha was not always happy during the first year of her marriage to John, but she was content. She lived in a wonderful home, wore good clothes and John was respected. Her hair was fashioned at the beauty shop. She was invited to many parties and was on the committees for the fair, the library, and the school board. She tended the flowerbeds, planted a small garden, worked part-time in the store, and kept the accounts straight. She made John breakfast every morning and her suppers were always delicious. They enjoyed evening walks and chatted with the neighbors to keep up on all of the local gossip, but were careful to never spread any gossip themselves. "It is not good business to take sides when you own a store," John said wisely.

Bertha stopped asking John if he had ever loved another woman more than he loved her. She felt cheated thinking about it, and her mood would turn dark as her mind would fill

129

with thoughts of sinister deeds. She decided she would try her best to please John, and in doing so, in time, he would love her more than anything in the world. Truthfully she did not know if she loved John. She really did not know if she knew what love was. She enjoyed the companionship with John. It seemed to give her a purpose but at times she was lonely, dreaming she would one day feel so deeply for John her whole life would revolve around him.

John pushed the consuming love for his first wife deeper into his heart. He knew he could never tell Bertha the truth. He could sense Bertha's deep jealousy and resentment. The first night of their marriage John realized that Bertha had a dark side – a side he never wanted to experience. He did all he could to please her – bringing her flowers, hugging her often, telling her he loved her, but still knowing his words were lies. It really made no difference. The love he held for his first wife sustained him, and, in his mind, it would sustain Bertha and him.

Even with the doubts and small deceits life was a comfortable routine. It was late in the second year of marriage that things started to change. Bertha and John were eating supper. Bertha had been quiet the last few days, but John had not inquired if something was bothering her. He was not one to dig into matters and avoided arguing as much as possible. When Bertha would get angry, he would remain calm saying, "Now Bertha, it will all be fine. Please relax?"

"John, I have to tell you something," Bertha said abruptly. "I am pregnant."

John jumped to his feet and swung her around several times. "Wonderful, wonderful," he cried happily. "I have so wanted a child."

"Now you put me down. We shouldn't be doing this in my state," Bertha scolded deeply relieved.

He kissed her tenderly on the forehead and for the first time Bertha thought John truly loved her.

Ever since Bertha knew she was pregnant she had been

worried. She had been afraid to tell John. They never talked about children, but they also did not take safe guards to not have one. Deep in her heart she feared a child would drive John away from her or that the child would steal all the attention he now lavished on her.

"If it is a boy we will name him John Adams Jr.," Bertha said.

"I would like to see my name go on," John said seriously.

"If it is a girl what do you want to name her?" she asked.

"I will name her Anna. I have always loved that name," John answered without hesitation.

"It is a lovely name, Anna Adams."

Bertha had no idea that Anna was the name of John's first wife.

Over the next several months John and Bertha turned the extra bedroom into a nursery. Each night in bed John held Bertha and reconfirmed the fact how happy he was that they were going to have a baby. Bertha felt safe in his arms.

John seemed happy. He was jovial at work. He would not let Bertha stand for long or work in the garden. He also took over the small chores of the house although Bertha would not let him cook. He showered Bertha with cut flowers and fussed and fawned over her. Bertha was so carried away by his devotion that one afternoon while John was at work she felt a deeper peace and contentment than she had ever felt in her life. There was nothing in the world that could harm her. "Maybe this is what love is," she whispered. "Giving and never taking. Maybe love is not something that just happens but it has to grow."

That evening when John came home Bertha said, "John, I love you," and it was the first time she meant it.

John smiled and kissed her as they embraced. But holding Bertha he only saw Anna as he replied, "I love you, too."

Bertha grew bigger and spent her time knitting blankets and little booties and hats. While knitting she pictured the face of her child looking up at her with nothing but trust and faith in its eyes. She could feel the lips of the child on her nipples and the little fingers gripping her hand. At times she would sing she was so happy. Although her voice was not good she carried a good melody and John, listening, would smile and tell her, "You will be a good mother."

All the ladies from town visited and brought jars of jelly and all kinds of canned fruits and vegetables. They told her about their children and how wonderful they were. A responsible mid-wife was contacted and she explained to Bertha, "Now you don't walk too much or eat too much. Drink lots of milk and eat a lot of vegetables. Then you will not get fat."

Bertha enjoyed the company and the gifts. All during this time her voice was silent.

At first it had been an easy pregnancy, with no morning sickness, by the seventh month Bertha was bloated and always tired. Her legs and feet were so swollen it was difficult for her to walk.

Bertha was sitting on the front porch and had a nauseating headache. It was an extremely humid and dark evening. Quickly approaching storm clouds flashed on the horizon. John was at the store doing inventory.

Paul and Thomas watched Bertha from the elm in the front yard. They had only appeared to Bertha the one time when she was on her way to Corydon, but they had been constant in their vigilance. Bertha felt a presence and peered into the darkness. "I know you are out there Paul and Thomas," she challenged. "Are you afraid to appear to me?"

Paul and Thomas's forms pulsated with the distant lightning flashes.

Thomas approached Bertha and stopped only a few feet from her. Bertha glared at the ghost.

"So you think you know love?" Thomas chastised. "You think your love is enough to hold John? He does not love you. He loves another more than you and always will."

"Who is the other?" Bertha demanded jealously.

"When you find out it will destroy you," Thomas warned and was gone.

A cold wind tore though the yard and within seconds large rain drops pelted the ground. Lightning blistered through the sky, followed by booming claps of thunder that shook the house. The wind swirled, moving the tree branches in a resentful dance. Bertha rushed painfully into the yard and was instantly soaked. "Who is she?" she demanded. "Come back and tell me who she is."

There was nothing but the rain and the lightning. Bertha hurried back to the porch. Her eyes absorbed the lightning, the voltage seared her heart. The baby kicked. Bertha put her hands on her stomach, another kick and another. With each kick Bertha could feel the will of the child and she shivered, not from being wet, but from what she felt from the child. "I will not love you," the child said. "I will steal your husband from you."

"I have given you life, and you will love me. I demand it," Bertha swore. "You will love me, or I will make you wish you were never born."

The baby kicked one more time and then was still. Bertha sensed it was afraid and she smiled. The lightning flashed and a strong wind swept the clouds away. The stars appeared bright and proud as if nothing had happened. Bertha abandoned the night and prepared for bed.

Paul and Thomas smiled over their malice.

The next day John knew Bertha was troubled. She was cranky and ill at ease. He was wrong thinking her bad mood was caused by the pregnancy. Bertha sat in a chair by the window and ignored him when he left the house for the store.

That evening though, when John came home from work, Bertha smiled. "I'm sorry for the way I was this morning," she said hugging John.

"I understand," John replied.

While they embraced the baby kicked in protest. Bertha ignored the kicks, holding onto John tighter.

"I can feel the baby kick," John said, breaking their embrace.

He kneeled down and put the side of his face on Bertha's stomach. Feeling the punch, punch, punch of the little feet he laughed.

Bertha pulled his head closer to her. The kicking grew stronger, hurting her. She wanted to cry out but she did not release John's head. "You will not win," she thought to the child. "You will never win."

The kicking stopped and John stood. "It will be good when the baby is born," he said, "and you can get back to a normal life. You have to be getting weary."

"Yes, it will be good," Bertha agreed, not divulging what was truly in her heart.

Anna was an easy birth with no complications. After the mid-wife had cleaned her she handed her to Bertha. "She looks exactly like John," the mid-wife said.

Bertha held the tiny child she had nourished. Instead of feeling love or hope she felt only resentment. I wish you would have never been born, she thought.

When John came into the room he took Anna from Bertha and every inch of John's face overflowed with happiness and joy. "Anna, Anna, my lovely Anna. How I love you!" John said. "What a grand life we will have. I will take you on picnics and even teach you how to fish. You will be the envy of all the girls in the county and every young man when you are older will want to have your hand."

A chill crept through Bertha's heart. John had never looked at her with such love. "Love is only an illusion," she muttered to herself.

Handing Anna back to Bertha John left the room so enraptured by his own bliss that he forgot to kiss Bertha or tell her he loved her.

Anna lay quietly in Bertha's arms. "You may leave us," Bertha told the mid-wife.

Bertha gazed at the baby. "I will curse you beyond your

death if you drive John from me. I will curse your children and your children's children," she vowed.

Anna cried and Bertha bared her breast. Anna suckled the dark resentment of her mother's milk.

Paul and Thomas appeared at the foot of the bed. "I will trade you my child if you leave the love of my husband alone," she said to them.

"We do not want your sacrifice," Paul said.

"You have already started to destroy yourself," Thomas said. "You will see us no more but we will always be watching you. We will be watching everyday, every night, every moment of your life and past your life. We will be there to witness your destruction and aid in anyway we can."

Paul floated over and kissed Anna before Bertha could react. Paul and Thomas vanished. A cool wind circled through the room twice and then entered Bertha. She shivered and fragments of dark fears entered her mind – fears she could not pinpoint or label, but were so intense they frightened her.

Anna stopped suckling, a deep furrow appeared on her brow, and she cried as if she already knew the pain life would hold for her.

Chapter Twenty-one

BARBARA

Faith is a belief that is not based on proof. But with proof could there be faith?

****

Barbara felt like a woman whose son had gone off to war – the fear was there but it could not be dwelled on. Life had to go on – even if only a show it still had to go on. Barbara started praying for Shannon and the prayers gave her a small amount of solace. She now completely accepted God although she questioned if He really had man's good intentions in mind.

One day Barbara thought about her father. It saddened her that she had not written him or gone to see him since her mother's funeral. It made no difference he had not tried to contact her.

Saturday morning Barbara decided she should visit her father. She phoned Katrina and asked if she would like to take a drive with her to Kirksville. Katrina's mother consented. "Barbara must be very lonely," Danyella said to Katrina.

When Katrina got to Barbara's, Barbara was wearing black slacks, opened-toed shoes, and a colorful, off-yellow blouse. "You look wonderful," Katrina said. She had expected Barbara to look worn and distraught.

"It gets better," Barbara agreed. "Not good but better."

They talked as Barbara drove.

"My father is an alcoholic," Barbara said. "I was raised very poor. Dad could never keep a job and my mother worked low paying jobs trying to make ends meet."

136

"I always count my blessings," Katrina replied. "I have always been comfortable and can pursue my life. It is all because of my parents. Sometimes I think it is all by chance how we are born. Some people are born into wealth, some into poverty, some sick and some healthy. It all seems so random and without a plan."

"I don't have any answers," Barbara said.

"Shannon doesn't either," Katrina replied almost sadly.

"Do you miss Shannon?" Barbara asked.

"I say a prayer for him every night and I think at times we share dreams and emotions although I cannot see him. One night I felt he was in deep distress as if he had done something that he knew would hurt me, and he did not know if I could ever forgive him. But I told him I would never forsake him."

Invisible to them Anna was in the back seat.

"Anna will protect him," Barbara said. "I know she will."

Anna smiled.

"I feel Shannon has to find his soul. He does not know if he has a soul," Katrina said.

"Did you ever try and tell him that?" Barbara asked.

"I can only support him. He must find out for himself."

"Are you sad, Katrina?"

"I don't know if you can call it sad. It is also not loneliness. How can I be lonely when Shannon and I are connected? I do not feel complete, but I am not empty."

Barbara tensed. "Mother, I know you are here. Show yourself. There is no need to hide."

A slight breeze circled through the car and Anna appeared in the back seat. "You will always be with Shannon," Anna said to Katrina. "You are a gift to him and although he will bring you sorrow, he will also bring you great joy."

Then Anna said to Barbara. "I am happy you are going to see your father. He is not well." Then she was gone.

"I have always wondered if ghosts are angels," Katrina stated. "Ghosts of people that no matter how many bad deeds they did they were good at heart and God sends them out to help people."

"I doubt if my mother is an angel," Barbara quipped.

"At least we know Shannon has allies," Katrina said.

"You are old for your age, Katrina."

"Your son has made it so," Katrina replied. "But it is not a bad thing. I would rather be the way I am and have witnessed the things that I have than to be like the others. At least with Shannon we have met a seeker in our lifetime."

Barbara felt comfort in Katrina's statement.

Parking in front of her father's run-down house nostalgia swept through Barbara. The peeling paint, the rain gutters in need of repair, the uncut and weed-filled yard, for some reason they all had their own beauty. It reminded her of a defeated army marching home to no glory, with no one to listen to their tales of bravery and sacrifice.

Barbara, not bothering to knock, and followed by Katrina, entered the house unannounced. The house was a mess. Gin bottles littered the tables and floor. Dirty clothes were tossed carelessly about. Her father was sitting on the sofa with a pint of gin in his hand. He had not shaved in days and his hair was uncombed. He was wearing a filthy pair of overalls with no T-shirt and bedroom slippers. The curtains were shut and the house was suffocating in gloom. "Barbara," her father slurred.

Barbara rushed around the room opening the curtains and the windows. Light filtered through the gloom. Fresh air drove away the smell of neglect and gin.

Katrina sat in a chair, not appalled, but saddened by Barbara's father's condition.

Barbara sat on the sofa but not close to her father. "Dad, this is Katrina, a friend of mine."

Her father's bloodshot eyes tried to focus.

"I've been thinking about you," Barbara said.

"I see ghosts," her father slurred, "but nobody believes me. They think I am nothing but a drunk."

Katrina and Barbara were both shocked.

"What ghosts do you see?" Barbara asked carefully.

Her father took a swig of the gin, coughed, and wiped his mouth with the back of his hand. "I see the ghost of your Grandmother Adams but she does not speak to me. She appears and watches me. I tell her to go away. Leave me alone. She stares at me with laughing eyes and a sneer on her face. It is like she is a buzzard waiting for me to die so she can eat my soul."

"And do you see others?" Barbara asked cautiously.

Her father started crying. Barbara made no effort to console him. "I see your mother. She comes almost every night. At first her image was dim, and she would try to speak, but I could not hear her. With each visit she took on more form and I can now see her face. She talks to me. She tells me she loves me. She tells me that one day I will find rest and will not have to hide behind gin. She tells me my sins are her sins. She touches me and it is like I am being touched by an angel. I feel alive, but when she goes all of my uselessness comes back, and I am filled with pity and a longing for death."

Barbara was happy Anna appeared to her father.

"But people do not believe me," her father continued. "They say I am crazy and only a fool drunk who is so lonely he has to believe in ghosts."

"The ghosts are real. I also see them," Barbara said.

Her father shut his eyes and rested his head on the back of the sofa. "In all my failings I have salvation," he muttered and passed out – the bottle of gin fell uselessly to the floor.

"Maybe it is I who failed you," Barbara said more to herself than to her unhearing father as she put the gin bottle next to her father. "If I was stronger maybe I could have reached out and helped you by letting you know being a father was more important than your job. If only I would have said, 'Daddy let's go to the park' or 'let's go for a picnic' or 'read to me' you would not have become what you are."

Katrina sat by Barbara and put her arm around Barbara's shoulder. "It is not your fault," Katrina said.

"I am not without blame," Barbara said.

Barbara kissed her father on the cheek.

Barbara drove Katrina around Kirksville pointing out places where she played when she was a girl. They drove by the old school which was being demolished to make room for a new school. New houses were being built on the edge of town. "Nothing stays the same," Barbara said. "Each day is just another day of history, another day that will mean nothing. Man searches for permanence but there is no such thing. No matter how tall the building, or how strong the wall, in time it will all topple to be replaced by another history, another group of people trying to find the same things, only under different conditions."

"Will we ever know the truth?" Katrina asked.

"I think we change the meaning of truth to fit our needs," Barbara replied.

They stayed silent for over half the way back to Kansas City. Then Katrina said, "I have been accepted to the University of Texas in Austin. Right after graduation I am leaving and will take two summer classes."

Barbara was both saddened and relieved. "What are you going to study?" she asked.

"Right now I am not going to pick a major. At times I want to be a doctor. At times I want to be a psychologist. Sometimes I want to be a veterinarian. I don't know. I have a few years to decide."

"It will be so thrilling for you. I always dreamed about going to college but I didn't go."

"You were chosen to have Shannon," Katrina said.

"You will have to write and call," Barbara said. "You are a great strength to me."

Barbara let Katrina out in front of her house.

Back home Barbara was sitting on the front porch as the sun was going down. "We each see the sun so we are always together," she said to Shannon. "We each feel the cool of the night."

Eight o'clock that night the phone rang. It was the sheriff

of Kirksville. "Are you the daughter of Anna and Darrell Harrington?" he asked briskly.

"Yes."

"I am sorry to inform you that your father was found dead at home late this afternoon. The doctor said he died from alcohol poisoning. We found a confusing note on the table with your name on it. Would you like me to read it or would you like to pick it up?"

"Please read it."

The sheriff cleared his throat. "It says, Barbara, Your mother has taken me to a better place. All is well. Love, Your father."

"Thank you, Mother," Barbara whispered.

After hanging up the phone she went outside. A shooting star had its short moment of glory. "Rest in peace," she said. "Forgive me as I have forgiven you."

Barbara, with the wishes of Anna, had her father cremated. She scattered his ashes on the edge of a corn field. Neither she nor her mother cried or felt deeply saddened. To Barbara her father's death was a blessing. Anna simply commented, "He is gone, not even a ghost. We will never speak of him. I hope he has found peace."

Her father had not written a will and there was no savings. Barbara donated the house and everything in it to the Lutheran Church in town. The Pastor was overjoyed. The gift gave her father one small moment of merit.

Chapter Twenty-two

SHANNON

What is a quest without a goal?

****

It took Shannon a full day to recover from his introduction to beer and passion. All day long he had dry heaves that were intensified by his guilt. That evening, feeling slightly better, he had soup at a cafe. At first he wanted to go where Millie worked but changed his mind. He felt that to Millie he was merely another faceless man she used in a vain attempt to try and cover her loneliness. He hoped she would meet a man one day who truly loved her and that her life would change. He did feel the deep pain of using another person and knew he would always carry the scar.

That night, while in bed, he flipped through his travel book *The Wilderness Areas of North America*. Each wilderness was inviting. Each held a mystique of its own. He fell asleep while looking at the photographs. When he woke up in the morning the book was not on the bed, but was on the chest of drawers open to Utah. There was a circle drawn around a small town in the far northeast corner called Dutch John. Flaming Gorge Reservoir and the Green River were close by. He had no idea who or what had moved the book and circled the town nor did he question the happening. But he understood without a doubt it was his destination. Without any fear or sense of foreboding he packed his belongings and walked to the bus station.

Buying his ticket Shannon's first bus transfer would be in Denver, Colorado. Then he would go to Cheyenne, Wyoming where he would transfer again for Green River, Wyoming and the final trip to Dutch John, Utah.

When the bus departed Kansas City there were only ten people on board. They ignored each other – lost in their own reason for being on the bus.

The bus rolled through the endless expanse of Nebraska – mile upon mile of hay and alfalfa fields interlaced with tall corn. Large herds of Black Angus cattle grazed on the lush grass. An occasional house could be seen and Shannon wondered what the people thought about in their isolation or if they worked so hard they had no free time to think – falling exhausted into bed each night, their minds burdened with the next day's necessities. The bus stopped at an occasional small town to unload a person and a few packages while another person and more packages were taken on – an endless cycle of coming and going.

The bus ride was relaxing to Shannon. The bus seemed to move with its own will, stopping when it wanted to, going on when it wanted to. The people boarding the bus and getting off were all uncaring. He, to them, was what they were to him – only a face, a face that would never be remembered.

When they stopped for lunch the few people on the bus filed out and sat at different tables without talking as if communicating would ruin their image of themselves or conversation would destroy their world. They ate hamburgers and hotdogs and roast beef sandwiches, washed down with soda pop and water. Then they were back on the bus. Most soon fell asleep as if the country the bus swept through was boring and not worth their time.

Shannon was dozing in and out of sleep when he heard distantly, "Shannon, Shannon."

When he opened his eyes a vague image of his Grandmother Adams appeared. A cool breeze swept over his face.

"Grandmother," Shannon said.

"Your destination is right," she said.

"How is my mother?" Shannon asked, his voice filled with concern.

"She is well. Upset but well. Do not worry about her."

"And Katrina? Please tell me she is fine."

"She knows your yearnings. She is with you more than anybody else. She is going to Texas to attend college. Your mother feels if she goes away Bertha may not find her."

"I miss Katrina more than I miss Barbara. It is like I have left a part of me behind. A part that I fear I will never regain," Shannon said.

"You are very fortunate, Shannon. Not many people feel for each other as deeply as you two do."

"Have you seen Bertha?"

"She watches you most of the time but when she leaves I have not been able to find out where she goes. I have a feeling she is controlled by something she has no power over and her desires are secondary to its. I also feel she does not know that she is being controlled."

"I know I am being guided but I do not feel manipulated. I wonder who is in control of Bertha."

"Maybe time will answer your question."

"Are there more like you Anna?"

"I see others but I cannot talk to them. They look at me with empty eyes as if they have lost all hope. I know they need help but what can I do? It is strange, though. Every so often I see two forms in the distance that are not like the others. They are dirty gray in color and one is slightly larger than the other. They never approach me but they watch me. I do not sense they wish to harm me and I think they are on a mission of their own desires."

"Can you tell Barbara I am okay?" Shannon asked.

A cool breeze touched his brow and there was no answer. Anna was gone.

It was almost midnight when the bus arrived in downtown

Denver. Shannon had a three hour wait for his connection to Cheyenne. The cafeteria was closed and there were only a few people in the station. An elderly black man dressed in rags ravaged through the ashtrays for long cigarette butts. The night janitor was sweeping the floor. His eyes were far away dreaming of what should have been in his life or merely wishing he had a better broom.

Shannon went outside to the loading area. Ten buses were lined up – restless silver beasts anxious for another journey. The stench of diesel fuel filled the air. Two men and a woman were washing the windows of one of the buses while another man cleaned the inside. They moved mechanically like robots – mindless, uncaring, going about their job for the only reason that they had to work.

Shannon sat on a metal bench. Its gray paint was covered with scratched-in initials and sayings – 'George was here – Frank loves Irma – Life sucks – Jesus saves – If you want a good time call.' All of the scratches were a small book. Shannon felt the emptiness in the scratches and he visualized weary faces – faces no longer believing in dreams but still searching for meaning.

Two bums walked behind the buses to a corner where there were several overflowing garbage cans. They rifled through the garbage slowly, picking out bits and pieces of treasure that they put in a plastic sack. The cleaning crew ignored them. A police car swung through the loading dock and slowed – the policeman not bothering the bums, their crime not worthy of his time or there was no room in the jail.

The bums shuffled over to Shannon. "You got a buck you could spare?" one asked. His breath was foul from wine.

Shannon gave them each twenty dollars. Smiles cracked their dry and grimy faces. "God bless you," the other mumbled and they shuffled off into the night counting their good fortune.

"Bless you," Shannon said to their backs but without thinking about God.

Back inside, several people, covered with coats, were curled up on the hard metal benches trying to sleep. The black man was gone with his cache of cigarette butts. Shannon saw a paper on a bench and sat down. Tornadoes ravaged the Midwest and left several hundred dead and many houses destroyed. A flood in China killed several thousand. A civil war in Africa left tens of thousands without food or water. An earthquake in Ecuador devastated a village. Shannon put the paper down. "The earth is our enemy," he said to himself. "Its only will is to destroy us. It is not a gift or a blessing."

Then he thought, maybe the earth is only trying to take care of itself and man is the enemy. Man pollutes her, ravages her, and destroys most of what she accomplishes. Maybe storms, volcanoes, earthquakes and tidal waves are the earth's armies trying to defend her from destruction. Maybe she has to destroy man or at least keep him in check so she can fulfill her true destiny.

The bus lumbered through the night. The outside lights from houses and stores flashed by in a whirl – each house encased in its own dreams. "I wonder how many of these people see ghosts," Shannon wondered.

They reached Cheyenne as the sun was rising. The rolling hills were bathed in purples and violets and small patches of fog clung tenaciously to the slopes in fear of the coming sun.

Shannon only had to wait an hour before he boarded the bus to Green River. He was amazed by the vastness of the land. It was as though he could see to the edge of the earth. An occasional dirt road meandered off into the distance. Parallel to the highway was a railroad track. A freight train hauling coal chugged by. The coal fueled the big cities with the spoils of the earth. Shannon imagined the miners – black faced and dirty, their lungs coated with killing dust, toiling day to day with little pay so that people could have heat and electricity, while the owners of the mines thought more about profit margins than their workers.

Shannon dozed off with his thoughts and did not wake up

until the bus stopped in Green River, Wyoming. Stepping off the bus many miles to the south were the mountains – gigantic gods that controlled all that was within their vision – bringing both man and living creatures to their knees in both fear and admiration. Shannon was both in awe and intimidated by their presence. The bus for Dutch John, Utah did not depart until morning and the ticket salesman told Shannon where he could rent a room close to the station.

"Where are you going?" the lady at the counter asked with a big grin as Shannon filled out the rental agreement.

Shannon informed her Dutch John and she looked at him warily. "You believe in ghosts?" she asked with a hushed voice.

"No," Shannon lied.

"A lot of people say the area over there is haunted and that there are ghosts living under the ground. At times they can hear their cries. Even if you don't believe in ghosts you be careful!" she warned.

Shannon relaxed on the bed in his room. He missed Katrina terribly and wondered what she was doing. He thought sadly about Barbara. Closing his eyes he fell into a deep and tormented sleep.

A giant man taller than the tallest pine tree grabbed Shannon by the ankle and started swinging him around and around above his head – faster and faster the giant twirled him until everything in Shannon's vision was nothing but a spinning and out of control blur. Shannon was both frightened and exhilarated with the sensation. The giant released Shannon and he flew out into a cloudless sky. First his face was to the earth and then to the heavens. Sticking his arms out as if they were wings he started to soar. He was free – weightless, not bound by the earth. There was no sound as he soared. A warm wind propelled him. He sailed silently through a cloud. The cool white inside of the cloud was a calming dew on his face. Coming out of the cloud below him were snow-capped mountains, rivers and tall trees. Sailing on he traveled over endless grasslands dotted with every beast known to man, over a frozen land of jagged protruding ice, and over a sandy desolate desert where no creature could survive. The wind carried him over an ocean. All the creatures of the sea came to the surface. He sailed over islands – the trees teeming with scolding monkeys and birds of every color in the rainbow. Then the sky started churning and Shannon was tossed violently up and down as if he was nothing but a nuisance. The blue sky turned gray and black. Diamonds shot through it with long shiny silvery tails and then disappeared. The sky was once again blue and calm. A tall jagged and snow covered mountain appeared below Shannon. The wind carried him and dropped him on top of the mountain where he could see in all directions for hundreds of miles. "See what you can see and tell me of your vision," his voice said to him.

But Shannon was suddenly blind. He rubbed his eyes, opened them again, but there was only blackness. "I cannot see," he cried out in fear. "How can I see when I am blind?"

"Even with eyes you are blind," the voice said. "I have given you all the signs but you do not see."

"Who are you? You are not God! Who are you?" Shannon demanded.

"I will take you to the river," the voice said. "You will travel down river for six days with only bread and water. On the seventh day you will rest by a boulder that looks like an old man and faces east over the river. On the eighth day you will cross the river and go to the top of the plateau that the rock face points to."

"What will I find?" Shannon inquired, feeling no fear.

A blast of wind pushed him off the mountaintop. He fell through blackness – forever falling, falling, falling. Shannon woke up drenched in sweat but he was not in bed. The sun was about to set and he was standing on the edge of a steep rocky cliff. More than five-hundred yards beneath him, down a jagged rock face, was a wide and beautiful river. The water was so clear that even from the top of the cliff Shannon could see boulders lying on the bottom of the river. The land around him was brown and dry. It was rock-strewn and spotted with gnarled juniper trees and a few sage bushes. He was wearing a white tunic belted at the waist with a rope, leather sandals, a leather canteen full of water hung from his shoulder, and a leather pouch containing two loaves of a hard crusted deep brown bread.

"You will spend the night here," the voice said. "Tomorrow you will descend to the river and begin your journey."

"Maybe I am not strong enough to accept my destiny," Shannon replied.

"You are stronger than you think," the voice said.

Shannon was not afraid but troubled. When it was dark he crawled under a juniper tree to spend the night. Hidden within the branches he felt secure.

The light from the half moon cast eerie shadows over the dry landscape. Shannon heard the distant and mournful cries of coyotes. He tore a small piece of bread from a loaf and ate. The bread was like none he had ever tasted. It was delicious and nourishing.

He was about to stretch out when a form began to materialize by the tree. Shannon watched apprehensively through the branches. Within a few moments the image was complete. "It was not my intention to deceive you," Millie, the girl who Shannon had slept with in Kansas City said to Shannon with a shy smile.

"You are not the deceiver," Shannon replied. "The deceiver was me. You needed a friend and I only thought about my own selfish desires and passion."

"I came to wish you well on your journey," Millie said.

"What are you?" Shannon asked.

"I was once again given life to test you."

"I failed the test for you, for myself, and for the one I love," Shannon said.

"You failed in only one respect. You let your passion rule

your actions which I know you will never do again.”

“Transgressions can never be forgiven,” Shannon said sadly.

“The test was also to discover if your heart was brave enough to admit remorse and guilt and to see if you possess compassion for others,” Millie said. “Your heart is good, Shannon. Do not judge yourself by your mistakes. No person is guilt free.”

“Are you well?” Shannon asked. “I feel a deep yearning in you.”

“I am as well as I can be,” Millie replied and evaporated into the night.

“I wish you all that is good,” Shannon said.

About to fall asleep he realized it was June 14th. It was his birthday. He was eighteen years old, but years seemingly had nothing to do with his age. He had the disturbing feeling that for him time possessed no meaning.

you. The time passes slowly but each day I feel you with me. I dream so of your embrace and the day we will be one in name. Your heart is always with me and your smile keeps me warm at night. I pray this letter finds you well and that I am still in your heart. God blesses us.

I am always with love, Anna

The walls of the basement closed in on Bertha. Paul and Thomas were in the corner but strangely they found no joy in Bertha's pain.

With trembling hands Bertha picked up another letter.

Dear Anna:

Soon my travels will be over. I have seen the world. Nowhere have I seen a sight more beautiful than you. I feel your heart with me at all times. I see you in the ocean and in the clouds and I feel the soft touch of your hand. It will not be long my love.

Love eternally, John

Bertha threw the vile shoebox against the wall. The heart beat pounded louder in her mind. "You must kill him," her voice taunted. "He loves another more than you. Your life is nothing. Your dreams are destroyed. He cares only for the child. The child he named after his true love. Anna, the love of his life."

That evening Bertha murdered John. She had no memory of picking up the knife or John's blood gushing from the stab wound. She did not remember the look of disbelief on his face as he fell to the floor. She did not remember ripping her engagement and wedding ring off of her fingers or throwing them at his dead body. She also remembered John's last words. "Anna. Anna. Finally I come to you."

Although Bertha could not remember the deed, she did see John's spirit leave his body – a stream of silver, radiant, released from life, spinning quickly toward the heavens.

Bertha also remembered the look of terror on her daughter's face when she rushed into the room. It pleased her and she laughed. After all, it was the child's fault.

After the murder, the voice stopped for many years. During her life in prison when she needed the voice the most it would not return. Even though she pleaded for it, her pleas almost prayers, it had abandoned her like her father and her brothers and John had. It left her alone in her cell. Thinking. Seething. Letting the demons grow, letting hate build to an undefeatable walled fortress. A place where no light was allowed, or reason, or love, or need – only darkness filled with voiceless evil faces, faces that became her friends and benefactors.

But the voice would return when there was not a single drop of good remaining in Bertha's body – when all good had been drained from her and turned into bitter dust – when Bertha was completely ready to do the voice's true bidding.

seem right."

"To be true to myself I cannot fight," Love said. "And although Hate attacks me every chance he gets we are of equal power and he cannot destroy me. That is why we each need a champion. You and Bertha will battle for the hundreds of thousands of souls of people that never loved or hated during their life times. Right now they are trapped beneath the surface of the earth at the location your journey will take you. Whoever wins will swing the balance of power to either Hate or me. The world will become a more terrible place than it is if Hate wins."

"I will not disgrace you," Shannon said. "But there is no guarantee that I will win."

"You will do what is in your heart," Love said. "I hope your choice is the correct one."

"You give me free will but you have guided me my entire life," Shannon said.

"I tried to give you choices along the way," Love replied. "But love must prevail. Without love everything is lost."

"Do you and Hate have form? Shannon asked. "I would like to see you."

"You will see us soon, but we are not what you would imagine."

"How many champions have you had?" Shannon asked.

"Far too many," Love replied sadly. "There are none that have understood my true meaning."

"Will I be the last if I am victorious?" Shannon asked.

There was no reply. Shannon answered the question. "There is never an end to war. One war only leads to another. There never has been or will be a lasting peace."

"Everything ends in time," Love said. "I hope beyond hope this is the last time."

"Do you love my mother or have you only used her?" Shannon asked.

"I love her more than myself. But like you, my love at times brings great anguish," Love replied and departed.

Shannon was both relieved and frightened with his new knowledge, now that he completely understood the dire circumstance of his responsibility.

Blue Jays scolded Shannon as he slowly descended the steep cliff toward the river. The going was slow and treacherous. Many times Shannon slipped, bruising his legs and knees and cutting his fingers. Chipmunks scurried from rock to rock, stopped and looked back at him when they were far enough away to know they were safe. A red-tailed hawk patrolled the cliff on the other side of the river.

When Shannon finally reached the bottom, the river was covered with shadows, only a few hours of sunlight able to penetrate the steep cliffs. The scent of the land changed. Gone was the dry arid incense smell of the top. It now smelled like the rocks he had put in his mouth as a boy – an earth smell, rebirth, life with water and shade.

The river was close to seventy-five yards wide at this point. It hurried around logs that had been snagged between large boulders, foaming in parts, smooth in others. Close to the bank, in small eddies, delicate water spiders pranced over the surface of the water, eyed closely by baby fish. Shannon sat on a flat rock next to the trail. The trail was wide and sandy for about fifty yards then turned right where it entered a stand of juniper trees before disappearing out of sight. Shannon imagined the trees were guards that guarded the sanctity of the river, allowing no one to pass that had bad thoughts or desires in their heart.

The river swept by only concerned with its own destiny. Its song was one of freedom and eternity, a world unto itself that did not need man nor want him. It was and it would be, as long as there was water. It would be home to fish and birds, insects and trees, things that meant it no harm, things that came to it only for sanctuary. A slight wind lazed through the canyon – moaning at times, sometimes whistling. A rock tumbled from the cliff and splashed into the water. If Shannon had not been there no one would have witnessed its fate. "But maybe its fate is not over," Shannon whispered. "Maybe its fate is not at the bottom of the river but somewhere where the river will move it – move it against its will, the rock's only wish to rest in the cold depths and be left alone, tired of the sun and the wind, the challenge of light and dark."

Shannon was suddenly extremely tired and lay on the ground without seeking shelter. The night with Millie, the grief from his selfish deed, the giant tossing him like he was merely a feather, the voice of Love that was his father, the descent down the cliff, the parting from his mother and Katrina, it all flooded over him

He slept deeply without dreams or feelings. Waking early in the morning it took him several minutes to realize where he was, there were only the sounds of the river, the wind and the singing of birds. His mind still halfway between sleep and being awake he started down the trail toward his destiny.

The juniper trees along the trail seemed to examine him as he passed undecided as to his intentions.

The sun was bright as he entered a corridor of cottonwood trees that extended before him for over a hundred yards. The trees were so thick he could only see patches of the river between their trunks. The branches were covered with puff balls of seed, soon to be released, some of them would find life on another part of the river but most of them would die, unfulfilled in dry cracks of rocks or blown to waterless parts of the arid, high plain.

Shannon knew all the smells around him from putting things in his mouth, but he had never experienced the actuality of them. The reality was much stronger, more intense. The cottonwood trees made him feel like he was an invader. He was unwanted in their world. They whispered, "Go back. Go back." He would only bring devastation and death.

Shannon was almost at the end of the tunnel of cottonwoods when Bertha materialized ten yards in front of him. She looked wilder than the last time Shannon had seen her. Her hair lashed out from her head as if charged with electricity. Her eyes darted from side to side frantically. Her form swirled like storm tossed clouds – the black hornets inside of her moved in a crazed frenzy. "Now you are a man," she said. "Your right of passage is complete."

"And you still are as lost as you always will be," Shannon said unafraid.

Bertha's eyes darted faster, the dark cloud of her form vibrated. "Your quest will end in disaster," she said. "You will see nightmares that will consume you. Your knowledge will be stripped from you and you will cry for my help."

"Do you know who the voice is that controls you?" Shannon asked.

"He is Hate. And I am his champion," Bertha said but with no pride. "After all this time he finally divulged his identity to me yesterday."

"My voice is Love. I do know Hate does not care about you, where mine does as he is my father. To Hate you are only an instrument of his wants and he will discard you when you have completed his task."

"All I want is nothingness. All I want is the relief of oblivion," Bertha said. "For your destruction it is promised me."

"You do not need your master to get what you want," Shannon asked. "Cast off your hate and you will find what you truly desire."

"I need your sacrifice. You must become like me. You are sent only for me."

"How can I be sent for only you? Hate did not send me. Hate did not educate me. Hate did not make me the way I am to save you. I was sent by Love, but not for your fulfillment to nothingness."

"You speak as if love is sent by God," Bertha said.

"Love and Hate existed before God. Long before man needed God, long before man needed worship."

"Then what do you seek?" Bertha demanded.

"I don't know," Shannon replied. "I only know we are

both champions and that we will battle.

"I will make you hate me," she vowed.

"Your complete life and death has been twisted so you would never appreciate love or kindness. You are a pawn that only seeks destruction of all that is good," Shannon accused.

"What would you want me to do?" Bertha asked.

"You must defy your master," Shannon said.

Several questions that she had never contemplated crept from an unknown source into Bertha's mind. They left her both confused and bewildered. If Shannon is the son of Love would he lie to me? Will Hate deceive me and not give me what I seek?

Bertha vanished to dwell on her dilemma.

Shannon took several steps and Anna appeared in front of him, her face was twisted in consternation.

"Do not worry, Anna. I know you cannot help me. It is not your fault," Shannon said.

"I could if I knew how," Anna replied. "I would not be what I am if it was not to assist you."

"Have you seen Barbara and Katrina?"

"I have informed them of the beginning of your journey," Anna said. "I told them they must stand strong in their love for you. It will not be easy for them. And you, you must never succumb to hate. No matter what happens you must not. If you do it will destroy you and you will become like Bertha. Once you let hate into your heart you can never banish it."

"What must I learn that I do not already know?" Shannon asked. "I contain all the knowledge of the world. I speak almost all the languages of the world. Yet I am not complete. There is emptiness in me deeper than being lonely. I feel it like a ravenous hunger, but I cannot eat enough food."

"If I knew, you would not be here," Anna said and vanished.

Shannon exited the tunnel of cottonwood trees. The sunlight bathed him and made the river sparkle. The water and the sunlight danced to a merry tune – each was content with themselves – not giving or taking – enjoying the other for what they were. In front of Shannon the path followed the river – steep hills were on either side. Shannon continued on. He wished to travel as far as he could before making camp for the night. He saw trout surfacing for insects, their red side's miniature rainbows as they splashed back into the water and he wondered if the trout was made for the insect, or the insect was made for the trout, or were they made for each other.

Shannon progressed around a bend in the river as the sun began to set. The western sky was a translucent red. There were three juniper trees on the right side of the trail. The ground was sandy and there was a circle of rocks with wood in the center ready to be lit. Several yards away there was a stack of firewood. Shannon realized he did not have any matches. The river ran smooth and tranquil as if it was resting. Shannon sat by the fire pit and observed the different colors of the sky as light gave way to the dark. He drank a little water and ate a small portion of bread. No sooner had it grown dark than the wood self-ignited. The firelight reached into the darkness – from the three trees gentle shadows came to life. The trees whispered to Shannon about their lives, telling tales of when they were only seedlings and their struggle for existence.

The fire enraptured Shannon. The stars magnified the night, brighter and more numerous than he had ever seen them. He stood and stepped several yards away from the fire and looked up at the stars. They were beautiful but also frightening. No matter how far man ventured into space there would always be more stars on the horizon, more mysteries that man would never solve. "I am one with all of you. I am the center," Shannon said to the stars.

"Then what am I?" a voice cut through the darkness, frightening Shannon.

Shannon saw, illuminated by the fire, the head of a large and magnificent trout sticking out of the water. "Answer my question," the trout said. "How can you be the center if I am also the center?"

"Every creature is the center," Shannon said.

"But maybe there is only one center," the trout replied before disappearing back into the depths of the river.

Shannon stacked more wood on the fire confused by the trout's statement. In the distance an owl hooted. The owl's cries carried through the night like they would go on forever.

Katrina's naked form appeared in the fire and then leapt from the flames – shocking Shannon. The sound of drumbeats reverberated through Shannon's body. Katrina started dancing. She moved with the drums, her breasts falling up and down to the rhythm, her hips swaying enticingly, her head tossed back toward the sky. Moaning and twisting, moaning again, Katrina looked at Shannon. Her eyes were wild and filled with animal lust. She circled Shannon, her pelvis inches from him. Bending she brushed his face with her breasts – her nipples were hard and erect. Shannon smelled the woman of her. His head swimming he reached for her, but she stepped back, laughing, mocking. "How can you want me when you have deceived me and been with another?" Katrina questioned.

"I am sorry. Dreadfully sorry," Shannon bemoaned.

"If you deceive than I may deceive," she replied.

Another form materialized out of the fire – a man, naked, golden like a Greek god, muscle's rippling and manhood upright. Katrina and the golden man moved to the heartbeat of the drums. Katrina swayed, enticing the golden man. The drums beat louder and louder, vibrating Shannon's heart. Perspiration dripped from Katrina and the golden man. The man grabbed Katrina roughly, demanding – no love, only lust in his desire, running his hands up and down her sides, holding her breasts. Katrina sighed and shut her eyes. Their hips met, plunging, plunging, the drums beating faster. The man's head sprouted horns. Katrina laughed, moaned, and grabbed the buttocks of the man, deeper, deeper. Her passion-filled eyes taunted Shannon. "You are no more," she gasped as waves of passion swept through her body.

The golden man, eyes red, nostrils flaring bit Katrina's breasts and her blood dripped to the ground.

Jealousy, disgust, and hate consumed Shannon. "No!! No!! No!!" he screamed while leaping to his feet and at the same time picking up a piece of firewood. With all his might he smashed the golden man in the face with the firewood. The creature fell, his head caved in, but his eyes still open. Smiling at Shannon he disappeared.

"Now see what you have done," Katrina accused with tears streaming down her face. She too vanished.

Shannon gasped for breath, blood dripped from the firewood onto the earth. With all his might he threw the wood into the river. When it landed a gigantic plume of water over thirty feet tall shot up from the river. Starlight shone through the inside of the plume and a deep voice from its depths jeered, "Now you will come to me. Now you taste of what I am. Now you know I am the most powerful."

Shannon fell to his knees. "I will not. I will not. It is not Katrina's fault. Do not punish her for my deceits."

Anna appeared. Her form was a deep purple. There was no anger on her face only compassion. She enveloped Shannon with her form. "Go from this boy man" she commanded the spiral of water.

The spiral sank back into the river. Shannon lay unconscious. Anna remained by his side until the first rays of the sun peeked over the eastern rim of the hills.

Paul and Thomas had observed everything.

Chapter Twenty-six

BERTHA

The first penitentiary's philosophy was that a man or woman would be incarcerated, given the minimal amount of food, basic clothing, and a Bible. The prisoners would spend his or her time in a barren, dimly lit cell with no ornamentation – allowed only a bed and a harsh woolen blanket. They were segregated from other prisoners and even contact with guards was minimal. It was believed that in time the prisoners would be so lonely they would yearn for God and thus be rehabilitated. It seldom worked – most prisoners only learned hate and resentment. The overlords forgot about caring and compassion. They knew nothing of the teachings they lived by.

****

Bertha's attorney tried to convince the jury that Bertha was temporarily insane when she killed her husband and she had no idea what she was doing. The eight men and four women convicted her of first-degree murder in less than an hour. The judge sentenced her to life in prison, plus twenty years, which made it impossible for her to ever be released.

Bertha was devoid of emotion as the Judge sentenced her. She stood stoically. Her mind somewhere off in another world as if the judge and the jury were not real. She had told them she could not remember stabbing her husband. But her words had fallen on uncaring ears.

As Bertha was being escorted from the courtroom by the bailiff she turned and screamed at the judge and the members of the jury, "I curse all that is righteous."

Bertha fully realized her fate when she was delivered to the prison. The women's penitentiary in Dubuque, Iowa was constructed out of three feet by three feet limestone blocks that had been cut years earlier from a nearby quarry by male prisoners from the state prison. Fossilized fish, sea shells, and other crustaceans were imbedded in the stones – frozen in time and space like the women entombed within the walls of the prison. The prison was surrounded on three sides by tree-covered hills that dwarfed the fifty-foot high limestone walls. Sunlight, even in the summer, only reached the prison for a few hours a day. On each corner of the outer walls were guard towers where faceless men with rifles waited for their chance to legally take a life. There was a steel gate to enter or leave the prison that swung open and shut mercilessly – the bars were as big around as a man's wrist. With shackles around her ankles and handcuffed Bertha passed through the gate. The sound of the closing gate rang with finality in her ears. Once inside the prison the shackles and handcuffs were removed. An unsmiling female guard ordered Bertha, "Take off your clothes," as four female guards with nightsticks watched.

Bertha stripped and every opening in her body was searched. Her head was shaved and she was sprayed for lice. A deeper anger than she had ever felt flooded her, but she held it in check. She was issued three dark blue dresses, three cotton panties, three bras, three pair of socks, black shoes that laced, toiletries with three towels, and a washcloth.

Before she was put into solitary confinement for one month the matron informed her. "You will be fed twice a day, four in the morning and two in the afternoon. I will bring you a Bible, but you get no writing material or anything else to read. If you behave during your solitary upon your release we will put you with the other prisoners. If you don't you can rot in solitary for all we care." Then she added sarcastically, "Enjoy your stay, compliments of the State of Iowa."

The cell was eight feet by four feet. The limestone walls

were painted battleship gray. There was a metal cot with a thin mattress and a small metal table both bolted to the wall, an army blanket with no sheets or a pillow, and a toilet with no top. The door was solid metal with an opening to slide a tray through with a tiny grate that also let in a sliver of light.

The metal door slammed shut. The sound of a key locking the door cracked through the gloom. It was then that Bertha truly understood her fate. Standing in the small particle of light that came through the grate she sobbed. Her sobs wracked her body. Collapsing on the bed she cried for over an hour. No one came to her aid, no one cared, no one would ever care – life was the walls around her – cold, silent, and unfeeling.

Bertha stopped crying and pressed her palms against the stone. "You and I are one, nothing can hurt us," she said resolutely.

The stone whispered back, "Take me into your heart. I will protect you."

Paul and Thomas appeared in the corner.

"You think this is your vengeance?" she asked scornfully.

Their answer was silence.

"You think I will fall to my knees and pray for forgiveness?" she sneered. "I would kill you both again and again, but it still would not erase the hate and destitution you taught me. There is no forgiving."

"We would forgive you, if you would forgive us," Thomas said.

"You two must have had a change of heart. Do you think you will find grace by forgiving me?" she asked. "There is no grace. There has to be love for there to be grace. There is no love. There are only selfish needs."

"We must show mercy," Paul said. "If not, there is no hope of being anything more than what we are now."

"Your mercy is too late, go from me," Bertha ordered.

Paul and Thomas came in and out of focus, as if in deep debate with themselves. A sigh floated through the cell and they were gone, leaving Bertha to her darkness and her oneness with the limestone walls.

Bertha pictured the knife in her hand – the knife driving into John like it was propelled by another's arm not hers. Smelling the sticky, sweet smell of John's blood she wanted to bathe in it, wash away the wretchedness of life. She slept, her arm against the limestone wall, absorbing the coolness and feeling faintly, distantly, the shadows of ancient life still alive in the stone – shadows that longed for death but were encased in their immortality.

Bertha spent the thirty days of segregation quietly. She ignored the guard when her food was delivered. When the Bible was slid through the grate, she pushed it back and heard it hit the floor with a dull thud. "You are only lies and deceits, fairy tales from an ancient people that have no bearing on our lives today. You belong with antiquity," she said.

When her month of solitary was over Bertha was assigned to be a cook. She ignored the other women but never bemoaned her existence or the fate that brought her to such desolation. She forgot about death. In a strange way prison was comforting. As long as she did her job, there were no demands, no thoughts of family, no searching for love. The days crawled by in limbo – no dreams, no wants, no birthdays, no need for friends, only the cold limestone walls that talked to her more and more as the time passed, overshadowing the need for her voice which seemed to have abandoned her.

There were fleeting moments when Bertha longed to be embraced and she would think about the house in Corydon, and she would remember John when they were first married. Sometimes she would think about Anna, and she knew she had done to Anna what Paul and Thomas had done to her. In her remorse, she would write Anna, waiting and waiting for a reply, but it never came and she would go back to herself and the limestone walls, talking to them at night, relishing the coldness like a lover.

There were also times that she felt a presence that was not Paul or Thomas. It was the shadow of the voice she had heard her entire life. She would call to it, "Speak to me. I know you are there. Do not play me for a fool."

But there was never an answer, although the voice always watched Bertha, observing her from the inside out, planting small seeds of mistrust and hate as it explored.

Bertha did not dream when she slept. There were no colors, no pictures of trees or birds, no longing for the real world. Her sleep was dark and shallow, always on the edge of wakefulness, as if she was waiting for something, never knowing what the something was.

The years tediously passed, one to one, two to two, ten to ten, nothing to differentiate one from the other. Get up and cook, walk around the yard for an hour and then back to the cell – spring to summer, summer to fall, fall to winter, over and over again, until it no longer mattered what season it was, or the date, or the year. Bertha's hair turned white. Her skin was pale and wrinkled, almost transparent, devoid of sunshine or wind. Dark hollow circles lived below her eyes – eyes that were never excited or shone with some small pleasure. There were no photographs or cut out pictures on the walls of Bertha's cell.

The evening after learning she had cancer Bertha imagined the cancer eating away at her body, cell by cell. She could feel the razor sharp teeth of the disease – the minuscule bites hurting, tiny spots of blood like trophies on its carnivorous smiling lips. She embraced the pain urging it on. "Faster, faster," she implored.

As the cancer progressed she was once again consumed by hate. The seeds of hate sprouted, grew, flowered, seeded and more seeds sprouted and grew, flowered and seeded. Every fiber in her body ached. Paul and Thomas's faces darted through her mind – Paul throwing rocks at her, Thomas's love for Ida. Her father saying "You are not born from love, you are not my daughter."

She remembered the stick crashing into Paul's head, the body being shoved into the river, turning face down, circling slowly in the eddy, sinking. She remembered the feeling of satisfaction, the beat of her heart as she watched the body. She remembered Thomas not seeing the knife until it was too late, the look of loss on his face as his love vanished. She remembered John's lies, the letters, Anna stealing his love, the blood, the satisfaction, the joy of it all. Destroy. Destroy. And the voice returned after all the years and Bertha understood for the first time the voice she heard controlled her and with a great realization she understood she had always been controlled. All the bad happenings in her life had been planned so she would become a tool for the voice and she seethed in hate for all that had happened to her, and all the people that had caused her pain, and especially for the voice that controlled her. "I hate you! I hate you! I hate you!" she screamed at the voice. "You will only use me for your own desires."

The voice replied. "You will fulfill me. You are my champion, but in life you will die slowly, the cancer lingering, relishing your pain and torment. You will cry out for death but I must teach you more hate, so much hate that there will be no shred of decency in you. You will be so consumed with your hate your mind will bury the knowledge of me so deeply you will not remember that you are my puppet. And when I do talk to you, you will think I am your redeemer."

"What are you?" Bertha demanded.

"I am the most powerful of all," the voice replied confidently. "I am Hate and you are my champion. You and I will destroy my sworn enemy Love."

"What must I do?" Bertha implored.

"You will make the person who my enemy loves the most hate and then you will kill him," Hate said and said no more.

Paul and Thomas watched unseen and they were frightened.

Chapter Twenty-seven

BARBARA

PSALM 37: Fret not thyself because of evildoers, neither be thou envious against the workers of iniquity. For they shall soon be cut down like the grass, and wither as the green herb.

****

Barbara had fallen asleep on the sofa. It was 4 a.m. when she was awakened by a pale dim light. An image of what time would do to her body materialized in the middle of the living room. Barbara had snow-white hair. Her face was folded in wrinkles and spotted with dark liver spots. Her eyes were mere slits in the sagging flesh around them. She was in a wheelchair – her legs were shriveled to nothing more than useless sticks and her feet were swollen and deep purple in color. Her breasts were absorbed into her body, gone forever, no remembrance of shape or touch or the feel of a child – no passion or longing or need, useless in their decay. Her fingers were bent and twisted, the knuckles large, stiff with arthritis, aching like they would explode at any moment. Her lips were mere lines of unsmiling gray, not comprehending or accepting her fate. "See how useless you will be," a harsh mocking voice cut through the room. "I will make you live long past your time. You will feel your bones rotting and beg for death, but I will make you live and experience every pain of old age. People will have to bathe you and you will wear a diaper, unable to stand or do anything for yourself. They will give you food through tubes. But your mind will be young, watching and knowing, trapped

175

in a body of decay."

Barbara could not take her eyes from the horrible image of herself, and she was appalled.

"But if you aid me, this is what I can do for you," the voice beckoned.

The image changed. Barbara was surrounded by old decimated people but she was young and beautiful. Her hair flowed to her shoulders, gleaming with life. Her eyes sparkled and danced. Her body was full, curving hips, graceful. Her legs were shapely. She smiled, happy and free, untouched by time or the fear of time. Her mind was light and carefree. A line of men came into the image. Some brought her flowers. Others diamond rings and gold bracelets or earrings that sparkled with her eyes. They humbly bowed to her, transfixed by her beauty. "I will show you the world," they each promised. "You will be my queen and everything you want I will give to you."

"What must I do?" Barbara asked hypnotized by her beauty.

"Only a small thing for the promise of beauty and no death," the voice said.

"What must I do?" Barbara asked again, her eyes riveted on her image.

"You must forsake Shannon," the voice whispered through the hypnotic haze of her mind.

Her image beckoned her, pulled at her. Barbara's mind reeled. The image once again changed back to Barbara as an old woman filled with pain, arthritis, and loneliness. "No," Barbara cried.

The image changed back, beauty, life, all desires and needs granted. "Come, all that you see will be yours," the voice taunted. "Say yes."

Barbara approached her image. "Come," the voice whispered.

Barbara reached for her image. First her finger, then her hand, then her arm disappeared into the image of her beauty. "Yes, yes," she murmured, but then a small portion of her mind rebelled.

Barbara yanked her arm out of the image. "No! No! I will never forsake my son!!" She screamed hysterically. "Go from me, all you promise is a lie!"

Her image vanished and Barbara felt weak. The haze left her mind. "I will make you forsake Shannon," the voice swore filled with fury.

Invisible hands grabbed Barbara by the shoulders and pinned her on the sofa. Hands groped her breasts – twisting, pinching, and hurting. Barbara fought back, but she was not strong enough. Hands dug into her thighs. The voice laughed. Her blouse was ripped off, the bra torn from her. Her dress and panties lay shredded on the floor. Cold, wet lips circled her nipples, sucking, biting. Barbara fought, but to no avail. Her legs were forced apart. Barbara stopped fighting and lay passively. "Do with me what you want. I will not forsake my son," she said through clenched teeth. "I am not the instrument for his destruction."

The hands holding Barbara released her. "I am not done with you yet," the voice swore and was gone.

Barbara was no longer frightened. She was angry. "You can return anytime you wish," she said. "Your threats will not work, nor will your temptations."

****

With a heavy heart Katrina decided to go for a walk. The night was calm and she wondered if Shannon was gazing at the stars at this same exact moment. She wished Shannon was beside her even if his mind was buried in some deep thought. She remembered when he was leaving, and holding her hand, and the deep love she felt emanating from him. She wondered what his search was really about.

On the corner there was a magnificent maple tree that Katrina had always been entranced by. It seemed steadfast and filled with wisdom and grace. Even in the winter when its leaves were gone and it stood naked to the cold it was magnificent. Katrina stopped by the tree. Lights from the houses filtered between its branches, casting the tree's gray shadow onto the dark ground. The earth and the tree were one – sharing, telling stories of time, laughing and crying together, all knowing to the perils of life but also not concerned over the consequences – content with whatever would be.

Katrina placed the palm of her right hand on the tree. The bark was rough and gnarled and stored years of unspoken memories in its cells, but it was reluctant to divulge the stories, knowing most of mankind would not understand them or, worse yet, would ignore them.

Katrina ran the fingers of her left hand tenderly over the bark. The tree seemed to sigh. Putting her cheek on the tree, she closed her eyes. "Oh Shannon," she murmured softly.

A breath rustled the leaves. A voice, low, not demanding, full of understanding, but also tinged with a deep sadness said, "Katrina, do not be alarmed. I mean no harm."

Katrina was startled but not afraid. It seemed the voice had come from the tree, and the ground, and the night, all at the same time.

"Who or what are you?" Katrina asked.

"I cannot answer that. It does not matter who or what I am or even if I am anything. But you must answer my question. It is of great importance to me. Why do you love Shannon?"

Katrina scoured her mind for the answer, but although she could feel the words, she was unable to express them. "I don't know," she finally said. "I only know I love him and I have loved him since I was a little girl and even before I was born. Shannon and I are and have always been."

"Do you question your love?" the voice asked.

"There is nothing to question," Katrina answered. "I do not have to understand my feelings for him."

"If I call for you because Shannon needs your help, will you come?" the voice asked.

"You know I will come. You do not have to ask. But answer me, is Shannon well?"

"He has been tested," the voice said. "And although broken hearted, he is fine. On his travels he will see and experience many things. They are only meant to educate him and aid in a major decision that he, and only he, must make."

"Is what you ask too much of a burden for Shannon to bear?" Katrina asked.

"I pray it is not so," the voice replied.

"At times I feel that something dark and sinister is trying to bend me to its will so I will help it to destroy Shannon and it is more than Bertha," Katrina said.

"You must be strong," the voice said.

"Can you tell Shannon I love him?" Katrina asked.

But there was no answer. The voice was gone.

Katrina touched the tree once again and said, "In the beginning was the word and the word was God," and she wondered who listened to God before man. For some reason she could not comprehend, she knew the voice she had heard was older than God – something so ancient it existed even before time.

Before school the next morning Katrina told Barbara about the voice by the tree and the summons for help. Barbara saw no need to tell Katrina what had happened to her.

Chapter Twenty-eight

SHANNON

What if there had been no fall from the Garden of Eden? Would it be necessary to have a God? And why did God not want man to have knowledge? Unless He thought man would be better off without free will or knowledge.

****

Shannon was up before dawn. Immediately the vision of Katrina's wanton nakedness and his deep anger as he struck and killed the golden man engulfed him. He had never before experienced anger and jealousy and hate to such a degree, but now that he had experienced them he was both deeply ashamed and disappointed in himself. It was with a heavy heart he started down the trail.

It was a wonderful morning. High above the hills an eagle circled and gray squirrels chatted from the branches of a lone pine tree that had miraculously taken root at an elevation it was not supposed to grow. Swallows, not yet driven off by the sun, dipped and darted barely above the surface of the water eating insects that were invisible to the eye. But even with the beauty around him Shannon could not rid himself of his gloom. He did not see the river, the swallows, the eagle, or hear the squirrels. His face was toward the ground, lost in the disappointment of his actions.

Shannon trudged around a bend in the river. There was a sandy beach over twenty yards long. The water moving sluggishly around the bend had over eons of time deposited sand, grain by grain, until it constructed a beach. Right after the beach the river narrowed and grew shallow, racing around huge boulders as it sped between two vertical rock cliffs, before turning abruptly and disappearing out of sight. Growing in the center of the sand beach, and only a few feet from the waters' edge, was a giant willow tree that was over forty-feet tall. The trailing graceful branches spread like an umbrella eight feet above the ground as though they had been trimmed by a master gardener and their sole purpose was to provide shade for a weary traveler. Shannon, saturated with his gloom, had already passed the tree when a feeble voice called, "Son, do you have any water? Please? I need a drink."

Shannon turned and there was an old man sitting under the tree. The man was wearing a floppy straw hat decorated with painted green leaves. His white hair hung past his shoulders, and his white beard reached the middle of his stomach. His moustache fell past his chin and there were tiny silver bells braided into each tip. He wore a faded, many-patched brown shirt, and dirty gray pants, and on his feet, sandals with no socks. Leaning against the tree was a walking stick with three smiling faces carved into it. The top of the walking stick was wrapped with leather and there were seven feathers attached to it by leather cords. The feathers were red, yellow, blue, green, orange, purple, and black.

Shannon handed the man his water skin. The old man drank deeply, water dripped down his chin and onto his shirt. "Thank you. Thank you," he said gratefully, handing the water skin back to Shannon – the bells on his moustache tinkled when he turned his head.

"I have bread if you are hungry?" Shannon said.

"I have no need for food," the man replied then asked, "Why did you stop and give me a drink when the river is only a few feet away?"

Shannon was perplexed for a moment. "I didn't think about it. It sounded like you were in need and it seemed the right thing to do."

"Sit, let us talk. I have not had company in a long time," the old man said, patting the sand beside him.

Under the tree Shannon's gloom slipped away as the shade cooled him.

"Shade is a great gift and a small gift all in one," the old man said.

"I have never thought about it before but you are right," Shannon replied, adding, "My name is Shannon."

"My name is of no importance," the old man said. "I cast off names long ago. They are only labels that people give themself to try and make more of what they are, when in truth we are always less than what we think we are."

"I do not know who or what I am," Shannon said truthfully.

"It does not matter," the old man answered simply.

"It does to me. I feel like a part of me is missing, a part I possess but cannot identify – a part that is the most important part of me."

"Do you think the fish in this river know they are a fish? Do you think this tree that is giving us shade knows it is a tree? Or the birds know they are birds? They do not worry about what they are or who they are. They follow their life's path without question, accepting all as it is meant to be."

"But they do not have feelings like we do," Shannon argued. "Their life is set out for them. It is an easy life to follow. They are not torn with decisions or rules."

"Then what is the difference between the creatures of the world and man?" the old man asked.

"We feel not only the physical but we also feel the mental," Shannon said. "Our dreams guide us or haunt us."

"Don't you think all creatures dream? We cannot put man's definition of dreams on other life forms."

"I suppose they must dream," Shannon replied.

"What feeling is the most important difference between man and all living creatures?" the old man asked.

Shannon looked at the old man closely for the first time

and noticed the old man's eyes. His eyes were shiny silver with no difference between the pupil and the iris and they were without depth, as though he could see from one edge of the universe to the other. They also seemed to know everything there was to know about Shannon.

"Who are you?" Shannon asked. "Are you a prophet?"

"It does not matter what I am. Now answer my question if you can."

"I suppose that the main thing that separates man from the creatures of the earth is that we have knowledge," he said.

The old man frowned. "Knowledge is only knowledge it does not redeem mankind or bring gratification. If all men were like you and knew all that man knows, what gain is there? Would they all be like you and not know themselves? Now answer my question. What is the greatest thing that separates man from all other creatures?"

"There is no separation," Shannon said.

"The main difference is that we can love," the old man said. "Do not forget this."

The man stood, picked up his walking stick in his right hand, and pointed the stick first to the east, then to the west, then to the south, and then to the north, and then to the ground. Then he dipped the stick in the water. All the carved faces on the walking stick started laughing, their laughter echoed merrily down the river. The man tapped the stick on Shannon's left shoulder, then his right shoulder, and then the top of his head. "Remember the answer and think on it, but maybe there are other creatures that love," he said as he started spinning the walking stick above his head with both hands. Round and round it traversed, faster and faster and faster, until the colored feathers melted into a glorious rainbow that formed over the old man. Then he vanished. The rainbow remained – one end in the river and one end on the sand. Shannon, in awe, touched the rainbow, feeling the texture of each color. The red was soft like velvet, the blue cool like the sky, the yellow happy, the green soothing, the purple deep and mysterious, the orange carefree and the black was the sum of all the colors, the guardian of faith. The rainbow, one color at a time, entered his body through his fingertips. Shannon heard the tinkling of two tiny bells and the old man's voice, "This rainbow is my gift to you for the drink of water. One day you may need it. On that day call for it. The rainbow will come."

The rainbow inside of him, Shannon was instantly overcome with a deep longing for Katrina and he remembered the first time they met in first grade and her words. "I have known you."

Each year with Katrina rolled through his mind like a silent movie. He remembered all she had been through with him, never questioning his behavior, never trying to guide him, always helping with a smile or a glance, a touch on the shoulder, always understanding. "Oh, how I miss you," Shannon lamented.

Shannon noticed there was no indentation in the sand where the old man had been sitting. He said to the tree, "Thank you for your blessing of shade."

Chapter Twenty-nine

BERTHA

People are not born with hate in their heart. Hate is taught and nurtured exactly like love or compassion. Good people cannot loathe those who hate. The really good people must learn to embrace those who hate. Then, and only then, will hate be defeated.

****

Bertha was on her deathbed in the prison hospital. It was a cold dank room on the fourth floor with only two barred windows that faced the eastern wall of the prison. Sunlight never entered the room, banned forever from existence. There were no bright and happy pictures on the walls, no flowers on the metal tables, no cards from well wishers. The doctor who administered to Bertha did his job remotely and with no emotion, letting Bertha know that she, as a prisoner, was the scum of society and not worth his time.

Bertha had written Anna, not out of guilt or because she wanted forgiveness, but for the first time in years she was lonely. Bertha waited tensely for a reply from Anna, but none came, and the feelings of hate returned, stronger than ever. She wrote a second letter filled with her bitterness and once again there was no reply.

The cancer emaciated Bertha. She was pasty gray in color and her hair was completely white. Her eyes were sunk back in her head, listless and uncaring. She longed desperately for nothingness, a place in the cosmos where there were no feelings, either good or bad, no feeble attempts to become something that she could never be, no thoughts of redemption or vengeance, no deep craving for love or friendship – only nothing.

The limestone wall outside her window reminded Bertha of her life. She had built a wall around herself nothing could penetrate. She remembered when she was a little girl – a girl who played with her doll, sang, and had no questions concerning life, only going from day to day happy and carefree in her games and dreams, but then the thrown rocks, the scorn, the blame for her mother's death. And she remembered the voice and the voice said, "This is what life will be for you. You will never be liked. You will never know love. You will walk in darkness and come to embrace the dark. I will be your only friend. You will be my soldier against my enemy and because of you I will be victorious."

Bertha remembered the voice growing stronger with each of her vengeful deeds. She did not think at the time the voice was more than her own thoughts, her own needs. "Come to me Hate," Bertha demanded. "Come to me now and tell me why you have made me so? What good am I as your champion?"

But there was no reply, not even a whisper in the back of her mind.

Bertha closed her eyes. Death was close. Her cells were shutting down and her heart was laboring. "Come to me Hate, please? I will embrace you," she sighed.

But even death mocked her, and she coughed, choked, gasped for breath when she no longer wanted to breathe, spat up blood that dribbled down her chin, which she did not bother to try and wipe off. What was her blood but vile, let it be her last mark of life, her testimony to mankind that they had made her bleed until there was no more blood left in her.

A tall, misty, faded-blue form drifted through the window and stopped by Bertha's bed. Bertha's eyes were closed. Her breathing was raspy and quick. "Bertha," it whispered.

Opening her eyes, a tiny smile creased her lips. "John, my husband," she murmured, her eyes closed for a moment and then opened again. "You gave me the only happiness I ever had in my life," she lamented.

"I have come to forgive you, and bring you rest," John said.

Bertha struggled to sit up, a small ray of warmth in her heart. "I love you," she was about to say, but all that came from her mouth was "I" before a blast of ice-cold wind swept through the room. Circling Bertha, it threw her violently back onto the bed. Bertha's eyes bulged with fear. "I...I...I..." she choked as blood erupted from her mouth and poured down her chin. Her head thrashed wildly from side to side.

John yelled, "Go from her, you who have created her misery."

But the cold bitter wind increased its fury and blew John out the window. Bertha screamed. "No! No! It is not what I seek!" And Bertha died, her body ridged, her arms outstretched – the blood on her chin frozen.

Bertha's spirit departed her body. She could not tell if she was falling or ascending. There was no light, only a blackness that was deeper and darker than any black she had experienced, so black nothing could emanate from it or penetrate it. Voices came from the black, menacing, low, the voices mocking and scorning Bertha, but also adoring her – words that caressed her one moment and then ridiculed her painfully the next.

From the black Bertha took form – a gray outline of her body filled with more hate and yearning than she had ever experienced during life. She cried out, "Where is my nothingness?"

Tiny blood-red sparks flashed in the darkness and then began shooting through her. They were the stings of angry black hornets, each sting produced more hate. Bertha tried to flee, but she could not move. There were more and more stings, more hate, until the pain was almost unbearable and Bertha moaned, crying out, "I will do your bidding. Command me."

The sparks vanished. The poison and hate filled stings stopped and became part of her.

A voice came from the darkness but not from one direction – from all directions. "You have done my bidding well," the voice said.

"Then where is my nothingness?" Bertha asked, not demandingly but humbly, almost begging.

"I am not done with you," the voice said. "When I am I will give you your release. I will destroy all that you ever were – every thought, every cell and every trace of life force that you possessed. Not even time will know you existed."

"What must I do?" Bertha pleaded.

"You must find one who must be of your blood. The person will be kind and filled with love and for your redemption you must make them hate – hate so much they will kill even though it is against all that they believe in."

"Are there others who will try and stop me?" Bertha asked.

"Yours foes are many," the voice answered. "But I must warn you. You will be refused more than once trying to find your redeemer. But when you find the right person, you will know and I will be there, although you will not remember me coming to you in voice until I wish it. Your own desires will guide you until the time comes. I will be like a dream in the back of your being you know is there but cannot see."

He did not tell Bertha that she would never be rewarded with her desire to be nothing.

The blackness disappeared and all around Bertha was light – a light so thin and translucent that every color in the universe shone through it – red and gold and green, mauve, and brown, orange and purple, pink and blue. Surrounded by the colors she started to descend feet first, but as she descended a deep emptiness entered her – emptiness more consuming than she had ever felt. She could not cry – there were no tears in her being to wash away the emptiness. She could not plead for help – there was nothing that could hear her. Deeper and deeper the emptiness filled her, until all her gray form was overflowing, and the emptiness starting spilling out into the light, droplets of black blood. Then, in defense or in retaliation, hate began to eat away at the emptiness and it left only parts of itself, hate for her father who had abandoned her, for Paul, and Thomas, and Andrew, hate for John who had deceived her in love and hate for her daughter. The hate gobbled at the emptiness and when there was only a small portion remaining the hate stopped gorging, leaving the last tiny bit of emptiness to always keep her hate burning and remind her of what her existence would be if she failed, an endless emptiness that would outlive even the stars.

Chapter Thirty

BARBARA

If everyone living on the face of the earth was a giver, giving to another person what they needed and receiving from another person what they needed, in time there would be no need for thieves to make the act of giving have grace – there would be only grace. If there was only grace there would be no need for Hell. Could mankind comprehend life without the fear of a hell?

****

Barbara was making herself a light dinner. She had not been hungry since her encounter with the voice, and the attempted rape, but she knew she had to eat. She had just finished making a tuna fish sandwich and she remembered how Shannon loved tuna fish

Bertha appeared in the corner of the kitchen. Her form swirled and convulsed upon itself in waves of everything detestable to man. Her eyes were nothing but evil. Barbara had never seen Bertha this way and was so frightened she dropped her sandwich.

"I see you fear me now," Bertha said with grim satisfaction.

"I fear more for Shannon than for me," Barbara forced herself to say.

"How mother like and noble," Bertha said.

"Who did you send to test me?" Barbara demanded, trying to shed her fear. "A voice came to me and offered me eternal life and beauty if I would forsake Shannon. I almost succumbed, but at the last moment I knew it was lying."

190

"I send no one to do my deeds," Bertha replied caustically.

"And then I was attacked," Barbara said.

"I have come to destroy you," Bertha declared coldly and with no remorse. "There is no more time for games and frivolities. I must hurt Shannon through people he loves."

Barbara knew by Bertha's tone she was about to die and she understood there was nothing she could do about it. Feeling no fear she clasped her hands together in prayer, "Our father who..." she began.

Bertha's image began to expand until it filled the entire room with her suffocating hate. Barbara fell to her knees in excruciating pain, "On earth as it is in heaven..." she groaned.

Bertha's hands circled Barbara's neck and squeezed viciously. Barbara clasped her hands tighter.

Barbara felt her spirit begin to depart her body. "Give us this day our daily bread," she barely uttered.

Bertha squeezed Barbara's neck tighter.

Anna suddenly dashed into the room. "Away, get away from my daughter!" she screamed as she rushed at Bertha. "She can do you no harm."

Anna was tossed away as if she was nothing more than a grain of sand.

Barbara fell on her side, her hands still clasped in prayer. "And forgive us our trespasses..." she wheezed.

Anna darted at Bertha once again, but Bertha's anger repelled her. Anna was completely exhausted. Her image faded to almost white and she lay on the floor like a discarded rag doll.

Barbara's last words barely escaped from her mouth before she died, "as we forgive those that trespass against us..."

Bertha released her grip from Barbara's neck and receded back to her normal size. "Where is your savior now?" Bertha sneered to the lifeless Barbara.

Unlike most deaths, Barbara's eyes were closed and her

face was peaceful, as if she was sleeping and consumed by a soothing beautiful dream. Her hands were still together in prayer and her last thoughts emitted from her fingertips, "And lead me not into temptation but deliver us from evil."

In only a few moments Barbara's body began slowly rising from the floor. Bertha gasped. Invisible beings unclasped Barbara's hands and her arms were folded gently across her breasts. Her legs were stretched out and her head centered, so her chin was directly in line with the center of her collarbone. Her hair was lovingly stroked into place. The body rose higher and the chimes of soft silver bells echoed through the room.

Bertha tried to vanish, but she was held in place by a power she had never experienced. Anna, still exhausted, painfully got up from the floor, and seeing Barbara's body suspended in mid-air she was mesmerized.

The ceiling of the house parted without noise or destruction. The bells stopped chiming and were replaced by harkening trumpets, their sound filled with joy. Barbara's body stopped rising. A bright beam of light came from beyond the sky and entered Barbara's heart.

Bertha covered her face with her arm in fear. Her arm was forced from her face. "You will bear witness," a voice commanded her.

The trumpets stopped, replaced by the aroma of frankincense and then, with no sound, the light and Barbara vanished. Immediately the ceiling closed.

A soft voice said to Bertha, "You may attempt to have my child but you shall not have the mother, now go from here and never return."

Bertha was cast out.

The aroma of frankincense lingered in the air. A voice said to Anna, "You will not seek vengeance. All is never what it seems. Go and learn love, and be peaceful in your heart."

Anna rested, slowly her strength returned and, with a deep sadness, she ventured forth to find Shannon.

Chapter Thirty-one

SHANNON

Only after death does one realize how much they loved the departed, but by then it is too late. Sow your love now. Supposedly in heaven you will not need it – for sure you will not need it in if there truly is hell.

****

Shannon had watched the clouds develop all day on the horizon. They started out white and fluffy and were now every shade of black imaginable. They had built up upon each other until half of the horizon was covered with their blackness. Lightning slashed through the clouds but it was still far enough away the sound of thunder was unheard. A cold breeze kicked up and the temperature dropped at least ten degrees. Shannon knew the storm would soon reach him and he hurried down the trail in hopes of finding shelter. By luck, he saw the mouth of a cave, no more than thirty yards up a boulder strewn steep hill. The cave entrance was as tall as a man and several feet wide. There was an eight or nine-foot sandstone ledge protruding over the entrance. Scrambling up the hill Shannon reached the cave a second before the wind whipped into a gale and raindrops the size of large pebbles pelted the ground. The cave was over twenty feet deep and the ceiling was at least ten feet tall. The top of the cave was covered with soot from ancient fires. Carved into the soft sandstone walls by the entrance of the cave were the figures of a deer, a hawk, a bear, and a stick man holding a spear in a throwing position. The floor of the cave was sand, having been deposited when the

193

river was deeper and mightier than it is now. There was also a stack of brittle firewood left by another traveler and a well-used fire pit.

The black storm clouds became interlaced with swiftly darting shreds of white that were the remains of tranquil clouds that had been captured in their futile attempt to flee. Thunder boomed so intensely that the ground under Shannon's feet vibrated. A lightening bolt flashed, striking the hill on the other side of the river and filled Shannon's nostrils with the burning smell of singed earth. Flocks of small blue birds were knocked about by the wind as they tried to escape – their fearful chatter lost to the wind. A lone dove flew over the crest of the hill and out of sight. The rain pelted the river so hard the water seemed to boil. Shannon retreated several feet deeper into the cool and safe interior of the cave. The pictographs of the deer, the bear and the hawk accepted him, while the stick man with his spear scrutinized him, trying to decide if he was a threat and should be driven off.

The wind intensified, bending the trees by the river almost to the breaking point, but with each lull the trees sprang back. Leaves were ripped off the trees and swirled through the air like thousands of shattered butterfly wings.

"Thank you for your shelter," Shannon said to the cave.

The sky was completely black when the wind suddenly died, the rain turned into a light steady drizzle. The earth lay in a purplish gray gloom. There was no sound except the patter of the rain and Shannon wondered what it would be like to be a raindrop, living in a watery world of both rejuvenation and destruction.

The river quickly began to rise. The once clear water was now muddy brown – feeder streams up river, gorged with the rain, had trees ripped from their banks. The trees, still green with life, raced downstream in the churning water, bobbing and turning with the will of the river. A tree swept by with a mother raccoon and her three babies clinging helplessly to it. The babies were yelping in fear. "Let them find safety,"

Shannon begged, knowing he could do nothing to help.

The mother raccoon's eyes seemed to bore into the back of Shannon's eyes. There was no fear or remorse in her gaze, only understanding. The tree rounded a bend in the river and disappeared out of sight. Shannon's hope, but also his despair, traveled with the tree and its desperate cargo.

The rain intensified again, cascading down so heavily it roared like a lion with its might. Rivers of water poured down the face of the hill, moving rocks and dirt and sand into the river.

Shannon imagined the primitive people who had carved the hawk, deer, bear, and the stick man watching a storm. They would be terrified, but also relieved with their safety, but they would also think the storm was a god – a terrible god filled with destruction and death, a god that they had somehow, with no intention, made angry, and now the god was pouring his vengeance down on them for being disobedient. "Why has man always needed gods of destruction?" Shannon asked. "Is fear so cherished we must embrace it instead of scorning it and driving it away from us?"

No answer came to his mind.

"Is pursuit of the truth only the pursuit of futility?" he pondered. "Or does every human have their own truth?"

He thought for a moment and decided, "It is impossible for every person to have their own truth. There has to be one truth to guide us, we must only find it, even if the one truth has different definitions to each person the inner meaning has to be the same."

The rain stopped, but the sky was still black, although not churning or in turmoil. There was not even a hint of wind. Everything was motionless as if caught between moments of time, undecided if it wanted to go forward or backward or stay forever in between, with no beginning and no end – trapped in the serenity of limbo, sighing in a land of rest. The silence, like a shroud, covered Shannon but it also drew him. Going outside Shannon looked straight up at the black sky, wondering if there was a purgatory this is what it looked like – a place to reconstruct one's sins, each soul wondering if they would do it all the same way if given another chance, and truthfully knowing, yes, they would do it all again in the same way, lying to oneself to cover transgression, making up reasons that made their sins not their fault but the fault of others. Shannon smiled ruefully at the thought.

The stillness intensified – a small white dot appeared in the center of the black clouds and started moving in a circular motion. Round and round the dot sped, growing larger with each revolution. It began to form a figure. At first the figure was misty and vague but then an ear, a nose, a strand of hair, an eye, until an exact portrait of Barbara's face covered one third of the sky. "Mother," Shannon sighed in wonder, "you are beautiful."

Barbara was happier and more serene than Shannon had ever seen her. Her eyes were sparkling. Her complexion was rosy, all care and worry had been scrubbed from her skin. Her hair was shiny and glowed with vitality and new life. Her smile came from within her, a part of her heart and her being. Barbara said to Shannon, her words melodious, the notes of songbirds rejoicing, "My son, you must never be drawn into hate, no matter what happens, no matter what you are told. Not over Katrina or me or any circumstance of your life."

"Barbara, I miss you so," Shannon said to the sky, his heart overflowing.

"I miss you also, but more importantly you must promise me that you will not be drawn into hate," Barbara said. "Now promise me."

"But why must I promise?" Shannon asked.

Barbara's face started to melt into the black clouds. "Don't go! Don't go!" Shannon pleaded.

"I am always with you," Barbara replied before her image evaporated into the blackness. "I do not know if I can not stop from hating," Shannon called to the black sky.

Feeling that someone was watching him from behind

Shannon turned. The carved pictures of the hawk, the deer, the bear and the stick man with his spear began moving. The hawk flew across the face of the sandstone. The deer ran and pranced not encumbered by the rock. The bear stood on its back legs, and the stick man lowered his spear and bowed to Shannon, accepting him. "I did not come to invade your privacy," Shannon said.

The figures stopped moving, once again embracing the stone. Shannon visualized a man with a crude sharpened stone scratching the figures into the rock, putting his soul into his art, wanting all of his known world to see his creations and wanting people of future generations to know that he had existed, if only briefly. "Maybe you were the first of your kind to ponder creation," Shannon said.

The stillness of the sky and the quiet were instantly vanquished by a resounding thunderclap, an icy blast of wind swept down the river. Hail, the size of quarters, erupted from the clouds, hit the ground like small cannon balls, and bounced back several feet as if it did not trust the earth, and only found peace in the dark clouds. The river took the bombardment, absorbing the ice like it was nothing. Within a few minutes the hills and ground were white from the hail and then the hail suddenly stopped, as though its few minutes of existence was only an accident, and now it wanted to do penance for the destruction it had caused.

Paul and Thomas appeared at the entrance to the cave and floated past Shannon over to where the stick man was. The figure of the stick man and his spear was vaguely discernable through them. Shannon was not afraid. A deep sympathy radiated from them. "What do you want?" Shannon asked. "I do not need your sympathy."

There was no answer, but the sympathy coming from them grew stronger, almost making Shannon shudder with its intensity.

"What do you want?" Shannon asked again.

"Do not do as we did," they both said in unison and were

gone.

Shannon was overcome with foreboding. What with Barbara's face and now the two aspirations something was terribly wrong.

Standing on the ledge, the black clouds were dissipating and patches of blue sky appeared. Soon the clouds were all gone and the sunlight melted the hail in only a few minutes. Several large flocks of birds flew over, not remembering the storm. Within another few minutes, the river was once again blue and clear, the mud swept far downstream like a bad dream. Taking a deep breath Shannon tried to drive his sense of foreboding away but was unable to.

A cool breeze swirled under the ledge and Anna appeared. She was dull gray, her form still – her face vague and washed with grief.

"What is wrong? What has happened?" Shannon demanded.

"Bertha killed your mother and she has been taken to the sky," Anna said sadly.

Devastated, Shannon fell back against the side of the cave. "Tell me how," he asked hollowly.

Anna told him the complete story, how Bertha had appeared and killed Barbara and how Barbara had ascended into the sky on a ray of light, and the voice that told her she should not seek vengeance. "I tried to help, please believe me but I am no match for Bertha's power," Anna said with dismay.

Shannon was overcome with his grief and then a deep resentment began to enter him. Anna sensed it. "No, you must not," she said.

Shannon shook, the resentment twisted through his body, tinged with particles of hate, hate that singed his heart and tried to overtake his mind. "I will destroy you and all like you!" Shannon yelled. "Come to me Bertha!" he ordered clenching his fist and shaking it at the cloudless sky.

"No! No!" Anna said and tried to move toward Shannon

but she could not move – something held her in place, but whatever the force was, she knew it meant her no harm.

Bertha appeared and floated a few feet from the edge of the cave. Her form was as black as the storm clouds had been, swarming with swirling tornadoes and hurricanes, splashes of hail and ice. The black hornets inside of her hissed with anger and resentment. She laughed. Her laughter was sinister and selfish. "I have killed your mother," she taunted Shannon. "She has died because you would not do as I wished. She died for your sins. Hate me and kill yourself in my name and I will not harm anybody else you love. Give me the nothingness I desire."

Shannon cried out, not words, but a deep guttural wail, the sound of armies clashing, of heroes slain. His temples bulged with the force of his angered blood shooting through his veins. Bertha laughed more. Shannon stepped to the edge of the cave. "Another step, fling yourself to your death. Give me what I wish and save others," Bertha said and motioned with her hands for him to jump.

"It is my entire fault. No one's but mine. I carry the blame," Shannon lamented.

Anna tried to holler "No" but the force holding her had also taken her voice.

The hawk on the sandstone attacked Bertha. Bertha tried to fight off the hawk but each bite hurt, each talon ripped at her form. The bear roared and flashed through the air, gashing Bertha with his long pointed claws. The stick man leapt into the battle, thrusting his spear in and out of Bertha. She cried out in pain. The deer watched ashamed of their actions.

Shannon yelled in his anguish. "I give you my sacrifice," and lunged out and away from the cave entrance.

But he did not crash toward the ground. It was as though he was standing on glass, suspended over the hill and death. An invisible hand grabbed him by the back of his collar and threw him to the back of the cave. He hit the wall with so much force it knocked the wind out of him, and he crumpled to the soft sand floor, gasping for breath.

The hawk continued its assault on Bertha. The bear slashed and the stick man pierced Bertha with his spear.

With a screech Bertha disappeared. The creatures returned to their wall, resuming their motionless form.

Whatever was holding Anna released her and she rushed to Shannon. Shannon sat up, dazed and confused he said to Anna. "I do not understand, please help me."

"I cannot help you. I only know you must not hate and you must not bow to Bertha's desires even though she killed your mother. It is not her or your destiny that is at stake."

Shannon stood and leaned weakly back against the cool wall of the cave. The wall was reassuring and solid. "I do not know if I can stop myself from hating," Shannon said.

Anna put her hand on his shoulder, knowing there was nothing she could do and vanished.

Shannon remained where he was until the sun started to go down and the cave grew dark. He put wood in the fire ring and the fire leapt to flame. He sat facing the mouth of the cave as the night reclaimed the sky. Looking out over the fire into the night, he thought about Barbara – all the things they had done, her great understanding of him and he had let her down. He had been too self-centered, lost in his own world so deeply he could not reach out and bring her love or understanding, and he was deeply saddened and felt useless – anything he did would not make a difference for him or anybody else. The stick man watched him intently. "I must hate my enemies," Shannon said bitterly. "There is no other way in life. I have no choice."

The stick man sighed.

Shannon neither drank or ate bread.

Chapter Thirty-two

BERTHA

If man has dominion over the earth and all its creatures, then what has dominion over our universe, and all the billions of other universes that are still forming? And what has dominion over man?

****

Bertha floated over a flat barren section of dry, alkaline land that stretched in every direction as far as the eye could see. The vague outlines of mountains to the east and west captured any rain that might have fallen on the plain, and left only a dry moisture-free wind, continually scouring the dirt and rocks. A few sagebrush and scattered clumps of gamma grass barely survived on the parched earth. Occasionally, there would be a pile of brittle and bleached bones – the remnants of antelope or deer that sadly wandered away from the safety of the grass covered meadows of the mountains.

The only creatures that inhabited the land were scorpions and spiders, nourished by eating those of their own kind.

Moans and cries of agony emitted from beneath the ground in the center of the desolation. The cries came from ghosts that had neither hated nor loved during their lifetimes and for millennium had waited for their salvation – a premonition having informed them their salvation was close at hand.

Bertha was still reeling with sharp, stabbing pains from the hawk, and with the tearing of the bear's claws, and the pricks from spear, but even with the pain she was furious, not at Shannon, who had almost succumbed to her will – she knew he would in time, it was inevitable. She was furious because she realized that Shannon had told her the truth – she was only a pawn to her voice. She also realized, without a doubt, that there was nothing she could do about it, but she was filled with questions. If she had been used how could she have her own destiny? Maybe the destiny she sought had nothing to do with what she truly desired. Maybe she did not want nothingness. There were times in her life when she had felt pity, and compassion, and traces of love, but they had been yanked from her – torn from her like they were a blasphemy. Even existing as she did now, there were fleeting moments when she questioned her hate.

"Come to me Hate!" she demanded.

But there was no reply to her demand.

Anna appeared no more than ten yards from Bertha. "Hate is a cancer that can never be satisfied and yet you hold it close to you like a lover," Anna said. "There can be no truth in hate. It only steals from you until you no longer know who or what you are and all you can do is follow its bidding."

Bertha's eyes bore into Anna's but Anna refused to look away or show any fear.

"I do not fear you, Bertha. I pity you," Anna said. "I have lost all animosity in my heart and I do not blame anyone or anything for what I did in life. Everything was my decision."

"And what will you gain with your new insight?" Bertha retorted

"Gain is not the purpose," Anna said. "It is how I feel. It gives me rest."

"You mean there is no satisfaction, only rest?"

"How can there be satisfaction when one concedes that they have done bad deeds by their own shortcomings and not by others?"

"You must hate me for killing your father and daughter," Bertha stated.

"I do not hate you now although I did. Now I see where I

should have written you while you were in prison. I could not love you but I should have shown compassion for your suffering."

"You know I murdered two of my three brothers," Bertha said.

"I know you did. Although it could not be proven I always knew you did. But even with all your deeds there is a small amount of good in all people. It merely has to be discovered. Maybe it is the last bit of good in you that makes you want nothingness. You are on the wrong quest trying to make Shannon your sacrifice. Nobody who is either alive or a spirit needs a sacrifice."

Bertha's last amount of fury ebbed. Her face grew empty as a night sky devoid of stars or moons. "Then what do I need?" she asked with resignation.

But before Anna could answer, a horrific tornado appeared from nowhere and engulfed them – a tornado filled with sand and dust and human skulls, skulls with their mouths agape trying to scream but unable to do so. Bertha and Anna were swept into the tornado. The sand and dust and skulls circled them, taunted them – faster, ever faster. A voice said to Anna, "You will come to my side. You have more hate in you than compassion."

"Never, never," Anna screamed defiantly.

She was thrown from the tornado as though she was an abomination to it. She landed back on the barren plain and watched the tornado race away from her, picking up more sand and dust and skulls as it departed. "Oh Bertha," she said, "I feel so sorry for you."

Paul and Thomas appeared in front of Anna, both forms somber. "Paul and Thomas," Anna said.

"How did you know us?" Thomas asked.

"I have sensed you many times and sensed you were Bertha's brothers."

"We have come as allies and friends to help Shannon," Paul said.

"We are like you. We have lost our hate and only feel guilt and remorse for our earthly actions. We can see how we aided in what Bertha has become," Thomas said.

"I fear we may be too late," Anna replied.

All three of them heard thousands upon thousands of moans and cries emitting from beneath the earth.

"What is this terrible thing?" Thomas asked.

"I think it is the end of the search and of all of our destinies," Anna said, and she departed to search for Shannon.

The tornado raced on, the dust and sand and skulls bombarded Bertha. Bertha heard through the tempest, "How can you question me? I have given you meaning. Do you not think I am the greatest of all that ever was and ever will be? Your deeds have made you my champion. But even with me as your guide they are your own deeds. I merely planted the seed. It was your own actions that killed your brothers and your husband and Barbara. From now on, you will hear my voice and you will obey. If you do not obey I will make you experience nothing but sadness and pain until the end of time."

The tornado stopped and Bertha was suspended high above the ground. All the pain from the hawk, and bear, and spear and the dust and the sand and skulls were gone. Her doubts and questions were erased from her mind. "Anna, I do not need your compassion," she said solemnly. "Save your compassion for Shannon."

Chapter Thirty-three

BARBARA

PSALMS 118-5-6-7: They have mouths, but they speak not: eyes have they, but they see not. They have ears, but they hear not: noses have they, but they smell not: They have hands, but they handle not: feet have they, but they walk not: neither speak they through their throat.

******

After Barbara was killed and ascended into the sky surrounded by a beam of light she had no idea what she was. She did know she was not like Anna or Bertha who had a physical form that partially resembled what they looked like while they were alive. Barbara could think, she could feel, but she had no form. It confused her, but it did not terrify her.

At times Barbara could see Bertha and Anna, but she saw them from all directions at the same time, as if her vision circled them. She could see Shannon and Katrina but she could not communicate with them. Even when her face had appeared to Shannon in the dark storm clouds, it was not really her – her essence had been pulled from her invisibility and made into form, but they were not her words that came from her lips – they belonged to another being who knew Shannon needed to see his mother's face. Barbara knew whatever the being was, it was very powerful, but it also had its limitations and at times it was afraid.

Even though she had no knowledge of what she was she did not question her state of being. She did feel a deep concern for Shannon but she refused to worry, understanding now that

205

worrying would do no good – deeds, not worry, would decide the outcome for all circumstances in life. She did have the strange feeling she was blanketed by a deep goodness – a goodness that kept her warm and safe, and, in time, it would keep others warm and safe.

She also knew that she would play an integral part in whatever Shannon was going through. What the part was a mystery but she was ready for the challenge.

Barbara had more concern over Katrina than she did over Shannon. She realized that in all truth she loved Katrina more than Shannon. It was a revelation to her, at first confusing, but then not. She also understood her love for Shannon in no way matched the love Katrina had for Shannon. Barbara's love for Shannon was nurtured by responsibility while Katrina's love for Shannon was nurtured for no other reason than the heart. She deeply wished one day Shannon would understand how much Katrina loved him and that she was a gift to his life, if only he would accept it.

****

The morning after Barbara ascended into the sky Katrina stopped at Barbara's apartment on her way to school, but there was no reply to her knock, even though the car was in its parking spot. That afternoon, she left several messages on the answering machine and waited anxiously for a reply. She then called Barbara's job – she had not been to work. In the morning, once again there was no reply when she knocked on the door. Worried, Katrina notified the police, who immediately came to the apartment to investigate. They got a key from the manager and searched the apartment, informing Katrina sternly she could not come in.

"There is nothing we can do," an officer told Katrina after the search. "There is no sign of any disturbance or foul play in the house. Maybe she is with a friend. In a few weeks we will put out a missing person's report if she does not return."

"But she would not leave without telling me," Katrina

said in protest.

Katrina's parents were not overly concerned, but how could they understand? They knew nothing of the ghosts. They knew nothing about Shannon. To make it worse Katrina could not confide in them. The only true friend and confidant Katrina had was Barbara and Barbara was gone.

The days passed and besides worry about Barbara Katrina's worry over Shannon increased. She found herself unable to concentrate on anything – her thoughts centered on only the bad things that could be happening to Shannon. For the second time in her life she could no longer feel what Shannon thought or needed. It was as though everything about him had been wiped from the face of the earth. There was nothing remaining of him, no soul, no heart, no tissue, all were gone to some far removed remote place he could never escape. Katrina was lonely but she did not cry - tears would do no good. She prayed for Barbara and Shannon, but her prayers seemed hollow, trapped, and unable to go beyond the walls of her mind, fearing if they did they would be destroyed.

The next night Katrina awakened, and succumbing to a silent compulsion, she dressed and snuck out her bedroom window. The night was calm and hazy. Barbara's apartment complex was quiet. Katrina tried the front door. It was locked. To her surprise Shannon's sliding door was not locked. The police must have left it open by mistake.

Entering she turned on the light. Shannon's room was neat as if he would return any moment. She could smell him in the fine dust in the room and the odor filled her with desire. She so wished he had slept with her one time before he left – skin to skin, touch to touch, heart to soul. What other true communication did a woman have with a man? Conversation was always taken in a different way than it was intended, only the speaker really understood what they intended to say, and the listener only understood their own perceptions of what was said. More often than not conversation was meaningless, but with touch and feel there was nothing more to understand – it was complete, an entity without the need for words.

Katrina explored Barbara's bedroom. The bed was made and all her clothes were in the closet. There was no odor or remnant of Barbara, not even the smell of perfume. The room seemed to have been swept clean of everything she had ever been or done as if she had only existed in a dream.

In the living room Katrina felt turmoil and confusion still clinging to the molecules of air. She stood as motionless as she could and slowed her breathing trying to decipher the feelings, but they were too faint – distant like starlight.

She entered the kitchen and immediately her sense of turmoil and confusion were gone. She had a feeling she had never experienced before. It was not a bad feeling but it was also not a good feeling, more a feeling of resignation, but without worry or fear or dread. The images of what had happened in the kitchen flashed through Katrina's mind. She witnessed Bertha attacking Barbara and Anna trying to save Barbara. She witnessed the ceiling part and Barbara ascending into the sky on a beam of light and she heard a voice cast Bertha out, "You may attempt to have my child but you will not have the mother."

"Oh Barbara," she lamented. But then the voice she heard by the tree said to her, "Katrina, Barbara is fine. Do not fret over her or fill your heart with worry."

Katrina became angry. "First you come to me and ask if I would come if Shannon needed help. Now you come to me and tell me not to worry over Barbara. All you do is cause confusion. What do you want with all of us? Why don't you just leave us alone?"

Instantly a strong wind picked up Katrina and swept her away. She shut her eyes, and then, after only a few seconds, she was set down. She opened her eyes. It was a beautiful day. The sky was blue and cloudless. A cool but not unpleasant breeze was blowing and she was sitting on a large, flat rock, high up on a ridge that had a few juniper and cedar trees growing on its sides. More than two hundred yards below her, a beautiful river twisted and turned through a gorge, the sunlight off of the clear water reflected back in silver rays, trying its best to return to their mother the sun. Imposing mountains were to the east and the west – their peaks were snow covered and Katrina thought they were diligent guards for the river.

Katrina had never seen anything so beautiful nor had she ever experienced such immense distance, and she understood why primitive people would have worshiped the sky and the mountains, finding them unexplainable.

She saw Shannon rounding a bend in the river, and she stood and waved her arms excitedly and called, "Shannon! Shannon! Look up! I am here! Look up!"

Shannon's gaze remained facing the ground, his footsteps were seemingly without purpose. Katrina could sense a deep heaviness in Shannon's heart and it swept through her, chilling her. "Shannon! Shannon! Up here, I love you!" Katrina called again. Her words echoed down the canyon.

Once again Shannon did not look up.

"He cannot see you or hear you," the voice said to Katrina. "But you may visit him in heart."

A sparkling silver halo emerged from Katrina's heart, hovered for a few seconds in front of her as if getting its bearings, and then in a flash of molten silver it sailed at Shannon.

A dart of silver shot at Shannon and he tried to turn, but before he could it entered his chest and circled his heart. "Katrina! Katrina!" he cried out. "I know you are here. Help me! Help me! I am lost!"

"I miss you, Shannon," Katrina whispered in Shannon's mind. "I am always with you. Even when you cannot feel me or when I cannot feel you, I am always with you."

"Barbara is dead. They would not let me be the sacrifice. It is my fault. I put myself above others," Shannon sobbed, tears of guilt pouring from his eyes.

"No, no! There is no fault," the silver halo replied.

"If I cannot love, then I must hate," Shannon sobbed. "It would be so much easier."

"I love you. I love you," Katrina's heart pulsed through Shannon. "If you cannot find your own strength have faith in me and use my strength."

The silver halo departed Shannon's heart and hovered in front of his face. Shannon reached for it with trembling fingers. He wanted to hold it, pull it back inside of himself. His hands penetrated the halo, into its center but he could not grasp it. He felt life, pulsing blood, a rhythm of time, and love – a deep soothing quiet love but he also knew he made the love worry. The halo shot away from him toward the top of the ridge above the river. He saw it stop by a large rock and then it was gone.

"Katrina. What am I without you?" Shannon sighed, falling to his knees.

He remained kneeling for several minutes, then standing he continued on his journey. The feeling of Katrina's love clung tenaciously to his heart, but it was not strong enough to push away the hate he held for Bertha.

Katrina was returned to Barbara's apartment. The room smelled of frankincense as if the spirits of the room were making an offering, but Katrina sensed they wondered if it was good enough. "I know you are trying to help Shannon," Katrina said.

"I am trying to help man," the voice said.

"Then destroy your enemy."

"I cannot. If I did, I would not be what I am."

"Then what are you?" Katrina begged.

"Shannon knows," the voice said and would speak no more.

Chapter Thirty-four

SHANNON

Being alone should not be tinged with bereavement or guilt. If it were true many people would not long for moments of solitude and the desire to learn the mysteries of self.

****

Shannon did not see Paul and Thomas following him. They tried to will his guilt and burning hate from him, to absorb the bad feelings, but it was to no avail. It saddened them that they too had felt what Shannon now felt, and they had let the feeling control them instead of driving it away.

Shannon also did not see or feel Anna. She floated above him, invisible, watching, guarding, trying with all her might to share the love she felt for Barbara with him.

Barbara was in all of the sky above Shannon – bits of pieces of self, scattered like sand in a sand storm but still one entity, still able to think and see and feel. Her being was held together by invisible threads that pulsed with the electricity of thought and sight. "Shannon drive the darkness from you. None of us can live without help. No one is perfect, not even God," she sighed to herself.

Shannon also did not see the cave creatures following him –the hawk, and deer, and bear, and the stick man with his spear, darting from rock to rock like ferreting spies, hiding so as not to be seen, but intently watching his every move.

Shannon trudged on, each foot set in front of the other, without knowing the destination, not guided by cause or duty or dedication – merely moving. Then Shannon remembered the words of the old man under the tree. "Remember your answer and think on it."

What was the question? Shannon pondered. What was the answer?

He remembered. The only difference between man and all the other creatures on the face of the earth was that man loved. Shannon realized this was not entirely true. There had to be other creatures that felt love for each other, but no matter man possessed the ability to love far greater than any other creature.

Shannon lifted his eyes from the ground and, looking straight ahead, his footsteps became lighter, not so immersed in darkness. "You must think on the good not the bad," whispered in the back of his mind. "We are all born to die. It is not the grief of Barbara's dying you feel. It is your own sadness. Rejoice in her life and let the goodness of others be your guide."

He once again started observing things around him – a large trout in a calm shallow stretch of water, two ducks flying along the river quacking to each other like whatever they were talking about was the most important topic in the world, a blue and green dragonfly resting on a tall thin strand of water grass, the grass bending with the dragonfly's weight, a long line of large red ants hurrying along and carrying small bugs and pieces of leaves like they were returning from a raid and a vengeful army was in hot pursuit. Four tiny white butterflies flew up out of the grass and circled Shannon's face several times, their tipsy flight made him smile and he wondered if they had any comprehension of life or if they merely enjoyed fluttering wherever the wind would take them – enjoying the journey but with no thought of outcome or consequence. "If only I could be so free," he said to the butterflies as they drifted away.

Shannon saw a half submerged tree, ripped from its home far up river by the storm and now beached in a foreign place. The leaves were still green. The roots protruded from the water as if the sky would bring them life once again. A few yards away, scampering up the hill was a mother raccoon and her three babies. The mother stopped. The three babies crowded around her. All eight of the black eyes scrutinized him. "I am glad you are safe," Shannon said. "Your plight saddened me. I could do nothing to help."

The mother stood on her back legs, her front paws extended in a gesture of thanks and then she started once more up the hill. The babies hurried behind her – not looking back.

Shannon wondered if concern had the same redeeming value as physically helping those in distress.

The speed of the river increased. In the distance Shannon could see a narrow canyon and could already hear the sound of rushing water. The trail narrowed to only a foot-wide ribbon as he entered the canyon. It clung precariously to the rocky walls that were so steep they never allowed the sunlight to touch the river. The temperature dropped at least ten degrees as the river sped around boulders the size of houses and then plummeted fifty feet over a ledge, leaving mists of water hanging in the air that would never dissipate, continually fed by the crashing water. Small darting flashes of red and yellow and blue filtered through the mist like tiny birds longing for true flight and form, but they would forever be held in the fingers of the mist like coveted fine jewels.

Shannon did not see Bertha materialize halfway up the cliff. Bertha did not see Anna, or Paul and Thomas, or sense Barbara, nor did she see the hawk, deer, bear, or the stick man with his spear watching her.

Once out of the canyon, the river widened into a calm pool over half a mile long, sluggishly but steadily continuing on its trip through a wide meadow. The trail was now sandy and inviting. The sunlight was once again alive, not imprisoned by the cliff walls. Blue-green vegetation grew several inches beneath the surface of the water, extending out over twenty yards from the bank. Schools of small fish hid in open pockets of the vegetation, not yet large enough or brave enough to venture out into the real life of the river. Gently sloping hills, about seventy yards away, were set back from the river. Tall green grass laced with wildflowers bloomed up to their base – yellows and blues, sprinkled with reds and whites. A flock of red-winged blackbirds settled in a scrub oak tree growing amongst the flowers, their songs raucous and carefree. Shannon heard a rock slide down the face of one of the hills. Looking up, a buck deer and five does ran up the side of the hill and darted over the top. A red-tailed hawk sailed over the rim of the hills, circled three times over Shannon and flew toward the south until it was merely a dark speck in the sky before disappearing.

Somewhere in front of Shannon a woman's crying sliced through the meadow, cutting the tranquility like a sword. Shannon could not see anybody but he hurried down the trail. With each step the crying grew louder. In front of a boulder larger than a man a lady sat cross-legged, holding her head between her hands – her face toward the ground, her tears staining the sand a dark brown.

The lady was in her early thirties and, strangely, she had Barbara's hair color, Anna's hands, and Katrina's eyes. She was wearing red short pants, hiking shoes, and a blue shirt and was tanned a rich brown from being in the sun. Her backpack leaned against the rock. "Are you hurt?" Shannon asked. But then, for an instant, he wanted to leave the lady, walk away like he had never seen her. What could he do? Another burden might overwhelm him.

Deeper sobs raked the lady's body, more tears soaked into the earth. You poor person, Shannon thought.

Saddened by her despair he knelt down on one knee. "I have some water if you are thirsty and food," he said abandoning his feeling of desertion.

The lady raised her head and looked sadly at Shannon. "I'm sorry," she said, wiping her tears with the back of her hand and tried to force a smile, which was to no avail.

Shannon could not think of anything to say. He sat and

faced the woman. The lady continued crying and Shannon felt the deepest sadness he had ever experienced – deeper even than Barbara's death, and deeper than leaving Katrina. He could barely breathe as the woman's emptiness and forlornness emptied into him. "I do not think I can continue on," the lady said between her tears. "I have no reason to live. Everything I love has been taken from me. I have nothing but myself. I have come here to jump in the river and kill myself."

"You can't do that. There is always a reason to live. We only have to look for it," Shannon pleaded with the lady.

Bertha wanted to rush at Shannon, circle him with her hate. "No," a voice that was not Hate ordered her "You must wait."

Anna felt the lady's sadness and wished she could cry, but tears were only in life. The stick man lowered his spear and bowed his head, remembering his own sadness – the ageless sadness of rock.

Paul and Thomas thought about the mother they had never known, but then they thought about the many children in the world who had been raised motherless and their sadness for them was great.

Barbara observed, forming no opinions.

"I am too weary to go on," the lady said. "I feel like my bones have turned to dust and can no longer hold me up. My mind is nothing but tears and my heart is empty with all of my losses."

Shannon wanted to tell her about losing Barbara and how in many ways he felt the same way, but there was no need to add to her sadness. "What have you lost?" Shannon asked.

"My husband died," the lady replied, her lips trembling as she spoke. "Thirty-four years old and he died suddenly. We had so many dreams, so many things we wanted to do. He was a kind and gentle man, so carefree and he loved me dearly. Now I have only memories and no dreams. It is not fair."

A cascade of tears streamed from her face to the ground. Her grief and desolation completely overcame Shannon and he started to weep – not only for her but also for all broken hearts, for all sad people. His tears fell to the sand and joined with hers.

Paul and Thomas's forms touched. Anna bowed her head. Barbara smiled with Shannon's gift of tears. The hawk, deer, bear and the stick man moved into a circle. The circle was complete, all giving all receiving.

"I must go. Let me go," Bertha pleaded the voice that held her. The voice ignored her and Bertha could not get away, even though her hate completely rejected the needs of the lady.

The lady saw Shannon's tears and reached out and took his hand in hers. "Thank you," she said and vanished.

Shannon, bewildered, stopped crying. The touch of the lady's hand was still warm on his hand. From the tear stained sand a dozen stems sprouted from the ground and budded, the buds gracefully unfurling into white blooms as delicate as fine lace and no bigger than a child's fingernail. Their sweet fragrance filled the air with hope.

"Find solace," Shannon wished for the lady and continued his journey.

<h1 style="text-align:center">Chapter Thirty-five</h1>

BERTHA

If there was something before God, then it cannot be destroyed by God. It must be the building block for all creation and the necessity for all gods.

****

Bertha was incensed by the flowers that bloomed from the tear soaked sand where Shannon and the lady had wept together. No sooner was Shannon out of sight then she started furiously ripping the flowers out of the ground. But the more she pulled the thicker and quicker they grew back, until what had been a dozen flowers was now over thirty. Then, as if to spite her, the flowers multiplied into thousands and carpeted the complete hillside, cascading over the top like a waterfall. Within a few moments' multitudes of monarch butterflies appeared over the flowers.

Bertha stopped destroying the flowers and remembered the flowers in the yard when she was married to John, and how beautiful they were in the early morning when they were still covered with dew. For an instant she felt sad, but the sadness was yanked from her before it grew.

"You must come with me," the voice of Hate said to her. "It is time. The true battle grows near."

The next thing Bertha knew she was high above the desolate mesa she had been swept from by the skull filled tornado. Bertha was in the exact center of the mesa, facing south. Beneath her was a perfect circle of barren desolate ground, so perfect it looked like it had been made with a compass. The circle was over a mile across. There was no sagebrush, no lonely clumps of gamma grass – not even a rock to soften the desolation of the circle. Emitting from beneath the circle she could hear thousands upon thousands of moans and sighs of anguish – the moans blended into a deep wail, begging for release but the earth would not set them free.

Love's voice said to Shannon, "Do not fear." He was instantly suspended next to Bertha over the circle of desolation, each of them unable to move or talk, only listen.

"I am here and I come in truce," the voice of Hate said from Bertha's left. The moaning from the ground abruptly ceased.

Love's voice answered from Shannon's right. "It has never been I who wishes to fight. I would settle for a truce and let those beneath the ground who wish to follow you do so, in return, letting those who wish to follow me be left alone by you."

"It is strange that you and I have always been. So many things we have seen together, so many different gods are because of us. It is too bad we cannot be one, it would have been so much easier," Hate said. "But even being what I am, I have come to respect you."

"You need me to exist. I do not need you," Love said. "But I have always wondered who created us?

"I do not care or ponder questions that cannot be answered. I only know that I and you are," Hate said. "Our beginning means nothing."

"And if your champion destroys my champion what will you have? You will have nothing to challenge you. You will have nothing to try and convert or destroy and you will grow bored," Love said.

Hate chuckled.

"If I win there will be no glory, only compassion," Love said, his voice tinged with sadness, "but I do not think either one of us can win. Man is not ready for any life without duality."

"It is only your failures that bring me gain," Hate gloated.

"That is true," Love agreed.

"But I must admit, this time you have a good champion, more so than any of your others," Hate replied.

"I have made many mistakes trying to make him ready. I tried to maintain his free will, but I think I would have done better by telling him the reason for his quest sooner, and at times I was too slow to come to his aid when you tempted him with your champion," Love said sadly.

"My champion has done well also, they are a good match. Her heart is almost as empty as mine," Hate said.

"It is a game neither of us would have to play over and over again, if not for you," Love replied.

"How many times did we fight before there was such a thing as mankind?" Hate asked.

"I cannot even remember the number of battles we had before we learned that by ourselves we cannot defeat each other," Love said.

Hate replied, sounding melancholy. "Yes, but they were great battles. You always running between the stars, me looking for you, finding you, great clashes ending only in stalemate, both of us afterwards off to lick our wounds, searching for our reason to be and finally finding it with man."

"And is our battle for the lost ones beneath the earth still the reason why we are here?" Love asked.

"That is what I agreed on. I have summoned my army. They will gather soon, Hate said."

"I have also summoned my followers," Love said.

"I must admit it is good to talk to you again, after so many millenniums," Hate said. "I had no idea the last time we talked that it would take us this long to find and train our champions."

"It is too bad that although we are so opposite we know each other so well, almost to the point where we can foretell each other's moves."

"My champion's victory will be great," Hate proclaimed.

"We will see after Shannon's day of rest."

"Go from me now. Put in your ears the wails of those below us. Soon they will all belong to me and you will have to run to a far corner of the universe for I will be the most powerful, and all the souls on the face of the earth will be mine."

"We will meet the morning of the eighth day," Love replied.

Shannon was placed back by the river. "I now know my purpose," Shannon said to Love.

"You are your own champion, you will do what you feel is best," Love replied.

"What have you done with Barbara?" Shannon asked.

"Barbara is and will be forever all of the sky."

"Thank you. I told her one day she would find a love as large as the sky."

"I wish it were not so. It was all I could do."

"I will destroy Bertha," Shannon vowed bitterly.

With Shannon's words Love was deeply saddened and troubled.

Barbara listened to Love and Shannon talking and a warm and caring feeling swept through her.

"You will not interfere with Shannon again," Hate said to Bertha. "The course is set. You will watch and observe and look for any weak point but you will not interfere. I command it. If you go against my will you will join the lost souls in the ground. You will have nothing but agony forever and never receive your wish for nothingness. Do you understand?"

"I will fight Shannon for your cause. Am I assured that after I destroy him I will receive my nothingness?"

"You will get your reward."

Bertha was swept from the desolate plain and floated high above Shannon, so high she was only a pencil dot in the sky, but she could see Shannon like she was only a step behind him. She also spied for the first time, Anna, Paul and Thomas, the hawk, the deer, the bear and the stick man as they followed Shannon and she laughed at their folly.

Bertha was not worried about Shannon and his pathetic army but she was worried about Barbara. There had been no sign of Barbara since her face appeared in the sky, and for some reason Bertha held a deep apprehension of Barbara.

Chapter Thirty-six

BARBARA

I am without form but I am. I see, I feel, I cry, I worry, I know of love and hate, bitterness and neglect. I know of all feelings but I cannot embrace them. I am without form but I am. What am I? Please? Tell me, even though it does not trouble me, I would like to know.

****

Being a part of the complete sky Barbara could see many things at the same time. She could see the orb ghosts of Paul and Thomas and the true forms of Anna and Bertha. But although she had heard the two voices that guided Shannon and Bertha, and knew they were Love and Hate, she could not see them. She decided that if everything on earth were destroyed the two voices would still be – the beginning and the end all in one.

She could also see the spirits from the cave walls and knew they were not on a quest for themselves but their mission was to help Shannon. She understood they were guided by some power greater than any spirit. She knew that their reward, if victorious, would be to return to stone until the stone was no more and their existence was erased forever from the mind of man.

Barbara started seeing hundreds of other ghosts drifting through the sky – ghosts of gray and silver, blue and light green, mauve and brown. Many of the ghosts were grotesque in manner and form and emitted pure evil as they twisted and churned through the sky as if they were possessed. Others were tranquil and seemed to be filled by a deep peace and serenity. They were all headed toward the circle of desolation. More and more came every day.

Barbara also watched Katrina. Katrina fought her way through each day listening to the demons that grew in her mind. She was becoming consumed by her worry over Shannon, playing over and over in her mind's eye the sight of Shannon as he cried out, "Help me! Help me! I am lost!"

Not being able to help Shannon Katrina reasoned her love for Shannon must be lacking in some way. What could she do without love? She was useless, unable to pray away the demons and, at times, even losing faith in prayer. What were prayers but pleas to the uncaring sky? Why does man pray to gods that do not listen?

At times Katrina was so despondent she tried to tell herself Shannon had never existed. He was like a drug induced dream she had fallen into so deeply that it had seemed real at the time, but now that the drug had worn off, the dream was fading back into the unreal. "What is my love if I cannot share it? Is it merely a curse? I would rather have not known love," she said bitterly.

Barbara's heart ached for Katrina. She wanted to console Katrina but she could not be more than she was. She could not connect the strings of her that encompassed the complete sky and make herself into an image, and her feelings were not able to penetrate through Katrina's worries. They were repelled, pushed away – her good thoughts and hopes vanquished to a land where they would do no good – useless in their intentions. So Barbara watched and hoped saying, "Do not lose hope Katrina. It is only a portion of time you must endure."

Barbara replayed in her thoughts the conversation Love and Hate had over the circle of desolation and she wondered how many champions they had each nurtured throughout time, neither being able to completely destroy the other, caught forever in a stalemate. She wondered what Love meant when it said, "Man cannot forsake its duality?" Didn't there have to be the opposite of one thing for the other to exist? But then Barbara decided no, it did not. There could be good without evil. There could be love without hate. And she asked herself, "Could there be God without the Devil?" And she once again answered, "Yes."

"Man does not need sin," she said to herself with great revelation.

With the thought a warm presence entered slowly through all of her vastness, ebbed through her until the entity completely filled her, not trying to possess her but become one with her – one heart, one mind, one being, and one spirit. There was a deep calm and peace in the entity but also a gentle sadness – a sadness not of grief or guilt but of caring and compassion and at its own failures – not blaming any being or person, only itself. "Maybe your dreams are unreachable?" Barbara said to the force within her.

"No good dream is unreachable nor should it be abandoned," she felt more than heard in reply,

"I know you cannot defeat your adversary and he cannot completely defeat you," Barbara said.

"One day one of us will win. In time there must be a loser."

"Is it this time?"

"I don't know. I cannot see the future but Shannon is stronger than my adversary thinks."

"My son is only a child. You have placed a great burden on him."

"He is the carrier of the gift and the gift can be a great burden. It is not an easy task."

"Will you save him?" Barbara pleaded.

"I do not know if I can. I can only hope. But he can save himself."

The force flowed from her, leaving some of it behind, embracing her. "If you lose I will sow your seeds," Barbara vowed. "And I will water and nurture them with the blood of my child and with the love and tears of Katrina."

Chapter Thirty-seven

SHANNON

JOB: CHAPTER 14-7-8-9-10: "For there is hope of a tree, if it be cut down, that it will sprout again, and that the tender branch thereof will not cease. Though the root thereof wax old in the earth, and the stock thereof die in the ground. Yet through the scent of water it will bud, and bring forth boughs like a plant. But man dieth, and wasteth away: yes, man giveth up the ghost, and where is he?"

****

On the fourth night after eating a small portion of bread Shannon was resting by a fire. The fire once again brought to flames by a miracle or magic. The sky was crystalline. The fire threw red shadows over the surface of the river. They danced like they were unborn dreams, not knowing if they would be good or bad and in their infancy, not really caring. Shannon thought about all the knowledge he possessed, knowing it was not all the knowledge of mankind. It was only written knowledge. What of the knowledge of the first man to make fire? What of the knowledge of the first man to make a bow and arrow? What of the knowledge before writing and books? What of knowledge when gods controlled the sky and the rocks and the plants – controlled all things, simply because there were no explanations that man had either made up or discovered? But then Shannon thought the old gods were all gods of fear, gods that had to be appeased and sacrificed to – gods that killed and destroyed and caused famine and drought, flood and tornado. But even the gods of the modern religions needed worship – the sacrifice of pain and suffering to find peace. "Thou shalt not take any gods before me," they all said selfishly in their own way.

Was it because of the gods there were ghosts? Entities caught in the void of knowledge and questions – believing and not believing, but unable to be accepted by either life or death or God.

But then, maybe, God had to take different forms during man's evolution so the people of each era could try and understand Him. Shannon thought of the first humans on the face of the earth – how frightening it must have been, chipping stone to make tools, sharpening sticks to hunt and for protection, sleeping at night to the sound of beasts that would devour them at any moment. He wondered what they thought when they sat at night gazing into a fire.

"My knowledge has done nothing for me," Shannon said to the fire. "In all of my knowledge there are no answers, only more riddles, more questions. How many questions are there in the universe to overwhelm me?"

Laying down Shannon quickly fell fast asleep. The fire turned to embers and slowly to cold ash.

Shannon dreamed a dream more vivid than life. There was a beautiful garden with no beginning and no end. Every plant on the face of the earth was in the garden, except poison ones and those with thorns or burrs or stickers. Each plant was covered with flowers – orange, red, purple, deep blue, crimson, violet, and every spectrum of light. Great trees grew up to the clouds, their trunks massive and their branches dripping with every form of fruit – all ripe and juicy, not harmed by bugs or worms or disease and never rotting. Animals of all sizes and types rested in the vegetation, their eyes peaceful, their spirits tranquil and their stomachs without hunger. Birds sailed through the canopy of trees – singing with song and contentment. Fish swam lazily in lakes and rivers.

Shannon and Katrina were in a small circular clearing in the center of the garden. They were both naked. The sky above them was a deep blue and calm having never known storm or tempest. The grass under their feet was cool and refreshing. Amongst the grass, white flowers grew – their sweet scent carried to every corner of the garden by the breeze. Katrina was gazing into the depths of the garden. The sunlight glided over her body, her chin cast a delicate shadow on her neck, her breasts. The shadow slid down her ribs like music. Katrina's eyes were ablaze with all that surrounded them – there was no mystery, no fear, only harmony. She breathed deeply all the scents of flowers and trees, fruits and vegetables. Shannon watched how her breasts moved with her breathing – how her stomach tightened and relaxed. He reached for her but she stepped away, smiling but not teasing, shy like a wren. "Am I worth more to you than all of this?" she asked, spinning in a graceful circle and pointing at all the wonder around them, her nakedness more beautiful than any living creature or plant in the garden.

"You are worth more to me than anything in our garden," he answered.

"And why am I worth more to you than anything in our garden?" Katrina asked.

Shannon wanted to lay Katrina down on the soft, cool grass. He wanted to be one with her. He ached his passion and feelings were so deep. He wanted to feel her skin molded to his so closely that he could not tell the difference between Katrina and himself. But, when Shannon tried to answer the question he could not. His words stuck in the middle of his throat like lies that, out of their own protest, want to remain silent, knowing if they became sound they would blaspheme the garden.

Katrina's smile faded from her face and, for the first time, her eyes questioned Shannon. "Tell me why I am worth more to you than all of this," she said again. "And I will gladly become one with you. You will share all the pleasure I can give. My body will be your solace and your refuge for eternity."

Shannon stepped toward Katrina but she retreated past the edge of the clearing – hiding her nakedness behind a bush. Shannon could picture her breasts and thighs, the curve of her back – her legs open to him. He tried to speak but once again there were no words and Katrina darted into the garden. Shannon chased after her but she was gone as if the garden had given her sanctuary. Shannon called forlornly, "Katrina! Katrina! It is not my fault! Please come back."

But there was no reply. He wandered aimlessly through the garden. The animals and birds ignored him. His desire and want grew. Everything he saw reminded him of Katrina. It seemed like he searched forever until he stopped in a part of the garden where the sun never reached the ground, only mosses and ferns grew underneath the trees, and he felt lonely for the first time – so lonely he started to shake and he cried out, "Katrina. Why have you forsaken me?"

Waking, the sun was about to clear the horizon. Shannon was drenched in sweat. The dream was gone, but the feeling of loneliness was etched so deep inside of him he wondered if it would ever go away.

Bertha, not far away, smiled. "She has always been your weak point. I was wrong thinking it was Barbara."

The sun sent its rays, golden and glorious, over the river. But the sun was useless. It did not warm Shannon or take away his loneliness, nor did it remove the visions of Katrina fleeing from him.

Shannon continued along the river, wearing his dream like a hair shirt, but not knowing what penance he sought or for what sin he must ask pardon. By midday he reached a portion of the river where the hills on either side were gray crumbling walls of ancient shale. The trail was narrow and uneven, treacherous in spots with the slick shale. Several times Shannon almost fell but regained his balance in time, avoiding cuts and bruises or a fall into the icy river. Fossils of small fish and crustaceans, incased in the shale, eyed him pensively as he passed, saying, "You too one day will be as we, merely parts of rock and dirt, empty of all life. Those in the future will not even ponder your existence or try to discover a reason for your being."

"At times I would rather be like you," Shannon replied to the fossils. "Your task is done."

Shannon entered a flat, open expanse, where the river divided and rushed around a pinion tree covered island that was only twenty or thirty yards from shore. The water was only a few feet deep between the island and shore. Shannon stopped and the island questioned him saying, "I have divided the one river and made it two and then I bring them back to one. Which is greater – the one or the two? Or, even divided, are they both the same?"

"All the living things on the earth come from one," Shannon said. "Whether the one is God or some single-celled creature, which in itself could be a god, and even though we all divide and go our own way, we are one and the same, there is no greater or lesser."

"Visit me," the island beckoned.

Shannon splashed through the shallow water. The current was strong and cold on his legs. The rock-strewn bottom was slippery from a light green moss that clung tenaciously to the submerged rock and made his progress difficult. "The island is only because of me," the river said. "I am not because of the island."

"You are only because of each other," Shannon said.

Shannon forgot about his loneliness and the dream of the garden, but as he stepped onto the shore of the island he suddenly could barely walk. His legs felt weak. His hands and his fingers curled into arthritic knots. The veins on his arms protruded deep blue under pale skin. His flesh sunk to thin fabric around his bones – the muscle gone as if not needed. Taking another painful step, his back bent over at the waist. He was unable to stand straight up or bend his head more than forty-five degrees to see where he was going. His breathing became raspy and short, his lungs begged for more air, but he was without the strength to fill them with the nourishment they needed. Shannon headed painfully toward the shade of a tree, the heat suddenly unbearable. He came to a small pool of water caught between two rocks and he saw his reflection. Gone was the boy-man, wrinkles creased his face like ancient tree bark, white whiskers, long and stringy, listlessly grew from his chin. His white hair was shaggy and hung past his shoulders. His eyes were set back in the wrinkles of his face, so far behind drooping eyelids that no color could be seen in them – only a gray emptiness – only a few worn and yellowed teeth remained in his mouth.

Shannon reached the tree and settled painfully to the ground. He leaned his back against the trunk of the tree – feeling like he never wanted to move again.

It was beautiful looking out from the shade of the tree across the river. A light breeze cooled him and took some of the ache from his joints and bones.

On the other side of the river, Anna, along with Paul and Thomas, the hawk, the deer, the bear and stick man watched Shannon. Paul and Thomas, who never knew old age, were confused by Shannon's state. To the stick man it meant nothing. Bertha circled high overhead and enjoyed his pain. Barbara, one with the breeze that cooled Shannon, whispered to him although she knew he could not hear her, "It is only a part of life. There is nothing to fear. Learn from it."

A person approached Shannon that was the image of Shannon as a young man. "What a child you are," Shannon said as he as a young man sat under the tree next to him.

"I do not feel like a child," the young Shannon said. "I feel as old as you."

"I understand now that most of my battles were merely within me, and what I sought was always within my grasp, if I would have only opened my eyes and heart," the old Shannon said.

The young Shannon and the old Shannon watched the river for several minutes. "It is peaceful," the old Shannon said with a sigh.

"I have never known peace," the young Shannon said. "All I feel is turmoil around me and within me."

"Peace is everywhere for those who seek it. You have tasted of it without knowing it."

"My problem is that I do not know what I seek," the young Shannon replied slightly dismayed.

The old Shannon looked the young Shannon in the eyes. "I know what you seek, but I cannot tell you. It is for you to find out."

"Where is Katrina?" the young Shannon asked. "I miss her terribly."

"I do not know. I lost her many years ago but I still feel her with me. I feel her in the breeze, and see her in a flower, and at night she lies down with me but she is only a dream, a vision that I carry in my heart and mind. I hope her life has been well and that she has forgotten about me."

"I do not want to spend my life without her," the young Shannon said. "I do not want to be old like you and be alone with only visions. Even if, in life, she died before me and filled me with sadness, I would still have memories. Memories can be held and cherished, dreams are only mist."

"Memories are all that we really have in life. Every passing sight or happening is only a memory," the old Shannon said. "We are, every moment to moment, only a photograph of what we were."

"I bet Katrina always thought about you during her life," the young Shannon said. "I bet you caused her much sadness."

"I dread you are right," the old Shannon said. "It was not my intent, but most of my intentions have never turned out the way I wanted. In my quest, I have always been too selfish, too occupied trying to find meaning in my own life."

"Maybe the meaning in life is merely to be alive and forget the questions," the young Shannon said. "Maybe we put too much credence in what we think we are or are supposed to be. Maybe if we tell ourselves we are nothing than we will discover we are everything."

"The search will come to you if you do not search," the old Shannon mused.

"If everything in life is a circle, it has to be true," the young Shannon said.

"I have never been one to dwell on simplicity," the old Shannon replied.

"In your years before you lost Katrina did you ever tell her you loved her?" the young Shannon asked.

The old Shannon shut his eyes. "No," he answered. "And that has been the source of my grief and sadness."

"I will not make that mistake in my life. I will also tell her you loved her but you refused to know what love was, or you were afraid of it," the young Shannon said.

When the old Shannon opened his eyes, his young self was gone. "What a fool I have been," he muttered.

Barbara, the complete sky, sighed.

Shannon rested his head back against the tree and the tree absorbed all of his mental and physical being. It pulled Shannon's old flesh and bones deep into its branches and roots. Shannon was the sap and the tree was Katrina. He was inside of her, feeling her warmth, her care, her protection, feeling her needs and desires, feeling her deep love for him, but also her concern and worry over him, and feeling the pain that her love for him caused her. "I did not know," Shannon cried out from within the tree, but his cries were absorbed by the bark and were unable to enter the sky.

"I did not know," he cried out again.

The tree expelled Shannon with his cry as if Shannon was a parasite that would steal all of the tree's goodness and waste it on some worthless pursuit.

Opening his eyes, Shannon was no longer old. He was once again young. Walking away from the tree he turned and looking back said humbly, "You have been a good teacher."

He waded across the river, leaving the tree and a part of himself behind.

Chapter Thirty-eight

BERTHA

Hate, of all the emotions, is the weakest. It only thinks it is the strongest because violence is its only defense. But with violence there is never a true victory. It only gives birth to retaliation.

****

Bertha, over the last two days, observed Anna more than Shannon. While she watched Anna her hate would ebb and a tiny fragment of a feeling she had known a few times during her life would creep into her. The feeling was almost a tear. She understood Hate knew all that she did and thought, but for a reason she could not understand, she had no desire to rid herself completely of the feeling.

She also heard strange questions that were barely audible whispers. Questions that she knew originated from some other force besides Hate. "How could you blame a child for your own shortcomings? How could you kill your brothers, even if they did you wrong? How could you kill your husband, who even if he was unable to love you the way you wanted, took care of you and fed and clothed you and provided a good home? How could you destroy Barbara?"

"It was not me alone," Bertha answered the whisper.

Then, in fear, Bertha would retreat back into herself, but still a few questions whispered through. "Would you not like forgiveness over nothingness? You still have time. You are form for more than one reason."

Bertha also wondered what her life would have been like

233

if she had held Anna when she was a baby – if she had taken the time to fight through her demons and not listen to the voice in the back of her mind. Maybe, in time, she would have defeated the feelings and found love for her child and in doing so she would have found love for herself.

With the whispered questions Bertha wanted to talk to Anna, not to attack her or hurt her but to talk.

"Maybe you only try to convince yourself you hate," Love said to Bertha.

"Go from me," Bertha ordered. "You are not my voice."

"Go back to the cave where the drawings of the stick men wait for their spirits and I will send Anna to you," Love said. "But I do not know how long your master will not be able to hear you or know you are gone. I can give you sanctuary for only a short time."

"How can I trust you?" Bertha questioned.

"Who else can you trust?"

Bertha was consumed with indecision but she departed for the cave.

Moonbeams filtered cautiously into the cave. Anna was in the middle of the cave – her image a soft gray, the moonbeams barely illuminating her.

"I only wish to talk," Bertha said.

Anna, for the first time, felt a tiny particle of need in her mother. "If you wish to talk to me, then talk, we do not know how much time we have," Anna said without malice or fear.

The moonbeams grew braver and filled the cave with more light. "I do not know why I wish to talk to you. Questions have entered me that I did not ask. A feeling searches for me that I do not understand," Bertha said.

"I fear you will never rid yourself of your hate," Anna said. "It is all you have ever known. But even hate yearns. It knows deep down that it can only be a failure and there are moments, even if they are fleeting, that it craves rest and peace and a warm touch on its brow."

"I have never known a warm touch," Bertha said.

"You never gave any either," Anna replied.

"How could I do what I never knew?" Bertha asked.

"Good is in all of us," Anna said. "Even you possess a small amount of kindness, you merely do not know what to do with it."

"What would kindness do for me now?" Bertha asked. "Or remorse?"

"It would give you and those that you have harmed peace."

"That could be true but I do not think I can run from my master."

"You cannot run. You can only disobey."

"It is strange. I hated you for so long during my life and now I wish to know you."

"I have forgiven all your trespasses against me and mine but I do not welcome you. I only hope that you will save yourself. I can do nothing for you but feel sad."

"I do not want your sympathy."

"Then what do you want from me?"

Bertha started to answer but, before she could say anything, the thousands of angry black hornets within her started stinging her savagely – each sting injecting more hate. Bertha's face contorted in pain and anguish, her lips curled into a sneer, her eyes turned into pools of smoke. The stinging increased. The buzzing of the hornets was a vicious tempest. Then the hornets swarmed and flew in a long black funnel out of Bertha's mouth and attacked Anna. "I will not hate," Anna screamed as they stung her again and again with their evil venom.

More and more hornets flew out of Bertha's mouth. Each hornet entered the world more hateful than the one before it. A whirlwind kicked up from the back of the cave. The whirlwind picked up Anna and fled with her from the cave, leaving the hornets and Bertha behind.

With Anna gone, no more hornets emerged from Bertha's mouth, but the hornets in the cave that had been attacking

Anna turned and swarmed over Bertha, stinging her hundreds of time, thousands of times, replenishing Bertha's hate. Soon, Bertha no longer felt the pain and she began laughing. "Fill me with your nectar," she cackled.

The hornets once again resided inside Bertha – their evil the essence of her hate. Bertha sailed out of the cave, she wanted to forget why she had visited the cave or that she had even seen Anna, but the faint feeling within her had not been destroyed and lingered like a distant and vague memory.

The whirlwind set Anna down between two boulders where she could see Shannon. Shannon was gazing into a fire. Anna was dazed and disoriented – her color faded and blotchy. Stings of hate festered on her form. "Please! Please! Do not let hate win," she whimpered.

Paul and Thomas appeared. "Go from her. You are not worthy," they ordered the hate.

The hawk, the deer, the bear and the stick man circled Anna.

Anna's color slowly came back. The stick man waved his spear triumphantly at the night sky.

Bertha, high overhead, released a blood-chilling scream. Shannon jumped to his feet, scanned the night for its source and saw Bertha silhouetted by the stars. Electricity sparked from her hair, and where her heart would have been if she were alive, molten blood-red rock dripped through the darkness, hissing angrily as it descended to earth. Her face was contorted with pain and misery. The scream reverberated up and down the river – creatures large and small cowered with its message. Shannon listened to the scream until it faded away to nothing. "You too, Bertha, even if you do not know it feel sorrow," he said and sat back down by the fire, his heart also molten rock in its own way.

Chapter Thirty-nine
BARBARA

S T. LUKE 6:27-28: "But I say unto you which hear, Love your enemies, do good to them which hate you. Bless them that curse you, and pray for them which despitefully use you."

****

From all directions, thousands of ghosts were now converging over the circle of desolation. Some of them came in huge groups, flying in swaying formations like swallows and bats, others in twos and threes, and still others alone. A gigantic gray cloud of ghosts shifted and churned over the circle of desolation and still more ghosts came.

The moans and cries of agony emitting from beneath the ground increased with each arrival. Those trapped beneath the surface of the earth beseeched the arriving spirits, but the clouds of ghosts ignored their cries, waiting for whatever or whoever had beckoned them.

Encompassing the complete sky Barbara's view of all things caused her to be in a sense of wonder. When it rained, the rain came through her, cool and refreshing. When the wind blew, it was part of her but did not force her anywhere. She experienced the feather touches of birds as they flew. She felt the wind as it caressed the trees and grasses. She knew clouds. She was one with the rivers and mountaintops, the deserts and the plains. She also was aware of cruelty in the life around her but she refused to dwell on it, and only acknowledged the good.

She knew there was something going on inside of Bertha that Bertha could not understand. It made Barbara wonder if it was truly possible for good to come out of something so evil. And if it was, did a good deed done by a bad person or bad spirit have more merit than a good deed done by a good person or good spirit? It was perplexing, but Barbara at times felt a deep sadness for Bertha that overshadowed all of Bertha's atrocities.

Barbara watched Katrina with concern and she tried, with all her existence, to put part of herself within Katrina but Katrina would not, or could not, accept her. Katrina had closed her mind and heart, trying to dispel the longing she had for Shannon. In many ways Katrina was in deeper peril than Shannon. Katrina was beginning to feel sorry for herself.

Since Love and Hate had met over the circle of desolation, Barbara had not heard them talk again. She wondered if they were like her, everywhere at the same time.

Observing Shannon Barbara no longer felt like his mother. Watching Anna, she no longer felt like her daughter. They, each in their own way, were part of her but she was so different now the bond had changed. Shannon was blood and tissue while Anna was form and spirit. Barbara, being all of the sky might not even be spirit. But it did not really matter, she was something and the something had no need of a definition to be.

Barbara observed Shannon beside the river. Anna followed Shannon, as usual out of sight. The hawk, the deer, the bear and the stick man were behind ridges on either side of the river. Bertha was so high in the sky she was not discernable from the ground. The voice of Love moved through Barbara, inaudible to all but her. "Shannon has done well," he said. "He has not turned back, although his heart is heavy."

"You gave him too much knowledge. The knowledge has only added to his burden," Barbara replied.

"It was necessary but it is not a burden he will always carry. I promise you."

"Why did you bring me a son with no father?" Barbara asked.

The voice pondered the question. "I am the father," it finally answered solemnly. "Fate has made it that I cannot fight my own battles. To do so I would destroy myself."

"You must sacrifice your own son?" Barbara questioned and experienced a deep wave of compassion for the voice.

"Not if he learns from his quest. If he learns, there will be no sacrifice."

"Why was I chosen as his mother?" Barbara asked.

"It was the love I felt when I first saw you," Love replied.

"You must tell our son what he must learn," Barbara said, now was not the time to try and make sense out of the mysterious birth of Shannon.

"I cannot. I can only guide and hope he learns well."

"Your load must be heavier than you can bear at times," Barbara sighed. "I feel like I should feel sorry for you but I know you do not need sympathy."

"You have been a good mother to my child," the voice said. "You have a grand and bountiful heart. Without guidance it must have been extremely difficult on you."

"Shannon has been a gift."

"He has even taught me," Love said.

"I feel so sorry for Katrina. She is lost in her love of Shannon and there is nothing I can do."

"I have visited her once. She must dig deep within herself and carry her burden for only a short time longer."

"Why can't you help her? Why can't you take away her fear?"

"There are many things I cannot do that I wish I could."

"Then love is not a god," Barbara said.

"No, thankfully, I am not a god."

"You are not a god but you are a good father," Barbara said

Chapter Forty

SHANNON

JOB 7: CHAPTER 6 - 11: "What is my strength, that I should hope? And what is mine end, that I should prolong my life?"

****

Traversing each bend in the river Shannon hoped to see the stone shaped like an old man's face he had been told he would rest by, but each bend was only another bend with no stone face. As Shannon trudged on, multitudes of ghosts flew over him, but paid him no attention. High in the sky, on the very edge of his sight, there was a circle of gray, like a building storm, where the ghosts congregated. "The circle of desolation is my destination," Shannon said. "They wait for Bertha and me."

Shannon knew many of the ghosts were his allies but many were also his enemies.

Shannon's mind was in turmoil over his dream of the garden, feeling Katrina had lost faith in him. He realized he had never given Katrina any reason to love him or truly have faith in him, so he could not blame her, he could only blame himself. But, what else could he have done with the circumstances of his life? "Where are you Love?" he demanded of the sky. "Now that all has been taken from me, where are you?"

Even though Love heard he did not reply.

"Nothing has been taken from you," Barbara answered although Shannon could not hear her, "if you would only look inside of yourself and not outward."

Shannon traveled all day immersed in his troubled thoughts. Toward evening he rounded a bend and saw a large lichen covered boulder over thirty feet tall. The boulder looked like an aged and haggard old man. Crevices swallowed the eyes, and the mouth was a deep slash in the stone, not smiling but also not frowning, caught somewhere in a land of no feelings. The face had huge, jagged ears, as if they could hear the plight of the world, and the nose was large and round. A small twisted cedar tree grew out of the top of its head. Anna, the hawk, the deer, the bear and the stick man rested around the tree. Paul and Thomas ventured toward the circling ghosts on the other side of the river.

Shannon hurried to the stone. The stone's eyes gazed through Shannon as if he was a nuisance and not worth one moment of the stone's time. The sun started to set and Shannon quickly gathered wood for a fire. He built a fire pit a few yards from the stone face. He noticed that the stone gazed due east, across the river, the eyes riveted over the top of the hill where thousands and thousands of ghosts circled.

With the dark, the fire leapt to flame by itself. After eating the last of his bread Shannon sat facing the stone. "You are like I am," Shannon said to the stone face haltingly. "You are unable to voice your emotions and feelings to the world, and you are trapped in your knowledge of time."

"I am not like you," the stone face said, the stone lips not moving, the eyes ignoring Shannon. "I have no emotions therefore feelings mean nothing to me. I do not care about time. There was time before me, and there will be time after me. You humans put too much emphasis on time. Your existence is too fleeting to even ponder it."

The flames from the fire cast ancient shadows on the stone face.

"It is because of me that my mother is dead. My guilt overwhelms me," Shannon said, unable to look at the stone face.

"Your mother would sacrifice for you again if she had to. Your guilt is unnecessary."

Bertha circled in the night sky, listening intently. Anna watched her from the top of the stone face, unafraid and resolute.

Shannon went to the edge of the river and stood with his back to the stone face. The river swept by, dark and cool, its image lost to the night but its path steady and not afraid. "I go to fight a battle for a cause that I do not know," Shannon said without turning around.

"You know the cause, you merely do not want to accept it," the stone face said.

"I feel even if I win, it will not be the last battle."

"In any battle, neither victory nor defeat is a winner," the stone face said. "A true victory will come only when both sides lay down their arms and vow to never take up arms again."

"Is that ever possible?" Shannon asked, returning to the fire.

"I do not know," the stone face replied. "All I truly know is that you love."

"You know nothing of Katrina," Shannon said to the stone face.

"I know more than you do of Katrina. I hear her sighs on the wind and feel her reach out for you, finding only emptiness in her search."

"I could only give her emptiness. If I do not know myself, how can I be of help to another?"

"Does man ever really know himself, when the riddle changes every day? Is that an excuse to not receive a gift from another? Or is it an excuse to cover up feelings you do not understand or are afraid to understand?"

"It is probably both," Shannon admitted.

"Then call to her, and tell her how you feel for her. Do not be afraid of what you are. She knows you better than any other in your life."

"I fear I will let her down," Shannon said.

"Let her be the judge."

But Shannon did not call for Katrina and went back to the fire.

"I know I go to where the ghosts congregate," Shannon said. "I am drawn to them and I know they wait for me."

"Do not let it worry you that you may fail," the stone face said. "There are many worse things in life than failure."

"If I die, I do not want to be a ghost. I wish to be the nothingness that Bertha seeks."

"There is no nothingness. Everything exists forever in one form or another. Even I, a non-breathing stone, am something and a part of life. In time, when I am worn down to sand, I still will be, and then worn down to dust, I still will be, always something new, but also always a part of what I was from the beginning, and what I will be in the future."

The words spoken by the stone face were confusing to Bertha.

"I have not done well with the knowledge that was given to me," Shannon said, placing more wood on the fire.

"You merely have not utilized it," the stone face said.

"I wonder at times what it would have been like to only think about trivial things and trivial pursuits."

The lips of the stone face seemed to smile.

"I suppose every person is caught up in their own quest, always wanting to be more than they are, searching for riddles to make more riddles, until they either solve the riddle or it destroys them," Shannon said.

The stone face did not reply. The fire popped, sending sparks into the sky that suspended themselves for a brief instant between earth and the heavens, and then dissolved once more to darkness as they fell back to earth.

"I have tried to kill myself to give Bertha her nothingness but Love would not let me," Shannon said.

The stone face remained silent but it seemed to ponder Shannon's statement.

Bertha circled closer.

"Maybe Bertha already has what she seeks, and she just does not know it," the stone face said.

Bertha stopped in mid-air, the faint feeling in her pulsing with need. The poisonous hornets inside of her were awakened by the feeling and stirred restlessly.

The stick man poised his spear. Paul and Thomas sailed back across the river and floated high above Bertha.

"You know you have many who follow you with only your protection in mind," the stone face said.

"I am the center," Shannon said. "The center of what I do not know but I know I am the center."

"When I was young and being formed out of the earth, I also believed I was the center," the stone face said. "But unless there is a perfect circle, there is no center, and there is nothing that is perfect. So how can you be the center?"

"Then, I am only a part," Shannon said, confused.

"Exactly," the stone face said. "A part of a plan that is so large no human being or creature can comprehend it or should even try. But every part is an integral part, no matter how small or large."

"Would you rather be like me or stone?" Shannon asked.

"I have no choice in the matter. I am content with what I am and I do not wish for more or less."

"What is the most important part of our lives?" Shannon asked.

"That is your quest, Shannon, the one your voice has sent you on. I cannot help you. I am only here to point the way to your destination, and give you one day of rest."

"Please help me," Shannon begged.

"I will talk no more. You must help yourself," the stone face said.

"No, talk to me, you must."

The eyes of the stone face sank deeper into the rock and ignored Shannon. Only the sound of the river disturbed the night.

Bertha sailed higher into the sky. Paul and Thomas

followed her cautiously. The stick man lowered his spear – the hawk, and deer, and bear rested.

Shannon placed more on the fire but the fire did not warm him, nor did the light from the flames lessen his burden.

He lay, facing into the dark sky, and when he shut his eyes he was instantly back in the garden. Katrina, all but her head, was hidden behind a tree. She was crying but also trying to conceal the fear in her eyes. Shannon was not far away in the center of a clearing. A ray of light knifed through the thick foliage and illuminated him. "Please do not be afraid of my nakedness," Shannon said, holding his arms out, hoping she would run to his embrace. "I come only in my need."

"You do not even know who I am," Katrina cried and ran away. Fleeting images of her nakedness as she darted through the thick foliage burned into Shannon's mind.

Shannon desperately pursued her but once again she disappeared into the garden.

Shannon opened his eyes. "Katrina, I need you," he called.

The stone face absorbed his cries and gazed to the east impassively.

"And she needs you," Barbara said from the vastness of the sky.

Anna flew up from the cedar tree on top of the stone face and stopped next to Bertha. "The hornets that came from you were not your fault," Anna said. "They were from you but not of you."

"I cannot change what I am when I do not know what I am."

"You cannot think only about yourself," Anna said. "Even though you have been a curse to Shannon he wishes you no harm."

"Go from me. You only cause me confusion," Bertha said, her voice not fierce or commanding but almost begging.

"Think on what I have said," Anna said and with a heavy heart returned to the tree on top of the stone face.

Chapter Forty-one

BERTHA

I f God treated all mankind like he did Job, how many humans would gladly become a crusader for Satan?

****

"I seek sanctuary once again," Bertha whispered to the night.

"Why do you seek sanctuary?" Love asked.

"I need to be one with my own thoughts," Bertha replied. "Can you control the hornets within me?"

"I will try my best."

Bertha was instantly transformed to the cave.

Looking out from the entrance to the cave Bertha remembered how cool and refreshing the grass felt on her bare feet when, as a little girl, she played in the backyard of Rebecca's home. "If only I would have died as a child," she said, "died before Paul and Thomas and Andrew threw rocks at me. I was not a bad person before then."

Bertha retreated into the middle of the cave. A dull gloom filled the cave, mingled with the smell of time. A memory gently flowed through her. Rebecca was hurrying away from Bertha's father's house with Bertha wrapped in a warm blanket. "You poor little thing, do not worry, I will take care of you and shield you from the world. It will be ok, if you let it," Rebecca said.

Bertha felt Mary's generous nipple brush her lips and the feel of the warm milk as it flowed down her throat to fill her empty stomach. She saw Mary's wide smile come in and out

246

of focus with her baby eyes. "She is an ugly little thing but in all things there is their own beauty," Mary soothed.

The baby Bertha smiled, not knowing of her mother's death, not knowing of her mother's cries, not knowing the force that had made her kick from the womb causing her mother such terrible pain. She was merely a baby, a baby with a smile, content with the gift of nourishment and the sound and touch of another human being.

Bertha blended with the dull gray of the cave letting the ageless smell of time settle into her. She thought of the stone face talking to Shannon. "There is no nothingness," the stone voice had said.

"How can I seek that which does not exist?" Bertha questioned.

The feeling that lay buried deep within her stirred, radiated small fingers of heat, but they were so weak they were unable to grasp anything to cling to and grow.

Another memory came over her – her doll, her lovely doll Naomi – her doll with golden hair and trusting eyes, the doll that consoled her and smiled at her and asked nothing in return. "I even destroyed my doll," Bertha said. "And she did nothing against me."

The feeling she could not define within her grew stronger.

Bertha remembered the first night of her marriage and how gentle John's touches had been. The touches were fleeting, yet exploring, timid in his deceit but not deceitful, searching for a love he had known, and not knowing if he could ever find a new love, but willing to try. Then Bertha rebelled against his soft touches, growing mad in her desire to possess him. She wanted to rip all of the old feelings out of him and make him only hers. She had made love like a harlot – uncaring, only out of necessity and her own greed, biting, scratching, taking all the gentleness out of John and leaving him wary of her. "I have made myself what I am," Bertha said. "It is no one's fault but my own."

But she had been so long with hate there was no sadness

or remorse in her, only truth, and Bertha felt that it was too late for the truth to make any difference.

She spent the rest of her sanctuary with no thoughts, for once in her existence experiencing solitude that was not forced by prison walls. As the first hint of dawn brushed the horizon, she sailed away, not looking back but also remembering the touch of cool green grass on a young girl's feet, and the one time in her life that she had truly smiled.

Chapter Forty-two

BARBARA

Who or what has caused hunger and poverty and war? It cannot be blamed on gods or demons. The blame lies only on humanity. We have the means to make life at least bearable for all. We, however, do not want to – it would destroy our kings and queens.

****

With the sunrise, thousands upon thousands of additional ghosts had joined the cloud of ghosts over the circle of desolation. The cloud was now immense, ghosts of all kinds and colors darted in all directions, making the mass swell and move like a gigantic swarm of bees. Some if the ghosts threatened others but they were ignored and their threats were not returned.

The voices under the ground wailed louder, but were still being ignored.

Barbara wondered if Love and Hate were like modern generals, receiving all the glory of battle but not fighting themselves, observing powerfully from distant hilltops while their soldiers shed blood only for blood's sake, then fleeing in fright if the battle ended wrong, uncaring to their dead followers, making up excuses to their kings as why their soldiers had been defeated, certain in their own minds they could not have been in error.

Love said to Barbara. "I cannot kill or maim or lay waste."

"Your son does not wish to fight," Barbara replied.

"If I could die, I would die for him, but for me there is

neither life nor death, nor for my adversary."

"Then why does Hate pursue you and force your hand?"

"It is all he knows. War of any kind is his pursuit, the apex of his need and desire."

"He must be very lonely," Barbara said.

"He does not know loneliness or compassion or remorse or pity or guilt. To him they are only the feelings of weak people, feelings that should be destroyed."

"Is he what has made the world what it is?"

"At times I think it is more my fault than his," the voice said. "There is never only one to blame."

"If our son is killed, what will he become?" Barbara asked.

"He will be on my right side forever, like you, a part of everything but not a part, only able to observe the world but make no changes, accepting what is but always hoping for what could be."

"I wish we were flesh and you could hold me," Barbara said.

No sooner had the words left her mouth than she was filled with a feeling so warm and fulfilling and caring that all thought was taken from her, and she was more than the sky, she was a portion of everything that had ever existed on earth – part ocean, part volcano, part fish, rock, tree, flower, insect, lake, even down to the tiniest one celled creature. Then, as quickly as the feeling had entered her, it vanished, and all of the sky that was Barbara sighed deeply, and the sigh flowed over the earth like a gentle rain.

Shannon was looking apprehensively at the cloud of ghosts. Barbara's sigh omitted from every direction around him. The circle of ghosts froze momentarily, both in awe and fright, then, timidly, began to move once again. "Mother, you are with me," Shannon said in relief.

Immediately after the sigh faded away Hate's voice reverberated menacingly, "Meet me as we agreed, all have arrived."

Every ghost over the circle of desolation including Bertha, Anna, the hawk, the deer, the bear, the stick man, and Barbara, heard the voice. The rushing river grew silent and the breeze was afraid to stir. The air hung heavy and tense.

Shannon noticed that there were no more ghosts arriving. The cloud of ghosts, as if on command, formed into a gigantic irregular circle blocking out the sun. Then, the circle separated down the middle into two halves – each half had the same exact number of ghosts. One half progressed to the eastern side of the desolation, and the other half moved to the western side of the desolation. Then, in strict military precision both sides, one ghost at a time, started forming into platoons – each rectangular platoon consisted of thousands of ghosts. As soon as one platoon was completed another formed beside it, until thirteen platoons formed the first rank, then another thirteen formed behind it, until they were lined up behind each other so deeply they extended to the eastern and western horizons. Each platoon had a single ghost in front of it, but no single ghost stood in front of the completed formations. Finished, the two armies faced each other. The ghosts were silent and stood at attention waiting for their commanders. Neither army possessed weapons of any kind. The battle would be fought hand to hand with animal savagery.

The cries and moans from the earth ceased. A deadly silence blanketed the armies.

Bertha, during the forming of the armies, observed Shannon. A strong gust of wind swept her up and placed her above the seventh platoon in the front rank of eastern army. She looked at the mass of ghosts and all the hate she had ever known screamed from inside her, but the tiny undefined feeling also remained within her.

"This is my champion. Is your champion ready for tomorrow?" Hate's voice called toward the western army.

Shannon was picked up and transported to the front and middle of the western army.

"My champion is ready," Love's voice replied from over

the western army.

"Tomorrow, at dawn, he will be destroyed," Hate gloated.

A tremendous pain stabbed into Bertha. It scorched her insides, ripped at her, tore at the feeble feeling she was unable to understand, but the feeling withstood the onslaught.

"What lie have you promised your champion for her loyalty? Have you promised her nothingness and oblivion?" Love asked.

Bertha listened intently. "She will receive her just reward," Hate stated.

"She does best not to trust you," Love said.

"Tell your champion to enjoy his day of rest. It will be his last," Hate said with a tone of finality.

The voices grew silent. The armies stood at attention. Bertha hovered over her army and Hate spoke only to her. "You will destroy Shannon tomorrow. You have no choice."

A steel cage materialized around Bertha. The bars were rusty and beyond time, and, even though a ghost, she could not pass between them. The cage was filled with her hate, and the hate of the army, and all the hate of the universe. It almost vanquished the tiny feeling tenaciously holding on within her. Bertha glared at the western army and vowed, "I will destroy you and I will receive my reward."

Shannon was transported back to the stone face.

Chapter Forty-three

SHANNON

Many people believe or do not believe that God created the earth and all its creatures in seven days. But it is an undeniable fact than on the eighth day man readied for war.

****

Shannon was sitting with his back against the stone face. The face's shadow was cool but brought no comfort to Shannon. "You have your day of rest," the stone face said. "Use it well, and reflect on all that you have been taught and experienced, and on all of the gifts you have received in your life."

"What of all my shortcomings?" Shannon asked.

"You should be smarter than to ask that question," the stone face said.

Shannon's world closed in on him. There was no stone face, no river, no sky, no trees, no Anna or Bertha, no ghosts of any kind, no voice, but there was Katrina – her smiling image was in the center of his mind but far beyond reach.

Shannon, like Bertha, was inside of a cage, only his cage was invisible. All he could do was look within himself. He thought about all the books and magazines he had read on religion, government, politics, history, and on and on. It seemed things never really changed – no matter how much wisdom one attained.

He thought about all the languages he could speak, but all of them were inadequate. Words were never enough to convey

253

true meaning.

He thought about all the worry he had caused Barbara and felt sad, but he also remembered the times he made her smile and how happy it made him feel.

Thoughts about Katrina made him both happy and sad.

Anna floated down from the top of the stone face and smiled at him. She was a deep, vibrant, blue. "It took me until death to know of love," she said. "I hope you do not make the same mistake."

"How can love overshadow mistakes and misgivings?" Shannon asked.

"Because it is gentle and forgiving, and never takes or misleads. It asks not for itself but for others," Anna replied.

"Will you be with me tomorrow?"

"I will be with you but you must win your own battle."

"How can I win this battle?"

"I do not know. That is for you to discover."

"If I fail, I want you to know I appreciate all that you have done for me."

"No. I appreciate all you have done for me," Anna said, and returned to the top of the rock face.

Shannon thought about his night in Kansas City with Millie. "Oh Millie," he lamented. "I did you wrong. I came to you only out of desire. I am a thief who stole from you when I should have given friendship and a smile. I only plunged you deeper into your loneliness."

He thought about the rainbow trout that questioned him from the river. "If you are the center of all things then what am I?" the trout had asked.

He thought about the old man with the bells tied in his moustache asking him what the most important thing was in life, and how the man had promised Shannon a rainbow whenever he needed it.

He thought about the sad lady who had lost all and was about to give up on life and how flowers had grown from their tears.

He thought about the mother raccoon and her three babies stranded on a log in the raging river, her only concern being her children.

He thought about his mother's plea that he must never hate, but he had hated the golden man, who had clawed and ravaged Katrina, and he hated Bertha for killing his mother, and he knew he must hate if he was to win the battle in the morning.

He thought about sitting under the tree on the island as an old man and talking to his young self, and how he wished desperately he would have told Katrina he loved her, if only once.

He thought about Paul and Thomas telling him to never do in life what they had done.

He thought about the silver halo entering his heart, and the feelings of contentment and wholeness that had swept through him, if only for a brief moment, and then, with its leaving, how empty and alone he became.

He thought about Katrina naked in the garden and how it had been his fault she hid from him.

He thought about all the dreams that had been more than dreams, more vivid than any moment in his life, dreams so vivid they were almost reality.

All of his thoughts filled his mind to overflowing – swirling thoughts, begging for answers. At times he wished he was unable to think. It would be a great relief to be like a tree or a rock or a river, to be with no comprehension of death, or sadness, or happiness, or hate, or love.

"What am I supposed to do with what I have?" Shannon called. "What is my true mission? You must tell me or I will fail you."

Barbara, all of the sky, could only watch her son. She could not embrace him or shed tears or convey her love.

Anna, the hawk, the deer, the bear, and the stick man with his spear also could do nothing. Paul and Thomas could not help. "In life, there can be no revenge," Thomas said to Paul.

Bertha, hearing Shannon's cry for answers, rattled the bars to her cage. She wanted to be released and destroy Shannon while he was weak and in need. She screamed so viciously all the ghosts of the western army cringed but held their ranks. The eastern army below her murmured with dark approval.

Shannon's mind swirled faster. "Why? Why? Why? Why?" he beseeched.

He shut his eyes and rubbed his throbbing temples and asked again, "Why? Why?"

A breath of cool wind circled Shannon. Opening his eyes, he was again in the center of the garden. This time though he was not naked but dressed, and the garden had changed. It was an overgrown jungle. The steaming heat was suffocating and unbearable. The trees were devoid of buds, fruit lay rotting on the ground, covered with maggots and flies. The flowers were limp and without color – all hope had been drained from them. The birds were hiding in the leaves, not singing, as if song was now a sin and would only lead to eternal damnation.

"Katrina, Katrina," Shannon called and headed in no set direction into the garden. But what were once clear paths were now tangles of brambles and bushes, all covered with thorns and burrs that tore at his skin and clothes – they ripped and cut and made him bleed. All animals large and small scampered away from him in mistrust.

"Katrina, Katrina," Shannon called feverishly. "I cannot help myself but I can help you."

His pleas were unable penetrate the garden and fell at his feet, useless and spent like wasted lives.

Shannon struggled on, first one direction, then the next, until there was no direction, only green tangles of vines and trees, the light only dusk above him. Swarms of biting insects emerged from the foliage and feasted on him, stinging, sucking his blood, leaving welts that ached and itched. "Katrina, Katrina," he called.

The sound of a woman sobbing echoed from all directions

at once. Shannon, turning in a circle, tried to locate the source but it was useless. He fell to his knees and covered his ears with his hands trying to block out the sound, but the sobbing only grew louder. "What have I done? What have I done?" he lamented and started crying.

Tears poured from his eyes, tears for Katrina, tears for his mother, tears for all the lost ghosts, tears for the lonely and lost and the disenchanted, tears for those in poverty and need, tears for the destitute, tears for those in war, even tears for Bertha. He cried harder, unable to stop, not wanting to stop. The biting insects retreated. As each tear hit the ground a tree in the garden bore fruit, another tear, and a flower bloomed, radiant with color, more tears, and the thorn and bramble bushes lost their thorns and burrs, and the paths of the garden were once again clear. Shannon cried on. Birds began to sing and fly, animals came out of their hiding. The jungle reduced its canopy, letting the sunlight filter through and filled the air with hundreds of misty rainbows. Still Shannon cried. Katrina's sobbing around him grew louder. Then, with one last tear, Shannon stopped crying and the sobbing also ceased. The garden was a chorus of bird song, butterflies, fruit, and flowers. The animals were tranquil.

Shannon was naked and on the edge of a clearing in the garden, the sunlight was bright but not hot. The grass under his feet was cool and as soft as velvet. Katrina emerged on the other side of the clearing, her nakedness radiant and proud. She smiled at Shannon and opened her arms for an embrace. They met in the center of the clearing, holding each other lightly. Shannon nestled his face into Katrina's hair and breathed deeply into his lungs the soothing scent of her. "I knew you would save me," Katrina whispered in his ear.

"O Katrina. I..."

Shannon's was once again sitting in the shade of the stone face. There were no questions swirling through his mind. He stared at Bertha in her cage and the door to his invisible cage opened slightly.

Chapter Forty-four

BERTHA

JOB 7 - CHAPTER 21. And why dost thou not pardon my transgression, and take away mine iniquity? For now shall I sleep in the dust; and thou shalt seek me in the morning but I shall not be.

****

Bertha thrashed like a captured wild beast inside her cage. Her normally empty eyes were blood red, so piercing that not even one ghost of the eastern army below could look at her without averting their gaze. But at the same time they drew strength from her just as she drew strength from them.

At times, Bertha's hate and anger would grow so extreme she would hurl herself at the bars but they repulsed her. The bars would ring like a death toll from the impact and make Bertha scream. The screams cut like razor-tipped arrows through the air, penetrating all that was good and well-meaning.

Randomly, the platoon leaders from the eastern army would fly towards the western army, stop short, and shout, "Your champion will be destroyed. Your beliefs are nothing. Join us."

The western army ranks would not waver or reply.

Moans and sighs intensified from the circle of desolation between the two armies. The eastern army was disdainful of the cries. The western army was saddened by their inability to alleviate, or in any way lessen, the grief of those trapped in the earth.

258

In the middle of the afternoon, a single ghost left the ranks from the front platoon of the western army. Beseeching pleas for it not to go followed it, but it took no heed. As it neared the front ranks of the eastern army, three ghosts angrily charged out to challenge it. "Leave him be," Bertha ordered harshly. "Whoever harms him, I will destroy."

The three ghosts, without protest, returned to their ranks.

The lone ghost advanced and stopped in front of Bertha's cage. "I am sorry I could not give you what you needed," the ghost of John her husband said.

Bertha did not attack the bars of the cage in protest. She hovered in the middle. Even with all her hate, a tiny flicker of the feeling she could not understand ran through her.

"I have not talked to Anna," John said, "but I have watched her. She led a lonely life but she has found herself now, and I am happy for her."

The eastern army grew restless.

"Why could you not love me?" Bertha asked, barely keeping her hate in check.

"There are many forms of love, some of need, some of companionship, some of loneliness, some of desire, some between children and parent. I loved you but not in the way you sought," John said with a tinge of sadness in his voice.

"Are you with your first wife?" Bertha asked. "The one you named our daughter after."

"She is with me," John replied. "She only wishes you had led a better life and means you no harm."

"Go from me, John. It is too late for me. There is nothing you can say that will stop me from destroying Shannon in the morning."

"Your side has won many battles but it will never know true victory," John said and with one last look at Bertha he started back toward the western army.

The eastern army hissed and screeched at him. Halfway between the armies, surrounded by the moans and agony emitting from the earth, John stopped, turned back toward

Bertha and waved. Bertha did not return his wave, the unknown feeling faded, and she screamed madly, "Go from me! You have come too late!"

The eastern army cheered with her pain and resentment.

Anna had not seen her father since his murder. She flew to the western army, calling out over the first platoon. "Father, father, I am here. It is your daughter, Anna."

They sailed to each other and embraced. "I have no words to explain how deeply I missed you," John said.

Anna felt her father's love. "I must return to my mission," she said. "But when all is done I will see you again."

She returned to the other side of the river.

"They forgive you but they do not love you," Hate said to Bertha.

"I know," Bertha said resolutely.

"The feeling you do not understand that stirs in you is only a temptation to drive you from me," Hate said.

Bertha was surprised by the statement, but tried not to show it. "I have no control over what enters me," Bertha said.

"Only my foe and I cannot be tempted," Hate said.

"What are the ghosts in the circle of desolation that we fight for?" Bertha asked.

"You and Shannon fight for the thousands of lost ghosts beneath the earth who knew neither love nor hate during their lives. The winner will bring all of these souls to his side, swaying the balance of power."

"I care not for your balance of power. I seek only what you have promised me."

"Then fight only for yourself and win for all that I seek."

"You cannot expect loyalty," Bertha said.

"I only respect treachery," Hate replied.

Bertha gazed across the river and she saw Anna and John, Paul and Thomas, the hawk, the deer, the bear, the stick man with his spear, the old man with a walking stick decorated with feathers, a lady, and, to her amazement, the ghost of Rebecca sitting in a large circle in front of the stone face with Shannon in the center.

"So your disciples gather each in their own way willing to forsake their own needs for yours," Bertha said. "Your death will be a good death, Shannon. Not like mine was. Your cause and your people will mourn and cry for you, and you will not have to seek redemption. You already possess it."

Bertha settled to the bottom of the cage, glared at the western army, and waited impatiently for the nightfall and the coming dawn.

The moans and cries from the circle of desolation increased in their longing.

Chapter Forty-five

BARBARA

If we come from the dirt of the earth, why do we look toward the stars in search of heaven? Is it because we have almost destroyed our home, and we know that one day in the future mankind's children will have to leave this planet because of our folly. It might be wise of us to save our home and give our children memories of us to be proud of rather than ashamed. No life wishes a journey caused by desperation with home only a memory that can never be visited again.

****

Barbara observed her son circled by the ghosts and spirits that had befriended him. The stone face was stoic, in constant vigil of the two armies. The cries from the circle of desolation between the two armies chased the clouds away, leaving nothing to impede the journey of the sun across the sky and its destiny with the dark. No one in the circle around Shannon was talking. They gazed intently at Shannon, not with sadness or grief but also not in adulation or praise, but as though seeing their own lives and experiences residing within him. Shannon was going to be the failure or fulfillment for each of them.

Within the circle, for the time being, Shannon felt safe and unafraid of the next day, but only half of him was in the circle – the other half remained in the garden, naked and embracing Katrina. But his thoughts of the garden were eerie and confusing. He had the sensation he had done all of this before, and that the garden was a necessary part of him.

Love spoke to Barbara. "They are a pleasing sight," he said observing the circle, "all teachers but also all students unto themselves."

"You are not a good teacher," Barbara said but not in scorn.

"There is nothing for me to teach that man does not already possess. They only have to accept me and they will teach themselves."

"Shannon's love for Katrina is great," Barbara said.

"He would not be my son and possess such a great love if I did not love you beyond any other," Love said.

"How could you love me beyond any other?" Barbara asked.

"I do not know. It confuses me. I watched you for many years and you became my dream, and now you are beyond dream."

"You have made me what I am and I feel warmer and safer than I ever have, but I cannot say I love you."

"You do not have to love me. I have made you all of the sky so that you are always around me. We are truly one, which no others can be. It has made me happy and one day you may love me."

"If I am never able to tell you I love you, you must know I feel that you are a great being," Barbara said.

"I do not wish to be great. I only wish to be," Love replied.

"You must go and bring Katrina here. It is her right to see Shannon, if this is to be his last day."

"I will go to Katrina for you and Shannon," Love said and departed, not knowing it was too late. They were unaware that Hate had been listening to their conversation.

Katrina was sitting at her desk contemplating her first dream about the garden. How could Shannon not answer her question? What was she to him? Although she had not wanted to flee from him, she knew she had to. In fleeing her nakedness had become an embarrassment to her.

The memory of their embrace in the second dream left her

the way she was now – sad, filled with longing but her hope rekindled, the touch of her skin against Shannon's skin etched into her mind, not ashamed of their nakedness, their nakedness a gift and more than a dream. Even though she could only reach out to him in dreams, she knew he thought of her and missed her, and needed her as she needed him.

"If Shannon is to die, you should die with him," a voice said to her that was not the voice she had heard by the tree.

"I would gladly die with Shannon or for him," Katrina replied. "Have you come for me now that his hour of need is near?"

Katrina was violently yanked out of the chair by unseen hands. A rough hewn wooden cross appeared on the floor. Katrina lashed out and kicked to try and flee but she was not strong enough. She was roughly laid out on the cross. Her arms were forced straight out from her body and her wrists were tied roughly to the cross beam with course hemp rope. Her legs were pushed together and her feet were tied to the center beam. A black hood was jammed over her head. She tried to scream but she had no voice. "You will get your desire, for love you will die," the voice said.

The cross was hurled into the sky and spun in slow clockwise revolutions. Katrina's heart thudded desperately in her chest. Her blood rushed from her head to her feet and back again. She was dizzy, lost, disorientated, her thoughts jumbled and filled with fear. Feeling like she could take no more, the spinning abruptly ceased, and she felt the cross being pushed upright. Cries and moans of anguish surrounded her, suffocated her, anguish so deep it cut into her heart so viciously she could not cry out or pray – only listen uselessly without the ability to do anything. The hood was yanked from her head. Her voice returned. "No! No! Please! God no!" she gasped.

She was suspended above Bertha who was locked in a rusty steel cage that floated at the front of an endless army of evil and sinister looking ghosts. The ghosts screeched at her, joyful with her plight. Bertha, eyes blood red as if her eyes were on fire sneered, "And so the lamb's heart has been given to me."

"Shannon," Katrina called desperately.

Shannon heard Katrina's cries and leapt to his feet. The cross above Bertha's cage was magnified in Shannon's mind a hundred times over so Katrina seemed to be only a few feet from him. "Katrina," he hollered in rage and ran toward the river, but the circle of his friends tightened so they were touching, and reaching the edge of the circle, their combined energies would not let him break the circle. "You must wait until the dawn," the stone face said. "You will not break the sanctity of the circle."

Shannon lashed out at his captors and ran at different parts of the circle but there were no weak points.

"You have broken our agreement," Love called but not angrily. "This is the day of rest."

"Did you ever think you could trust me?" Hate replied.

"Even you should have some honor."

"Victory at any cost is the only honor," Hate responded, and a curdling laugh pierced through the sky.

The army of the east cheered. The army of the west sighed deeply.

"You must let me pass," Shannon pleaded to the members of the circle.

"The circle is not our will," Anna said resolutely.

"Then whose will is it?"

"Yours, only yours."

Love, the father of Shannon, the savior of Barbara, unheard to the rest of the world, cried.

Chapter Fourty-six

SHANNON

S T. JOHN 15: CHAPTER 15 - 12-13: This is my commandment, that ye love one another, as I have loved you. Greater love hath no man than this: that a man lay down his life for his friends.

****

Anna, John, Paul and Thomas, Rebecca, the old man with bells in his moustache, the lady, the hawk, the deer, the bear and the stick man circled Shannon and would not let him go to Katrina.

Shannon was close to rage. His hands were clenched into fists. "How can you be my friends and keep me confined?" he demanded from the center of the circle.

The circle remained steadfast and no one replied.

"I will not sacrifice Katrina for any cause," Shannon said, glaring at each member of the circle. "I will forsake all of you and Love if need be."

"Would Katrina sacrifice for you?" the stone face asked.

"I would not want her to," Shannon said, taken back by the remark.

"I asked if Katrina would sacrifice for you?" the stone face repeated.

Katrina was no longer crying but hung limply on the cross, her head sagged forward as if in deep thought. "She would sacrifice for me," Shannon answered quietly.

"It is sad when love is not returned," the stone face said.

"How can I tell a person I love them when I do not know

my future?" Shannon demanded.

"No man or woman knows their future yet many love," the stone face said.

"Now there is no way I can defeat Bertha," Shannon said forlornly.

"Then let your foe defeat herself," the stone face said.

"How? Please tell me how?" Shannon begged.

"I do not know. I am only stone."

"Then what good are you to me?"

"The same that you are to me."

Katrina raised her head. "I am with you. It is all that matters," she called to Shannon with no fear in her voice.

No energy, either angry or peaceful, remained in Shannon. There were no questions, no answers – no hope. He was lost. He fell to the ground praying the earth would devour him, take him from this place, but it refused and he closed his eyes. Shannon felt he had been a failure in all he had ever done, and that he would be a failure tomorrow.

Barbara tried to take Shannon's emptiness from him but she could do nothing. The circle did not waver and not one of them moved to assist Shannon.

The stone face watched the two armies. He was neither happy nor sad. He would still be stone whatever the outcome in the morning. Both armies were silent, waiting, no scouts were sent forth to survey the enemy.

Shannon kept his eyes closed until the sun started to set. The last sunrays of the day combined into one large ray and centered on Katrina. The rays circled her, framing her in a gold and silver aura that defied defeat.

When dark came the sunray remained on Katrina and illuminated both armies in a golden shadow. The cries and moans emitting from the earth ceased.

A single sunray separated from the glow and arched from Katrina's heart, danced through the darkness and touched Shannon gently in his heart. The ray connected the two and Katrina smiled at Shannon. Her smile was unafraid. Shannon smiled back. "I understand," he said with a sigh. "I finally understand."

With its purpose complete the sunray dissipated into the darkness.

A rose bush materialized next to Shannon and burst into flames. Inside the flames the rose bush remained green and covered with crimson red roses. The scent of roses filled the air. "I will not desecrate the circle," Shannon said to the figures surrounding him. "I had no right to try to escape and destroy your unity."

"Without you we are not a circle," Anna replied.

Shannon bowed to the burning rose bush and called. "Come to me Love. It is time."

The flame leapt to the sky and Shannon was transformed to the top of a mountain. He could see forever, even past the curve of the earth. There were mountains and oceans, lakes and rivers, forests and deserts, islands, all the creatures of the earth. "All that you see I have not given man," Love said. "I am not a part of creation. I was before creation, although creation is because of me."

"Father, do I die tomorrow for your sins?" Shannon asked.

"If you die, it will not be for my sins, it will be for my failures."

"I thank you for a wonderful mother and Katrina."

"They both have been a joy to me but Katrina was not a gift from me to you, she is her own gift. A gift you have always had."

"I also thank you for my life."

"You have done well, Shannon."

"Now you must tell me why I must fight."

"You fight for the spirits beneath the circle of desolation who neither felt love or hate during their life time. Whoever wins gets their souls. Hate and I are equal in power. The winner will gain dominance over the earth."

"If I lose, you will have to hide and the world will be in greater peril than it is," Shannon said.

"My son, why do many not come to me?"

"With all my knowledge, there is no knowledge that can answer your question."

"I hope you understand why I cannot fight my own battles. Do not hold it against me."

"I understand," Shannon replied.

"At times I think my complete existence is merely a selfish pursuit and I try and be God."

"Your pursuit is noble and if there is a God you must make Him smile."

"I do not know, my doubts are many."

Shannon was back inside the circle, the rose bush was still burning – the scent of roses flowed across the river and surrounded both armies. Katrina was still bathed by the sunray. Sitting with his back to the burning rose bush Shannon gazed at Katrina and waited for the dawn.

Chapter Forty-seven

BERTHA

A wild beast in a cage never forgets its freedom. It will wait restlessly for however long it takes for the opportunity to maim or kill its captor. The beast knows that death is its last remaining freedom.

****

Bertha's mind wandered. She remembered waiting under the bridge, the peaceful sound of the river shattered when the stick crashed into Paul's head, his body turning slowly in his watery grave, not knowing or understanding what had caused his death. But now, Bertha held no great satisfaction with her deed. What if she would have waited for Paul and talked to him? What if she had told him she was sorry he did not like her and what she really needed was a friend?

She thought about Thomas, murdered at the height of his love for another? Did he still yearn for his love? Did the lady, now grown and probably married to another, at times miss Thomas and think about him?

The feeling in her that she could not understand stirred.

"Bertha, I would like to talk," Katrina beckoned from the cross.

"The battle is tomorrow and whatever you say will make no difference but I will talk," Bertha replied.

"You do not have to destroy Shannon," Katrina said. "Why would you want others to suffer like you?"

"I have no choice. To end my existence I must destroy Shannon."

"You do not always hate," Katrina said. "I know at times you feel other emotions that you try and hide from your master."

"I feel nothing," Bertha lied.

"Then why does Hate keep you caged?"

"Your love is also a cage in many ways," Bertha said.

"Oh Bertha, I feel so sorry for you. True love is never a cage."

"But it is filled with sadness and longing," Bertha said.

"Yes, but it is never filled with resentment or hate. The sadness and longing only make love stronger, they do not build cages."

"I read once when I was young that those who truly love must have had to hate to really know love," Bertha said.

"I do not think that is true. Hate is the void that is caused by the absence of all feeling."

"All people have hated something at one time or another."

"But it is rejected by those who want love."

"I was not strong enough to reject it," Bertha said with a tinge of remorse, "and now it is all that I am."

"You cannot lie to me, hate is not all that you are," Katrina said.

"It is strange Shannon and I are about to battle for souls that knew neither loved nor hated during their lives. I wonder how a person could have not known either," Bertha contemplated.

"They buried their feelings so deep within themselves they became lost," Katrina said.

"I would rather have been like them and let somebody else fight this battle," Bertha said.

"Shannon will not fight you," Katrina said.

"To save you he must fight. He has no choice."

"To be what he is, he must not fight. He and I will be together when we are truly spirit and not trapped by our bodies and the needs of life. Your master, no matter what the outcome, will not let me go. I am doomed."

"What good is love, if there is no life to enjoy it?" Bertha asked.

"It is everything. It does not need life it transcends time and the stars."

"As you have become resolute in your love, people also become resolute in their hate," Bertha said.

"Love does not intentionally harm," Katrina said.

Two ghosts made their way from the western army. "No harm will be done to them," Bertha ordered her army.

The ghosts stopped several yards from Bertha's cage. One advanced to the edge of the cage. "My father, look what you have done to me," Bertha spat, her anger rekindled.

"I was not kind enough to love you," her father said. "I have regretted it for all of my time. You were in need and I put my selfishness before you. I come to ask your forgiveness."

Bertha lunged at the bars. Her words spewed like snake venom. "I can never forgive you. I was of your blood and you cast me out."

"I cannot forgive myself but I will do nothing more to harm you," her father said. "But please? Do one good deed and do not harm Shannon."

Bertha darted around the inside of the cage, her anger and hate flying off of her in sparks each time she hit the bars. "Go from me," she ordered her father. "You were the seed for my hate."

Her father sadly returned to the western army.

The other ghost approached the cage. "My child," she said.

Bertha was shocked by the sound of the ghost's voice. "Mother," she said tentatively.

"It has been so long," her mother said. "So very long."

The fire in Bertha's eyes dimmed. "I meant you no harm. I was only a baby."

"I know that now. What you did to me was not you. You had no control."

"I never thought of you during my life," Bertha said. "I

blocked you from my mind."

"I have never had a moment in time when you were not in my thoughts," her mother said.

"I have come to ask for your forgiveness for the curse I placed on you."

"There is nothing to forgive, Mother. I will do you no harm."

"I suppose you will not listen to me either and not harm Shannon."

"It is too late, Mother."

The ghost returned to the western army. Bertha watched until her mother disappeared into the ranks.

"In another time and another place you and I could have been friends," Katrina said.

"There is no other time or other place," Bertha said. "The days do not turn back and give us other chances."

"Yes, but the future does," Katrina said.

"Shannon will be easy to defeat, your kindness will not protect him. I will talk no more," Bertha said and turned her back to Katrina.

But Bertha found no satisfaction in her words. And the fragile feeling deep within her pulsed ever so slightly.

Chapter Forty-eight

BARBARA

THESSALONIANS 5 - CHAPTER 5 - 15: See that none render evil for evil unto any man; but ever follow that which is good, both among yourselves, and to all men.

****

Barbara observed Shannon. His back was to the burning rose bush. Barbara hoped he finally realized the path he must follow and had come to terms with it. Anna, John, Paul and Thomas, Rebecca, the hawk, the deer, the bear, the stick man with his spear, the old man and the lady were not looking at Shannon, but sat in the circle around him mesmerized by the burning rose bush, as if the bush possessed all the knowledge of the world – the knowledge of gods and dreams, souls and spirits, the things books could not explain or come close to capturing their true meaning.

Katrina ignored the pain that racked her body and held no remorse or sadness in her heart. Her love for Shannon radiated in the glow that surrounded her. Even the army from the east was quiet and subdued by her grace and courage.

"Can I speak to my son one more time?" Barbara asked Love.

"It is only right," Love replied. Hate did not interfere.

A delicate, blue-gray swallow landed only a few feet from Shannon. It tilted its head lovingly at Shannon. "It is good to see you Mother. I have missed you," Shannon said with a caring smile.

274

"You have never been out of my sight, Shannon. I only wish to remind you that you must never hate?"

"But I have felt hate, and hate still lingers in me."

"Has it entered your heart?"

"Not yet but at times it rages and almost wins."

"For yourself, if for no other reason, you must not let hate conquer you."

"How can I save Katrina if I do not hate my enemy?"

"I love her like my own daughter but she is only one part of the whole. You must remember that."

"Is not one part as important as all of the parts? Without the one there can be no whole."

"That is for you to decide."

"I want you to know that I love you, Mother," Shannon said. "And I wish I could have told you earlier."

"I always knew you did but it is good to hear it."

"I am proud to be the son of Love, although I do not think I can make him proud of me."

"Pride is of no great importance to your father. It means nothing to what he is. Those who follow him do not need pride."

"Why did he choose you as my mother?"

"He felt my need and he said I have a good heart."

"What worries I have caused you," Shannon said.

"You were born out of and into love, Shannon. There is always worry over one you love, but the worry is not caused by love. It is caused by the strife we place in life."

"I have been blessed with a good life," Shannon said.

The swallow hopped onto Shannon's knee. "Go with my blessing my son," Barbara said and flew away. She was absorbed by the complete sky as soon as she passed the outer edge of the circle.

Shannon gazed at Katrina. Her eyes beseeched the heavens, and even in extreme pain she seemed tranquil and serene. Shannon followed her line of vision. The night sky was cloudless. The stars were beacons of hope. Katrina's glow merged one with the starlight, proclaiming, "The dark will never win. I am not afraid of your treachery. Look at my radiance. It is a gift for all who will partake of it and I ask nothing in return."

"What will Shannon do tomorrow?" Barbara asked Love.

"He will do what he feels is right, but no matter what course of action he takes, it will be a heavy load on him."

"What if he makes the wrong choice and loses the battle?"

"There will be you and I remaining to try again."

"How can you love me when I do not know if I love you?"

"I love all things, all creatures, even those who wish to destroy me, but I love you more. I can do no more. It is what I am."

"At times it must be extremely lonely for you."

"It is never lonely but sadness is never far away."

"You needed Shannon to for knowledge, because you do not possess it," Barbara said.

"Feeling is not knowledge, but I also know now that knowledge can be unfeeling. It is not the answer to happiness or contentment. I am the only answer, but perhaps I am too simple for modern man. Man seems too complicate life so."

"They always have."

"I wish they would not complicate their spirit also," Love said.

Shannon peered deep inside the burning rose bush. "There are flowers in flames," he said. "There is rebirth in destruction. Therefore, there has to be love in hate."

Turning from the bush, Shannon smiled at each member of the circle around him. "Thank you, each one, for what you have taught me and for how you have protected me. I will always hold you within my heart. Now you must leave me. I wish to be alone."

The old man with the bells in his moustache and his feathered walking stick stood. "Thank you for the drink of water," he said, and started spinning his walking stick around his head until the red, yellow, blue, green, orange, purple and black feathers were a blur. A rainbow shot from the stick and circled Shannon three times before it raced across the night sky to Katrina and became one with the glow circling her. With his gift of the rainbow the old man vanished.

The lady stood. "Thank you for your tears. They are the flowers of the earth," she said and disappeared.

The hawk, the deer, the bear, the stick man all stood, bowed, each in their own fashion, and disappeared, the stick man left his spear imbedded in the ground as a testament to his loyalty.

"Thank you for teaching us to forgive," Paul and Thomas said and drifted toward the western army.

Anna approached Shannon. "Thank you for giving my daughter the love I never was able to give her." She also headed for the western army.

Rebecca said before departing. "You have no knowledge of me but it is of no importance. I came in hopes Bertha might change."

Shannon was alone. "To all of you in my life please forgive me my trespasses," he said to the burning rose bush.

The spear the stick man had left behind disappeared.

Shannon gazed at the North Star, and he thought about Mohammad, and Buddha, and Confucius, Allah, he thought about Jesus and Gandhi. He thought about God. He thought about the twelve apostles and all the martyrs of all religions and beliefs. Then he asked the burning rose bush a series of questions. "Have all their sacrifices accomplished anything?"

"Has it stopped war or greed?"

"Has it stopped poverty or misery?"

"Has it made all of mankind brothers?"

"Has it given us charity and compassion?"

"Does love and hope prevail only to lose?"

Then he asked, "Have they created more good than bad?"

The bush divulged no answers but the flame grew taller, the smell of roses an offering to the night.

Chapter Forty-nine

SHANNON

ROMANS 12-9, 20: Let love be without dissimulation. Abhor that which is evil: cleave to that which is good. Therefore if thine enemy hunger, feed him; if he thirst, give him drink: for in so doing thou shalt heap coals of fire on his head.

****

Bertha saw Anna head toward the western army, "Anna, I would like to talk to you," she beckoned.

"You will not talk to Anna," Hate commanded.

"You will not tell me what to do anymore," she said defiantly.

"Without me you are nothing," Hate said with disdain.

"Without me you are also nothing," Bertha replied fearlessly, and then ordered, "Now go from me until the dawn."

Bertha felt Hate's displeasure but there was no protest.

The army under Bertha stirred restlessly. Katrina, from the cross, smiled at Bertha.

"Anna, I wish to talk to you," Bertha called again.

Anna stopped in front of Katrina. "Love is not the cross you are bound to," she said.

"I know," Katrina answered. "Love is not a cross."

Anna then turned to Bertha and said, "Even you should not be in a cage. It only causes more hate and grief."

"How can you not hate me, Anna?" Bertha asked even though she had asked before it still confused her.

"To hate you, I must hate myself, and, even though I do not like what I was, I do not hate myself any longer."

"Katrina, will you hate me when I destroy Shannon?" Bertha asked.

"I cannot. I will pity you."

Bertha pointed at the army below her. "All of them are like me," she said, "but I am the strongest. I can even defy my master."

"It is such a waste," Anna said. "So much has been lost and destroyed for your master's will."

"We are all beasts," Bertha said. "Love is only a dream."

"No, mother, we are not all beasts," Anna replied, "and love is not a dream."

Bertha felt the strange feeling in her stir. She pointed at the western army. "Your army has no fight in it, no will to destroy, and yet I feel no fear from them."

"They possess a bravery you will never know," Anna said.

"I want to understand how you are able to forgive me Anna," Bertha almost pleaded.

"By watching Shannon and Katrina and learning about love. They caused me to look inside myself and not outside. I had to tackle the demons that I created in my self-pity. To forgive myself, I must also forgive you and hope you find peace."

"There is nothing left inside of me that I can examine," Bertha said. "It has all been expelled."

"There is a tiny feeling in you that I can detect," Katrina said. "If you let it, it will give you what you seek."

"Only in victory will I get what I seek," Bertha said but not resolutely.

"You will find no satisfaction in your victory and your reward will not be for what you search. There is nothing more to say. I wish you well, and I feel sorry for you." Anna said and rejoined the western army.

"It was not I who brought you here," Bertha said to Katrina.

"I was brought here by your master to make Shannon fight you," Katrina said.

The distant feeling inside of Bertha stirred and caused her to wince with indecision.

"Do not fight the feeling, embrace it," Katrina said.

Bertha grabbed the bars and started shaking the cage. "Bring the dawn and deliver the lamb to me so I may drink of his blood," she screamed.

"Bring the lamb, bring the lamb," the eastern army chanted.

The ghost of Rebecca cautiously approached Bertha. "I was not worthy of you," Bertha said to Rebecca. "You only gave me kindness and I deceived you."

"I only hope you find a small portion of peace in your existence before the end and I hope you understand I only meant you well," Rebecca said and turned toward the western army.

Bertha could not speak and the tiny feeling in her stirred again.

Shannon, after hearing Bertha's screams and the eastern army chanting said, "It is sad but I can do nothing for them."

"Only by example can one teach," the burning rose bush murmured and disappeared. For a few moments the fragrance of rose blossoms lingered in the air like a distant memory.

Shannon faced east. The horizon was a black purple – a color guard for the dawn. "The end of your quest is within you," the stone face said to Shannon.

"I know that now."

"Go with my blessing and may your heart be strong."

Shannon walked resolutely to the edge of the river. He pointed at the river with his right hand and the water parted, forming two walls of water over seven feet tall. Shannon passed through to the other side of the river. As soon as he was once again on land the river united.

The horizon turned a pale red. The cries from the ghosts from beneath the circle of desolation resumed – moans filled with every sadness and grief possible. The eastern army chanted, "Bring us the lamb. Bring us the lamb."

The western army responded in one peaceful note. "AUM" they sang.

Bertha flew in a rage inside her cage. Her eyes were pits of nothingness, her color turned mid-night black and glistened with sparks and flashes of electricity. The black hornets inside of her were so outraged they circled in one mass of buzzing destruction.

The golden glow evaporated from around Katrina. Shannon and Katrina became one being in thought and mind. There was nothing else, no armies, no desolation, no approaching new day. "Do not make us two," she called to Shannon. "Do not destroy what we are or will be."

Shannon stretched his arms toward her. "Know that I have always loved you. I loved you before we were and I will love you when our flesh is no more of this world."

Katrina's smile radiated to Shannon. "Before time and until the end of time I have always loved you," she called back.

Bertha's rage grew – lightning flashed from her form and made the air crackle and hiss with killing electricity.

"Bring us the lamb. Bring us the lamb," the eastern army chanted louder.

The single clear note grew louder from the western army, "AUM."

A sliver of the sun rose above the horizon. It illuminated the eastern army first then swept over the circle of desolation before basking the western army with all its glory.

Chapter Fifty

BERTHA

"**Y**ou have heard that it was said, 'Eye for eye, and tooth for tooth.' But I tell you, do not resist an evil person. If someone strikes you on the right cheek, turn to him the other also. And if someone wants to sue you and take your tunic, let him have your cloak as well. If someone forces you to go one mile, go with him two miles....You have heard that it was said, 'Love your neighbor and hate your enemy.' I tell you: Love your enemies and pray for those who persecute you..."

****

Shannon proceeded to the center of the desolation and stopped exactly between the two armies. He bowed to the rising sun. Then he bowed to the west, then he bowed to the north, and then he bowed to the south.

The cries and moans from the circle of desolation grew in intensity, filled with desperation and longing.

The sun cleared the horizon. The sunrays burst forth, bringing light to the day, and then, like their birth had been a mistake, the rays retreated back into the sun – the sun was a bright yellow orb suspended in a dull gray sky. The sun rested on the horizon for a brief instant and then moved quickly through the gray sky until it was centered directly over Shannon. A ray of light came down from the sun and circled Shannon.

In front of Shannon, and extending to the outer edge of

the circle of desolation the crust of the earth vanished, leaving a deep and wide cavern. Thousands and thousands of ghosts almost devoid of all color floated in the cavern, they twisted and turned like a gigantic school of lost and forsaken fish. Not one form could be differentiated from another – none of the forms touched, forbidden to even share their grief.

Their pleas of anguish drifted into the sky and made Shannon overwhelmingly sad.

Barbara, all of the sky, was consumed with their pain. Thunder rumbled where there were no clouds. The gray sky boiled, not knowing if it should try to help the cries, or repulse them back into the belly of the earth before the moans overpowered it, and the sky would never be allowed to be blue again.

"Silence," Shannon ordered the ghosts.

Their cries ceased immediately. Thousands of tormented forms beseeched Shannon. "I am not your redeemer. Only you can redeem yourselves. I have only come to show you the way. You have two choices when this day is over. You can go east or you can go west. You can either embrace Love or you can embrace Hate."

The hole closed in upon itself – no sound emitted from the circle of desolation.

The light circling Shannon drew back into the sun, but the sun remained where it was, staying directly above Shannon. The gray sky was still. The eastern army stopped chanting. The western army's flowing note ceased. The plateau lay silent as if it had never known sound. The cage around Bertha disappeared. Bertha floated free in front of her army and then flew directly toward Shannon, stopping a few feet from him. She glared at him without speaking. Shannon smiled sadly at her which momentarily confused Bertha.

A crystal sphere so clear that it was almost invisible, fifty cubits in circumference and perfect in all dimensions, appeared over the western army. An identical sphere in size, only shiny black crystal, appeared over the eastern army. The spheres of Love and Hate, silently and without casting a shadow, moved toward the center of the circle of desolation. Each sphere stopped above and directly behind their champions. Bertha and Shannon turned to their sphere and bowed their heads and then faced each other again. Without warning the black eastern sphere rammed with all its might into the western sphere, the impact was louder than thunder and made the ground shake, but it was repelled. The western sphere was not phased or moved from its position. Again and again the eastern sphere attacked, hitting the western sphere from different angles, in the middle, from below, searching for a weakness, only to bounce off the western sphere each time. Faster and faster it attacked. Sparks flew in the gray sky from the contact, each attack louder, until the sky rumbled in one continuous thunderclap. With one last attack and again being repulsed, the eastern sphere moved once again above and behind Bertha. "You can never destroy me," the western sphere said. "You can deceive my followers to your side but you cannot destroy me."

"And what have you done with your precious Barbara?" the eastern sphere taunted. "I have searched for her but cannot find her."

"She is where you can never find her but she can always find you."

"My champion will spare your son in exchange for the ghosts from the circle of desolation and Barbara. She does not love you, as you love her."

Barbara was instantly filled with an all encompassing love for Shannon's father. A rainbow-filled tear slid down the gray of the sky and landed between Shannon and Bertha. The tear transformed into a blooming white Lily.

"There is no trade," the western sphere said.

"What are you that you would forsake your own son?" the eastern sphere implored.

"He is not forsaken. He has his own free will."

"And you Shannon. I will release Katrina if you forsake

your father," the eastern sphere challenged.

"When this day is done we will be in a better place," Shannon said to Katrina.

"I look forward to the stars," Katrina replied. "We will make the heavens glow."

"I will not forsake my father," Shannon replied to the eastern sphere with a deep heaviness in his heart.

"Thy will be done then," the eastern sphere replied.

With no other words the two spheres disappeared.

"And now it is only us," Bertha said with finality to Shannon.

"From the moment of my birth it has been us," Shannon replied. "I saw you even as I was being born, but I want to ask you for one favor before you destroy me."

Bertha's eyes glowed, her mouth twisted in agony. "What is your favor?" she forced herself to say.

"I want to bid my army farewell."

The eastern army resumed chanting. "Bring us the blood of the lamb. Bring us the blood of the lamb. Bring us the blood of the lamb."

"AUM" softly replied the western army.

The chants of her army swept into Bertha. The black hornets started buzzing in anticipation within her and started stinging her with their venomous hate. "Say farewell to your army," she stated. "Then I will give no more quarter."

"Thank you. Somewhere in your being you know of kindness," Shannon said.

A feeling stirred in Bertha and made the hornets stop buzzing for a brief moment, but then they resumed stinging her.

Bertha sailed over her army. The ghosts screeched at Bertha. Every screech shot through Bertha, awakening more hornets, more stings. Her form grew darker and darker. "I am the killer of the lamb," she proclaimed.

"Bring us the blood of the lamb. Bring us the blood of the lamb," her army answered.

Bertha hovered in front of Katrina. "Oh Bertha," Katrina lamented.

Bertha tossed her head back and thousands upon thousands of hornets erupted from her mouth. The hornets circled above Katrina in a dark, buzzing, sinister cloud. "You will not feast on love until I command it," Bertha warned the swarm.

The swarm buzzed louder and several hornets dove at Katrina. Quicker than light Bertha reached out and smashed them. The swarm retreated.

Shannon, holding his head high, approached his army. The spirit of "AUM" drove away any fear he possessed. The sun stayed centered over the circle of desolation. He stopped before the army and held up his arms for silence. The "AUM" ceased but its echo continued rolling gently through the sky until it rolled over the curve of the earth, soothing all creatures in need.

"There will be no destruction because of me. I want you all to go back to where you came from," Shannon announced to his army.

A whisper of disbelief rippled through the army's ranks.

Anna floated up above the western army. "I speak for all," she said. "We are here from our own free will. We will fight with you."

"There is no victory in war," Shannon answered. "War only begets more war. Now please go and keep my father's blessing alive."

Not one ghost from the eastern army made a move to leave.

"Do as my son wishes," the clear crystal sphere of Love said from the gray sky with great pride and admiration.

The army sighed, ghosts began reluctantly rising from the ranks and flew to the north and south and west, not one ventured east or looked back.

Bertha and the eastern army, seeing the exodus, grew quiet and perplexed. Even the hornets stopped buzzing.

"Shannon, I knew you would do the right thing," Katrina said with a deeper love than she had ever experienced.

"Cowards, stay and watch the death of your champion," the voice of Hate commanded.

Hate received no reply.

Soon, all except one ghost from the western army was gone. Anna said to Shannon. "We protected you, only to prolong your slaughter. It does not seem right that Bertha will win."

"What happens here today will not be the final outcome," Shannon answered.

"Do you ever see a day when love will rule the world?" Anna asked.

"Perhaps after time, when our spirits have known eternity," Shannon said. "Until then it will always be a struggle."

"Oh, Shannon, it is so sad."

"It is not all sad. I will sit on the right side of my father and Katrina will be with me."

Anna departed.

The eastern army began chanting again. "Bring us the blood of the lamb. Bring us the blood of the lamb."

The hornets above Katrina buzzed but none were brave enough to attack Katrina. Bertha flew toward the center of the desolation. The slight feeling that Bertha had both tried to explore and repulse stirred ever so gently in her being. Bertha landed in the center of the desolation.

Shannon's eyes never left Katrina as he advanced toward the center of desolation and his fate. "I love you, I love you," his eyes spoke.

Chapter Fifty-one

SHANNON AND BERTHA

Mathew 26:52 – "Put up again thy sword into his place; for all they that take the sword shall perish with the sword..."

****

The sun released it rays from of the center of desolation, driving off the gray sky and replacing it with a deep turquoise blue. The sky became dotted with powdery white clouds – the clouds wise tranquil faces that gazed down on Shannon and Bertha.

Shannon smiled at Katrina one last time and then looked directly into the emptiness of Bertha's eyes and said calmly and without fear, "I will not fight you Bertha. I will not resist in anyway. I am sorry, but I cannot give you your nothingness by becoming what you are. I can only truly help you if you come to me."

He let his arms fall passively to his sides. His hands not formed into fists.

"You are a true champion. You have learned and understand the truth," Love said with a heavy heart to Shannon.

Every evil of all time flashed through Bertha. Venomous snakes slithered and hissed inside of her. The swarm of hornets left Katrina and formed into a deadly circle above Bertha. The earth around Bertha and Shannon began to rumble and large cracks and fissures cut through the circle of desolation. The ghosts beneath the ground, who had known neither love nor hate, did not cry out but listened intently.

Barbara murmured, "Shannon, with the sacrifice of your flesh, you are greater than your father."

"Destroy the son and champion of my enemy," Hate commanded Bertha.

The earth rumbled louder and the cracks and fissures in the earth grew larger.

"Bring us the blood of the lamb. Bring us the blood of the lamb," the eastern army chanted.

Stretching her arms away from her body, lightning shot from Bertha's fingertips. Her eyes filled with the evil of ages – tarantulas and scorpions and snakes writhed inside of her. "You will hate me," she screamed at Shannon and stuck him violently across the face.

The blow cut Shannon's cheek to the bone, blood streamed down his face. The attack stunned him and almost knocked him down, but he straightened back up, keeping his arms by his sides. "I will not fight you. I can only pity you and with my pity I can offer you love," Shannon said.

Bertha struck Shannon again across the face, only harder. Shannon fell to the ground. He staggered to his feet, straightened back up and turned his head, offering Bertha his other cheek. Bertha struck him with all her might, his head snapped sideways but he remained standing. Blood poured from both wounds on his face. Turning his head again he said weakly, "I will not resist you, Bertha."

The earth rumbled. The cracks and fissures grew larger. A low murmuring came from the cracks – the words indiscernible but the thoughts deep and complicated.

"I will destroy that which you love the most," Bertha screamed at Shannon. She flew into the air and pointed at Katrina. "Bring me the heart of the lamb," she ordered.

The cross shook as if it was being held in the clutches of an invisible powerful force and then circled over the eastern army. Ghosts shot out of the ranks, diving and screeching at Katrina they scratched her arms and face until she was bleeding from hundreds of wounds. They clawed and ripped her clothes until her garments hung in tatters. "I will not forsake you, Shannon," Katrina cried painfully.

Shannon's love poured out to Katrina. Tears spilled from his eyes, mingled with his blood, but he could not help Katrina.

The cross moved away from the army, to the exact center of desolation, stopped and then settled to the earth, remaining upright directly between Shannon and Bertha and directly beneath the sun. Katrina faced south, the right cross beam cast its shadow on Shannon, the left crossbeam cast its shadow on Bertha. "Do not blame them for they know not what they do," Katrina whispered in agony.

"They are what they are only because of our own failings," Shannon said.

"And I am on this cross only because of my love and joy," Katrina said.

The earth rumbled deep in the folds of its heart. The cracks and fissures in the circle of desolation grew larger. The murmurs grew louder and more intense. The clouds grew darker but still hung motionless in the sky. The sun remained constant in its vigil.

Bertha ripped off what remained of Katrina's cloths, throwing them to the ground in disgust. "Look at what you have caused," she screeched at Shannon.

Katrina, through all her pain, gazed at Shannon with love. Shannon wanted to look away but he could not.

Bertha laughed hysterically.

"He will never hate," Katrina said to Bertha, unashamed of her nakedness.

"Now you may feast," Bertha said to the hornets. She faced Shannon and leered at him.

The hornet's buzzing increased and a wave separated from the mass and attacked Katrina. Katrina held back a scream. After each hornet stung Katrina it instantly died and fell to the ground having not even left a welt. Still the hornets attacked, wave after wave, their buzzing angry, their dead meaning nothing to the next wave. On and on they came until they were all dead and there was a heap of dead hornets at the bottom of the cross that almost reached Katrina's feet.

Bertha was stunned. The leer on her face was replaced by disbelief. The emptiness in her eyes receded – the snakes, tarantulas and scorpions within her started biting and stinging themselves. Paul and Thomas appeared over the western horizon and sped to the circle of desolation, one stopped on Shannon's left the other on Shannon's right. "We beg your forgiveness," Paul and Thomas said in unison to Bertha.

"How can you not hate me?" Bertha asked in a weak voice. "It is impossible."

The murmuring in the ground increased, their voices transformed into one sound. "AUM" resonated out of the ground. From every crack and fissure in the desolation ghosts began emerging.

Bertha grew pale. The snakes and tarantulas and scorpions in her were now dead, the last remaining creature having killed itself. "Go back, go back," Bertha feebly tried to order the rising ghosts. She covered her ears with her hands in an attempt to wipe out their song.

More and more ghosts came from the earth. Thousands upon thousands and still they emerged, rising higher and higher into the sky until they almost touched the sun. Their "AUM" covered the desolation and swept gently over the eastern army. The eastern army was transfixed as more and more ghosts came from the earth until the ghosts far outnumbered the eastern army and still they came. Then one last ghost emerged from a crevice behind Katrina. He floated between Bertha and Shannon and, with his back to Bertha and bowing to Shannon, he said, "Your father's way is the only way. There is no redemption in hate."

The crevices in the earth began to close. A wind kicked up, sweeping the heap of dead hornets into the crevices. The earth healed and all the ghosts that had emerged from the circle of desolation formed behind Shannon and Paul and Thomas.

The eastern army was stunned into silence.

Another ghost sailed over the western horizon and stopped by Bertha. "John, you once again return," Bertha said.

"I forgive you," John said.

Anna returned. "I forgive you," she said to Bertha.

Bertha faded to a light shimmering gray. A warm feeling grew in her that had devoured the dead bodies of the snakes and tarantulas and scorpions. She tried to speak but her growing feeling could not be formulated into words.

Rebecca returned. "I forgive you," she said. "Please forgive yourself."

"I forgive you," Anna, John, Paul and Thomas said once again.

"My father holds no malice," Shannon said. "There is no past. There is only the future."

A black crystalline sphere appeared over the eastern army. It cast a dark menacing shadow over the land. "Bertha, you will not forsake me," Hate commanded. "They only deceive you. Only I can give you what you seek."

Bertha crumbled to her knees, the feeling inside of her comforting, but she could not draw strength from it, it had been abandoned for far too long. "He has only used you," Shannon said to Bertha.

The clear crystal sphere of Love moved over the army of his new followers. It cast no shadow.

"I have been so lonely," Bertha sighed.

John glided over to Bertha and embraced her. Their forms molded into one. "Oh, John," Bertha sobbed but there were no tears.

Anna glided over and joined in the embrace.

"Please forgive us, Bertha?" Paul and Thomas asked again.

"I have forsaken love," Bertha whispered. "It did not forsake me."

Another ghost came from the north and joined in the embrace. "I should have held you when you were a child,"

Bertha's father said.

"You hold me now," Bertha replied softly.

John and Anna stopped their embrace and stood by Shannon. Bertha's father still embraced his daughter.

"Go from me now," Bertha told her father.

Her form was now almost white. "I am the cause of all my wrong," she said. "Please forgive me, as I forgive all of you," and a single tear formed in each of her eyes. The black sphere of Hate trembled with rage hearing Bertha's words, "Destroy them all," he commanded his army.

The front ranks of the army started to advance toward the circle. The new western army advanced toward them. The out numbered eastern army hesitated and stopped. "Do as I say," Hate ordered, "or I will abandon all of you and you will wander the earth forever lost and with no purpose."

The stick man with his spear materialized between the two armies. He pointed his spear at the eastern army and then he broke the spear over his knee, tossed the two pieces to the ground, and vanished back to the sanctuary of the cave wall.

"Bring me my rainbow," Shannon called.

A complete rainbow spread from behind the eastern army and extended over the western horizon.

"There is no victory for hate without resistance," the clear crystal sphere of Love said to the black sphere of Hate.

"Do I not have a worthy champion?" the black sphere beseeched his army.

No ghost rose up from the eastern army. "Then, vengeance is mine," Hate swore and without warning a black arrow shot out of him, traveling so fast that it could barely be seen it impaled into the left side of Katrina. Katrina cried out with the piercing pain, her body became rigid, her eyes shut, and her head fell – the life force barely remaining within her.

"No, no," Shannon cried, running to the cross and reaching up to hold Katrina's feet.

Katrina's blood covered Shannon's already blood splattered face and chest. She could barely open her eyes.

Gazing down at a grief-stricken Shannon, she whispered, "My blood is your protection."

"What have I done?" Shannon sobbed. "What have I done?"

"It is done," Katrina said and died.

Barbara – all of the sky, moaned in agony. The sun paled.

Bertha's form changed from white to crimson. Her eyes flamed, hotter and more intense than the molten rock in the center of the earth. "It is all because of me. I should have loved you all," she said to Anna, John, Paul and Thomas, Rebecca, and her father.

Shannon could not move. He possessed no hope or love or will. He was devoid of all feeling like the ghosts that had lived under the circle of desolation. "My sacrifice has been too great," he beseeched Love. "In all your mercy you must destroy me."

"I cannot," Love said with the deepest sadness he had ever experienced.

Anna, John, Paul and Thomas, Rebecca, and Bertha's father tried to embrace Shannon but he lashed out at them. "Go from me I do not seek condolence," he ordered. "I have destroyed all that is good around me."

Barbara, all of the sky, wished she was no more. The heartbreak of her son was more than she could possibly bear.

Anna held her arms out beseechingly to Bertha as if there was something Bertha could do. The feeling inside of Bertha stirred and soothing warmth spread throughout her entire being. She gazed at the eastern army, then at Shannon, at the crystalline orb of Love, and finally at the other ghosts, and it was the first time she really understood what they truly were. She bowed her head toward her daughter.

Bertha floated up to the lifeless Katrina and touched her gently on the forehead. "I give you all of my forgiveness. I give you my fleeting glimpse of love," she pleaded in a caring voice devoid of all hate and malice.

Lightning flashed through the sky. The dark clouds

formed into one. Three raindrops fell from the sky and landed on Katrina's forehead.

Shannon turned away from Katrina and fell to his knees. All was lost. Another raindrop landed on Katrina's forehead.

Anna, John, Paul and Thomas, Rebecca and Bertha's father turned away from the cross.

Another raindrop landed on Katrina's lips.

"I denounce all that is hate," Bertha swore to the lightening.

The sky erupted with rain. The blood was washed from Shannon and Katrina and mixed with the dry alkaline soil.

A thunder clap erupted that was so strong it shook the ground as if with vengeance.

Hate shot another arrow at Katrina but Love intercepted it, casting it to the ground like vermin.

Katrina's eyelids fluttered. Her chest barely moved. She inhaled a tiny bit of air. She breathed deeper. All the wounds on her body were healed by the rain – disappearing like the evil that they were. She opened her eyes and seeing Bertha she murmured as if waking from a deep sleep, "Bertha, now you know of love."

With the sound of her voice Shannon turned in wonder. The ropes holding Katrina undid themselves and the cross vanished. Katrina stayed suspended in the air. A purple smock appeared and covered her nakedness. She then settled gently to the ground. Shannon embraced her. "My love, my love," he sobbed.

"I promised I would never forsake you," Katrina said.

"How can I thank you? I will do anything," Shannon said to Bertha.

"There is no need for thanks," Bertha replied.

"You have my blessing, Bertha," Love said.

Bertha faced the eastern army. Holding out her arms to the sky lightning arched from the dark clouds, striking her – thunder rolled over the plain. "Now you will feel my vengeance," she yelled at the black sphere and like a blazing comet she shot at him – all of her remaining hate burning out of her as she advanced. "I come to you with love," she cried.

Bertha crashed into the black sphere but there was no sound. The black sphere rolled on its axis, stunned and baffled, a tiny hole having penetrated its side. The hole healed within an instant after impact. "Now I am part of you forever," Bertha laughed, flying around the inside of the sphere.

Bertha lost all form and became a pure essence of love.

The black sphere wailed – a tiny distant feeling inside of it made it wonder and question all it had ever been.

The earth suddenly opened up in a perfect circle beneath the eastern army and it was pulled into the abyss. The hole closed up so quickly none could escape. The black sphere, alone, bellowed, "It is not finished," and vanished.

Moans and cries of agony emitted from the new center of desolation. Shannon and Katrina still embraced. The new ghosts of the west that had been lost in the circle of desolation rose up in a great cloud and then dispersed in all directions except east. "Now we can rest," Paul said to Thomas and they faded from view.

"I am not yet worthy," Bertha's father said, sailing to the north.

"My purpose is not done," Anna said to Shannon and Katrina before heading south.

Rebecca smiled and said nothing as she departed.

The white crystalline sphere started to expand, larger and larger until it was a fine crystal mist that sparkled from horizon to horizon. Then Love said to Shannon, "I take from you all of your knowledge of this world. You are no more or less than what you would have been."

The crystal mist blended into the sky. "I've found the love I always sought," Barbara said as the mist and she became one.

Shannon held Katrina tighter. "How could I not have told you I loved you?" he asked.

"Love is not words," Katrina replied.

Then everything was dark.

Chapter Fifty-two
BERTHA

Peace be with you.

****

Bertha was without form and no larger than a particle of dust. She had no memory of her life or her afterlife. She was a tiny seed of love – a seed patiently waiting to grow inside of Hate that contained all that he longed to destroy – a constant question, a constant source of turmoil, a feeling that although distant and vague would never go away – a feeling he could never completely destroy unless he destroyed himself.

Bertha had not found nothingness. She had found her true destiny.

Chapter Fifty-three

BARBARA

Life is not all questions. It is also filled with answers.

****

"And where are Shannon and Katrina?" Barbara asked Love.

"They are back from where they came."

"And you and I are all of the sky. We are one to each other like no other two can be."

"It is wonderful," Love replied.

"Yes, it is wonderful," Barbara said.

Chapter Fifty-four

SHANNON and KATRINA

Death shall not be my keeper nor life my house
I live in the home of love and do not fear.

****

The garden had not changed. It was beautiful. Every tree on the face of the earth grew in the garden. All the trees were covered with ripe fruit even though there was no hunger in the garden. Every shrub and bush grew in the garden and none had thorns or burrs. Every animal lived in the garden with no animosity between any kinds. Singing birds filled the air, their songs always joyous. There was no sickness or death. The air and sky were tranquil with never scorching heat or freezing cold. There was no sin or greed or hate or mistrust, no longing or sadness or treachery. Contentment and peace and love ruled supreme.

In the middle of a clearing a single apple tree grew that was constantly bathed in a golden light. The tree produced only one apple at a time and it was sweeter and more delicious than any other fruit in the garden. Shannon and Katrina, both naked, were sleeping beneath the tree.

When Shannon awakened he knew he had been dreaming, but try as he may he could not remember the dream. "It is of no matter," he finally admitted and gazed lovingly at the sleeping Katrina.

Katrina's face was peaceful and even in sleep she smiled. "You are beautiful and I love you," he said.

Katrina stirred. "Why do you look at me so?" she asked

Shannon feigning annoyance.

"Because I love you."

"You do not have to tell me all the time. I know you love me."

"For some reason I feel I must tell you all the time."

"In truth I never get tired of you telling me."

"And do you love me?"

"Of course I love you."

Shannon stood and while helping Katrina up he noticed a golden ring on her little finger. The ring had two tiny hearts no larger than a teardrop engraved on it. "Where did you get that ring?" he asked puzzled.

Looking at the ring Katrina was confused. "I do not know," she replied, "but I like it. It is pretty and I do not want to take it off."

"It is pretty," Shannon said. "There is no need to take it off."

"Look," Katrina said pointing at an apple core beneath the tree. "Did you eat the fruit from the tree? I have told you never to eat of this tree. It is too beautiful."

"I don't remember doing so," Shannon said truthfully.

"It does not matter. The new apple on the tree is more beautiful than the last apple," Katrina said. "Would you like to eat this one?" and she started to pick the apple and hand it to him.

"No. Do not pick it. You are right. It is too beautiful to eat."

"Maybe another time," Katrina said.

Holding hands they walked out of the clearing.

"I feel like I have been on a journey but I cannot remember where I was or what I did," Shannon said.

"Do you feel like you have been on many journeys?" Katrina asked.

"Too many journeys," Shannon replied.

"I feel the same way," Katrina said.

"Maybe we both ate the apple and it was not as good as it

looked," Shannon said.
    Smiling, they embraced.

THE END

9 780578 984261